I0457777

Fate Intended

COULTER MEN BOOK 3

ELIZABETH SECKMAN

This is a work of fiction. Names, characters, places, and incidents are products of the author's imagination or are used fictitiously and are not to be construed as real. Any resemblance to actual events, locations, organizations, or person, living or dead, is entirely coincidental.

World Castle Publishing, LLC
Pensacola, Florida

Copyright © Elizabeth Seckman 2013
ISBN: 9781629890425
First Edition World Castle Publishing, LLC December 1, 2013
http://www.worldcastlepublishing.com

Licensing Notes
All rights reserved. No part of this book may be used or reproduced in any manner whatsoever without written permission, except in the case of brief quotations embodied in articles and reviews.
Cover: Lindsay Anne Kendal Graphics
Editor: Eric Johnston

Acknowledgements

Thanks to my husband and kids for putting up with the insanity (and take out!) that goes hand and hand with getting a book to the publisher. And many thanks to said publisher, Karen Fuller, for putting up with my insanity, and to the rest of the WC team…Lindsay Anne Kendall for giving me cover love and editor, Eric Johnston for his support and encouragement.

Special love to my betas! Kari DiNardo (Stacey Leichliter lost her copy, so uh, thanks for nothing…LOL), Betsy Helmick, Cathy Loy, and of course my mom, Caroline Hartman. You guys get to wade through the rough stuff and I thank you for your patience!

To my fabulous writer friends and critique partners, I am forever in your debts. Celeste Holloway for giving the chapters and good start; Tammy Theriault for catching every head pat, nod, and swallow; Emily King for providing polish and smart advice; and Annalisa Crawford for insisting the red wine be taken out of the fridge.

And last, but not least…thanks to Loretta Baker for the pecan pie that nourished me through the edits, and the wine for the celebration when they were done!

I love you all! God bless and thanks!
Elizabeth

Dedication:

To my mom, Caroline Hartman, for being my most loyal fan.
Love you Mom.
And to my dad, Ken Hartman, for being my guardian angel. Miss
you Dad.

Elizabeth Seckman

Chapter 1

After spending a year in America, Jane figured she would die of boredom. It seemed logical since she spent every single one of her days the exact same way: cleaning all day, watching *Jersey Shore* reruns at night. But hey, she was lucky to be free, right?

The hollow metallic tick of the chrome wall clock echoed in the room, knocking Jane out of her reverie and instantly setting her nerves on edge. She glanced at the time and bit her lip. Six minutes past a safe escape. Her scrub brush whipped round the smooth curves of the porcelain bowl. Swish, swish, flush. Good enough, at least for today. She dumped the clothes from the hamper into a canvas laundry bag, straightened a crooked rug with her toe, and scooted from the room.

Silence persisted. Peace lingered. She might make it out unharmed.

She hustled through the hall, so close to the safety of escape that her breathing calmed and her shoulders relaxed. As she made her way to the door, a thumbprint on the hall mirror caught her eye. She spewed a few curses as she polished the mirror with her shirtsleeve and stepped back and looked it over. Perfect. As she turned again to leave, muffled voices filtered in from the hallway. They were moving closer and closer to the apartment door.

A wave of queasy warmth washed over her. Her heart raced and sank simultaneously. The lion, or, more appropriately, the lioness, approached the gate. At Forrester Apartments, service was number one and the owner of this unit demanded Monday morning

1

cleaning between 7 and 8 AM. Jane didn't arrive until after 7:30 to clean the two-bedroom space. Wiping sweaty palms against her puke green tunic, Jane gathered her supplies, the dirty laundry, and moved it toward the door.

The voices came closer. One woman, one man. The bitch and *him*.

Jane looked herself over in the now polished mirror and cringed. She looked like hell. She wore no makeup, and the black circles under her eyes accentuated her pasty skin tone. Her hair was flat, and her overgrown roots cast a thick shadow at the base of her bottle-blond hair. Dropping the laundry bag to the floor, she did what she could to be a little more…well, a little less, hideous. She fluffed her hair and pulled it into a ponytail, slapped her cheeks, and bit her lips for some color. Taking another look, she groaned.

The key slid into the lock. She jumped as if shocked by the sound. "Damn dream," she spat looking over her shoulder and considering for one crazy moment about jumping out the fire escape window. She could exit unseen…as long as she didn't trip. She imagined being discovered by *the bitch* with her shirt flapping over her head, blood rushing to her face as she dangled by her feet from the windowsill. Jane shuddered as the image fleshed out in her mind: horns would honk, maybe even the police called, as DC traffic crept along the street where residential buildings lined up like tiny institutions for the criminally wealthy. Every building looked the same—simple brick structures; each sported a brass plate street number and a hunter green door canopy. Nothing set one building apart from another. *Well*, thought Jane, *all but Forrester Apartments, it could have a cleaning lady dangling from its fourth floor.*

That would never do, so she shook her head and abolished the thought. She was an adult…a Sarkhov…and she would act like one.

As the doorknob turned, she grabbed the bag of laundry. She grimaced and braced herself against the wall of the narrow foyer hoping to be invisible when the door swung open. But no matter how small she made herself, Jane was in the way as Olivia Higgins brushed past her. They hit shoulder to shoulder and Jane stumbled a bit before catching her footing and returning to the wall. Mr. Perfect caught her arm. Smiling, he asked, "You got it?"

Her throat went dry and her mind blank, but somehow Jane managed a nod.

Olivia, the sultry lioness, was simply beautiful. Her honey blond hair was never out of place. Jane was certain a 5 AM fire would catch Olivia perfectly put together. The woman wasn't human. She had the perfect life. Money, Harvard law degree, the world's best man...

Jane sighed.

Olivia was without a single obvious flaw; she was totally enviable. And that was totally unfair, because Olivia was mean. She was a people-snubbing, black-hearted goat wrapped in swimsuit model flawlessness. In Jane's way of thinking, it was cosmically unjust for such a nasty woman to get such a wonderful life. Jane wished beyond all current wishes that the woman would break a leg while out on her morning jog, get fat, depressed, and then break out and become all zitty and horrendous looking. That was what she deserved. Jane grinned at the thought of a bloated, miserable Olivia. Then she frowned as she admitted, at least to herself, what really got under her skin was that she had *him*.

Jane hugged the bag of dirty clothes to her chest. *He* was the epitome of male perfection, and he was twisted around the she-fiend's perfectly manicured little finger.

It wasn't fair. Jane knew he would be happier with her. Admittedly, she knew very little about him. Like where he grew up...where he worked...or even what his name was, but she knew him better than anyone else did. She also knew from months of watching and dreaming that he was, beyond any shadow of a doubt, meant to be with her.

The time they spent together—in Jane's very active imagination—was perfection. He knew exactly what flowers to buy, what her favorite chocolates were, and he would playfully kiss her after teasing her with a joke.

Her heart understood that the quiet, sensitive man hid a secret daring that he let no one else see. She looked past the disheveled blond hair, and beyond the wire-rim glasses to eyes which sparkled with a spirit of adventure. Jane wanted to reach out to him and tell him they were meant to be together, that she knew they were soul mates. Even if he didn't know she existed.

Her musings were stopped short as Olivia pulled her gym clothes off as she walked down the hall. Perfect body too, Jane thought with a grimace. Breasts not too big or too small, solid abs and exercise-tightened thighs. Sighing, Jane headed for the door. She supposed Olivia hadn't seen her if she stripped down to her bra and panties right there in the foyer. Jane crept to the apartment door and twisted the knob. "Ms. Mitchell! Where are you going?" Jane jumped at the sound of Olivia's bark.

Jane's mouth hung open.

"Yes. You. May as well take these to be laundered. Good God, you think I stripped right here for my health?" She tossed the gym clothes onto Jane's bag, waved her off, and then turned her attention back to Mr. Perfect. "This discussion is over. These fantasies of yours? They're just that...fantasy. You have a good job; a bright future. I honestly don't know what the hell has gotten into you lately."

Mr. Perfect brushed past Jane as he followed Olivia into the living area. Jane caught a whiff of his scent. Subtle and clean; citrus and musk.

Jane's cheeks flamed. She was smack in the middle of what was evidently a fight. Sure, they weren't screaming and yelling like normal people, but Olivia's voice was clipped and Mr. Perfect looked flushed and, dare she hope...irritated. She stood momentarily stunned, her heart fluttering at the hope of a relationship-ending battle. Her eyes met his. Her heart yelled, *I understand. You need to be free.* But her mouth said nothing. She imagined throwing the dirty clothes at Olivia and grabbing Mr. Perfect's hand and shouting, *Come! My love will save you from the succubus!*

The lioness turned on her with a roar. "A little privacy. Please!" She pointed to the door as she said to Mr. Perfect, "Good God, I know her English is horrible, but I didn't think she was retarded too.

4

Don't they have schools in where she came from?"

Jane fled without shutting the door properly, so she could hear Mr. Perfect's smooth voice whisper, "Liv, how can you treat her like that?"

"She's the cleaning lady, *Rowan*."

Jane didn't want to hear any more. She ran down the hall toward the elevator. She looked over her shoulder as she spastically punched the button willing it to come quicker.

Olivia's door opened. Jane's heart skipped a beat. She jabbed the button again. The light blinked and the door binged and slid open. Jane rushed forward, bumping into Mr. Little as he tried to exit. The bag of groceries the old man carried spilled across the floor.

Jane blinked away the frustrated sting in her eyes. "I'm so sorry, Mr. Little. I'm clumsy. Hurrying and not watching where I go."

"It's all right, Jane." Mr. Little held the door as Jane bent down and bagged the groceries. As she worked, Mr. Little leaned on his cane. "I know all about being in a hurry." He laughed. "Why, did I ever tell you 'bout my days as a fighter pilot in WW 2?"

"I thought you were a medic." Jane stood and handed him his groceries.

Mr. Little laughed. "That was in the beginning. I learned to fly a bird to impress a girl."

"Ahh, that's so sweet and very romantic. Mrs. Little must have been a special—"

"Now, don't go telling Mrs. Little. I didn't date her until after the war."

"Oh." Jane's surprise took her eye off the bag of groceries for just a moment, and in that moment, Mr. Little dropped them again.

"Oh, I went and did it again. Damned arthritis."

"It's all right." Jane crouched down and started refilling the bag.

*****

Trip found Jane in the hallway kneeling on the floor stuffing groceries into a bag as she listened to Mr. Little's various accounts of his service during that great war. Mr. Little gave him a wink and a thumb's up. Trip shook his head and frowned at the old man.

Jane put the last item in the bag for the second time and stood, handing the groceries over very carefully. "Here you go."

"It's these hands. Useless damn things."

"Accidents happen to everyone." Jane assured with a sympathetic pat on the back.

"They happen to some more than others," Trip grumbled.

Mr. Little's grin offered no remorse as he gave Jane's bottom a pat and shuffled along to his apartment.

Jane jumped, letting out a surprised, "Oooh."

"You realize Mr. Little's only clumsy when you're around?" Trip said.

Jane slowly turned and looked at him as if he spoke a foreign tongue. Her mouth hung open, and she kept glancing over her shoulder at the elevator. Trip shifted from one foot to another, then cleared his throat and offered a simple, "I'm sorry."

Jane's head tipped to the right and she looked even more confused. "Sorry that Mr. Little is clumsy?"

Trip shook his head. "No, I'm sorry about Olivia."

"Oh." Jane's eyes widened for a moment, before returning to normal. She shrugged and shook her head. "It's nothing."

"No, it's not. There's no excuse for Olivia's behavior. I'm sorry you had to be on the receiving end. She's mad at me. Not you."

"I'm used to her…umm, unfriendliness?" Jane said retrieving her bag of laundry off the floor.

Trip's eyes narrowed, and he crossed his arms over his chest. "Well, I'm not. I've never seen Liv this pissed." Trip reddened. "Sorry, I mean angry."

"Really?" Jane bit the side of her cheek.

Her blue eyes caught his attention. They were so dark he would've mistaken them for brown if he wasn't so close. And her skin was smooth, even without make up. He hadn't realized just how pretty she was before. He had to admit he was as guilty as Mr. Little about not getting beyond the curves of her petite body to notice her face. His cheeks flushed, burning with his thoughts. She

6

was too young, couldn't be much older than eighteen.

He mumbled yet another apology, and added a lame "Yeah. Usually she's sweet."

"Really." Jane's nose wrinkled.

"I take it she's not so sweet around you?"

Jane fidgeted as the redness on her cheeks spilled down her throat. Trip couldn't believe how upset Olivia made her. Maybe he was lucky to have seen this side of Liv before making the relationship exclusive. Olivia's treatment of Jane stunned him. He couldn't imagine anyone finding fault with the girl. She was kind to everyone. Even pervy old Mr. Little.

"I've never seen Liv be so rude. And how she treated you? Like I said, that was my fault. I guess I stepped out of line."

"Stepped out of line?" Jane asked, her eyes squinted, head shaking in thought.

"It's a figure of speech…meaning I disobeyed."

"Oh, I see," Jane answered, awareness growing on her face.

"Evidently Olivia Higgins is not one to be crossed."

"No, no she's not. She is…." Jane struggled for the right word, "powerful?"

"Bossy as hell evidently."

Jane smiled. The elevator dinged, alerting them the emergency stop button was still pressed. Jane situated the laundry bag on her hip. "I should…I need to drop this off for laundry."

"Of course." Trip stepped onto the elevator with her and closed the doors. Jane stared at her pink Converses.

"Which floor?" he asked.

"Basement," she croaked. They rode in awkward silence.

*****

When the doors opened, Jane squeaked a good-bye and bolted. She tagged the bag with Olivia's room number and tossed it in the gurney. She held her hands to her hot cheeks.

Mr. Perfect probably thought she was an idiot. She couldn't think straight with him so near. How could she not realize what *stepped out of line* meant? Having him close made her brain work like pudding. She shook her head and grabbed an empty laundry bag from the hook. Turning to leave, she jumped at the shadow cast by a man in the doorway.

Trip smiled down at her. "That was quick."

"Just had to drop off."

"Well, I still feel bad. Let me buy you coffee?"

Jane chewed her cheek. She really needed to work, but she really wanted be with Mr. Perfect. Her heart fluttered. If she said no, she could miss her one opportunity. Jane pointed to the little break room across from the laundry room. "I suppose I could take a few minutes."

"Excellent!" Trip allowed her to lead the way, but stepped ahead as they approached the coffee maker. He grabbed two cups and filled them both. "Cream or sugar?"

Jane shook her head.

Holding up the can of powdered non-dairy creamer, he grinned. "You sure, only the finest fake milk in DC?"

Jane laughed as she took the cup. "Black is good."

Trip leaned against the counter. "I really am sorry about how Olivia treated you."

Jane answered quietly, barely above a whisper, "You said that."

"Yeah, but I really mean it."

"I never doubted you," Jane said, her eyes locked on her Converses again.

"It's just that 'sorry' seems lame after all you went through."

"I am unharmed." She flashed him a quick smile, then offered, "It's okay. You are forgiven for being in bad company, Mr.?"

"Trip. Rowan…actually, but I hate that name, so since I was a clumsy kid, my family called me Trip, and it stuck. So call me Trip. Trip Coulter."

"Well, thank you for the apology. It repaired a horrible day. *Spa' sibo,* Trip Coulter."

Trip cocked his head, "You're Russian? That was Russian, right?"

"Yes, I said thank you."

"Your accent, it's a little different."

Jane nodded. "My mother was British, my father Russian. I

grew up in London until I was eight, then to live with my father, then to college at Oxford." Jane swallowed hard, then added, "In England."

"Of course. Impressive. So, if you've been to Oxford...hmmm."

"Why am I scrubbing toilets for bitchy women?" Jane smiled.

Trip shrugged. "Not that, just good to know you're...well, you're not...I mean, you're an adult."

"Of course! I turned twenty-three in June. I spent three years in school, and I have many hours to my credit, but no degree. I was never a very serious student. But being in school seemed like the adult thing to do."

"I understand," Trip said casually, then grinned and added, "No, that's a lie. I was always a serious student. Never partied...too busy studying."

"Oh, I never partied." Jane shook her head. "Poppa would have brought me home fast. I just didn't study. I suppose if I'd realized I would have to get a job later, I might have made better decisions. Funny how little I thought of ever having to work when I was a girl. I suppose I was a bit of a spoiled dreamer. Always a dreamer. Always a fool."

"No, not a fool. Being a dreamer is a good thing. I think that's part of the world's problem.... Adults don't dream enough. It's like as a kid, you plan to be...to do...whatever it is you love. Because, as a kid, you don't care about whether or not the money is good, or even if the idea makes sense.... You just know, you're going to do it. But then, everyone tells you to grow up. Be sensible. And you do. You work...every day...doing what's safe...then you realize: damn, life's half over and I'm stuck."

"You are stuck?"

"Hypothetically speaking. But let's say I was stuck, but then, I got the chance to do what I want to do. Like it fell in my lap. I call that fate."

"You believe in fate?" Jane asked softly.

"I guess. I mean, hell, I never dreamed my day would go the way it has, that I would follow you to the basement laundry and tell you crap that I couldn't, in a million years, explain to Olivia. Which is really weird; but it feels natural."

Jane swallowed. Her heart screeched, *YES! YES! I knew it. Fate made you for me!* Again, her lips made no sound, but she did manage a nod.

"So, you don't think I'm crazy?"

"Oh, no. I think…." Jane moistened her lips and swallowed the heart that was trying to plant itself on her sleeve. "I believe you must live to be happy."

"Yeah," Trip echoed. "Got to do what feels right. What is right for the soul."

"Exactly," Jane agreed.

"I'm not sure if Olivia sees life that way."

Jane wasn't surprised. Olivia was an evil harlot. The only thing she knew about life was how to suck it from someone else's soul. Titling her head to the right, Jane offered a little smile and an, "Oh?" She was shooting for a look of innocent curiosity—he wasn't ready to know the hard truths.

"No, we definitely see things differently." Trip shook his head slowly as if he was piecing the puzzle together. "As a matter of fact, that's what we're fighting about."

"About life?"

"Sort of. You see, this summer, I spent a couple of weeks fishing with my brothers, and I realized: both of them are happy. I mean really happy. They love their wives, love their jobs. I mean if you gave them a magic wand, they'd change nothing. They've got it all. It got me thinking, am I happy? Well, I'm not unhappy, but I have to admit, to myself at least, that I'm not…"

"Excited?"

"Yes. Excited. Nothing in my life makes me eager to start a day."

"And you want that?"

"Yeah, so I quit my job and started a new one. The pay's half, I'll have to be totally retrained, and it involves a lot of overseas travel."

Trip leaned against the wall, so close his arm brushed against hers. She shoved her hands in her tunic pockets and willed herself not to pass out. All of this was almost too much for her hopeful heart to handle. She *knew* they shared a connection, and now...here he was...pouring his heart out to her, because she understood him. And no one else did. It took all of her might to say without an eager quiver in her voice, "These changes? They will make you happy?"

"I think so. I mean I haven't felt this good in years, you know? You'd think me being happy would make Olivia happy, but she's furious. Told me if I go through with *my insanity*, it's over."

"Oh." Jane tried to hide the joy that bubbled through her. "So what will you do?"

"I'm sticking with my plan. And Olivia will either adjust or move on."

Jane nodded as her mind sang—m*ove on, move on...to me!*

Trip paced the hall. "It's not just Liv. My decision has everyone pissed at me, but I can't help how I feel. It's *my* life, right? I have the right to be in control of it."

"Yes!" Jane bounced on her heels. "You must...always follow your dreams."

"Yeah! I refuse to quit living before I've ever even started. I don't have to explain to people...it's not like I have kids or a wife or..." He slapped his hand to his forehead and groaned.

"Worried about Ms. Higgins?" Jane offered. "I'm sure, eventually, that she'll come to understand." *Or not. Hopefully the latter.*

"No, not her. It's Eve. Damn." He tugged at his floppy blond hair. "How the hell could I have forgotten about Eve?"

"Oh, I see," Jane answered, her heart sinking to her toes.

Chapter 2

Her spirits sagged as she looked Trip over more critically. Her brows knitted together as she tried to imagine him as a womanizer. He didn't seem the type, but honestly, she had no record for comparison. She'd never, in her twenty-three years, been on a date. As a matter of fact, with the exception of the one in front of her, no man ever made her want to take the time. She picked at the chipped plum paint on her thumb nail. "So, you have another girlfriend?"

Trip's look of surprise by the question was instantly replaced with a grimace. "No. Not a girlfriend. Eve's my new puppy."

Jane had to stifle a happy dance, but she couldn't control the grin that spread from one ear to the other. "Ahh, you have a puppy?"

"Yeah, and I was going to ask Olivia to dog sit, but she took the first part of the news so badly, she'd probably take my head off if I asked her for a favor. But then I guess I have to ask her, I don't really have any other…"

"Leave her with that witch? The poor creature." The words tumbled from her mouth and only stopped when she clasped a hand over her lips.

Trip's laugh came like rapid fire.

Jane felt the heat of humiliation from head to toe. She had been doing so well, playing the game of appearing neutral.

Trip gave her shoulder a squeeze. "Oh, hell, don't look guilty, she deserved that."

"I still shouldn't…."

"Don't worry about it. You're just being honest. I admire that."

Jane nodded, removing the hand that covered her lips, but her eyes remained wide.

Trip studied the ceiling a moment before speaking. His words didn't really seem to be directed at Jane; it was more like he was thinking aloud. "I hadn't planned on getting a dog, but one day I left for work and there was this little dog rooting through my trash. It was like she came out of nowhere. I gave her the sandwich from my lunch and left her sleeping on my porch. When I came home, she was still there waiting for me."

"Aha…Eve."

"Exactly," Trip said. "And just like the original Eve, she is causing complications. I don't know what to do with her while I'm gone. I'd ask one of my brothers, but they live out of state, and there's no time. My mother's definitely *not* a dog person. I could call a kennel, but she's so small."

"I could keep her, if you trust me," Jane asked, her voice timid, with just a touch of anxious quiver.

"I couldn't ask you to do that," Trip answered with a shake of his head.

"Really, it's no problem. It's what I do; I help people…here in the building. I mean I clean and get laundry; sometimes even groceries. It's really no big deal."

"But it's a pup, not a load of laundry. Pups can be a lot of work."

Jane waved off his concern. "I know dogs. I have a little white poodle dog named Frosty. I'm sure he'd love the company."

Trip's eyes lit up. "You would seriously do this for me?" He barely waited for Jane to finish nodding her head before he added, "I'd be forever grateful, and I promise I'll pay you."

"No, really. We are now friends, no?"

"But it's too much. This is definitely a family-level inconvenience I'm asking for. I'll be gone three months."

"Uh, well, I…I really don't mind. I love puppies. Can you bring her by before you leave?"

"Well, she's in my car, in the parking garage."

"Oh, poor puppy!"

It was Trip's turn to flush and look embarrassed. "She's not been there long. I planned on bringing her up to L—"

Jane grabbed his arm to interrupt him. She didn't want to hear the name *Livia* on his lips again. She was Olivia. Livia was a sweet person's name…or a nickname given to a chum…and Jane didn't want her to be either. "I trust she is fine. Can I meet her?"

"Yeah, I have to leave tonight. If that's okay?"

Jane nodded. "Of course!"

"Man. Really?"

Jane nodded.

"Thank you." He grabbed her hand and shook it. "You don't know how much this helps me. And I mean it, I'll pay you. Eve's cute and all, but I know how much work she is."

"I will enjoy it," Jane assured. He kept hold of her hand, which made her heart beat quicker. And she would see him again! At least once, when he picked up the dog. Jane bit her lip to subdue a goofy smile. Her wild imagination raced as fantasies spun like cobwebs filling her eager brain. They would talk and laugh over stories about the dog. He would see how right they were for each other and see what a bitch Olivia was in comparison to her sweet self, and before she knew it, he would kiss her. A timid kiss, but one filled with passion. He would tell her how lucky he was to fall in love with her. Jane's meanderings were interrupted when the hand he had latched onto was jerked toward the elevator. Her body followed.

As the doors opened, he dropped her hand and made the gentlemanly offer of letting her in the car first. The ride to the first floor was quiet. Jane pressed her body against the cool wall and wondered what it would be like if touching him was a natural condition, rather than a freak moment of emotion. She wanted that. She wanted to reach out and fix the piece of hair that was left sticking up after all his worrying.

But she couldn't.

He wasn't hers.

As the doors opened, he led her through the garage, telling her about his dog as he walked. How he called her Eve because she came out of nowhere.

"And I took her to the vet, but she'll have to go back for the rest of her immunizations." Trip's pace slowed. "I never thought of that." He seemed to lose some of his enthusiasm.

"If you have her record, I could take her to Frosty's doctor. He is close by."

Trip nodded. "Yeah, I brought it. And I mean it about the money. You won't have to pay for anything. I really appreciate this. I've only had her a week, but she gets under your skin, you know?"

Jane nodded and felt her heart lurch. She completely understood loving someone you barely knew.

He unlocked his car door. Jane smiled at the Subaru sitting among all the Mercedes in the lot. Trip really did have his own humble style. As he pulled the door open, a wagging, whining bundle of fur wiggled its way from under a blanket. Trip scooped her up and turned her to Jane. She was a Beagle still young enough to have her puppy pot belly. From her floppy black ears to her black-tipped tail, Eve was adorable. No wonder Trip rescued her without hesitation.

Heck, Jane was already deep in puppy love at first sight.

Eve licked Trip's cheek as he held her against his shoulder and scratched her ears. Looking down into the pup's big brown eyes, he said, "Now, Eve, this is Jane. She's going to take good care of you. What do you think of that?"

The dog whined and kept wagging her tail.

Jane reached out and scratched the dog's chest. "Hi there." Trip handed her over. Jane laughed when she, too, was bombarded with puppy kisses. Jane lifted her face out of range. Her laughter rang out in the hollow garage as Eve tried even harder to give her kisses. "She's the most affectionate pup I ever met."

Trip smiled as his eyes lingered on Jane for a moment. He shifted his weight and crossed his arms over his chest, leaning against his car. "She definitely likes you."

"Either that or I taste good." Jane kissed the top of the dog's head and hugged her a little closer. Trip stared at her a moment longer, then cleared his throat. Jane talked to the pup in purring tones.

Trip shifted again and rubbed the back of his neck. Clearing his throat, he said, "I, uh, really can't thank you enough."

Eve continued to lick at Jane's chin. Jane had to strain her neck to avoid getting French kissed by the pooch. "She is so sweet. I think we will be good friends."

"I think I may get jealous."

"Oh, silly, she will still love you. I promise." Jane giggled and tucked the pup against her body with her tail under her arm. Eve whined and wiggled, looking at her temporary mistress.

Trip rubbed his jaw and mumbled, "Wasn't her liking you that I was jealous of."

"Pardon?" Jane asked, unable to make out his words.

Trip's cheeks flushed and his attempt at replacing his original comment came with a bit of a stutter. "I said you must be sweet?"

His comments filtered into her mind slowly, almost escaping cognition. As they made sense to her, she couldn't help but let out a little squeal. "Oh, you are a sugar talker, Trip Coulter."

"Sorry. That was…." Trip ran a nervous hand through his hair.

Jane bounced on her heels. She wasn't an expert, but she was pretty sure he was flirting with her, and she definitely wanted him to know it was fine with her. She added quickly, "No. Don't feel bad. You can sugar talk me; I don't mind."

"Sweet talk," Trip said as he stared down at Jane. A quiet study of each other passed between them. Trip broke the silence with a quiet declaration. "Scratch that. Sugar talk is better. Much more you."

"Sweet talk, yes, sweet talk. I am not so smart about your phrases, but I like them. They are fun. I like to learn them, but mess them up so much." *Especially when you're around and my brain is slow*, she thought.

"You're actually, very good. Very impressive."

"Why, thank you. And thank you for letting me watch your puppy."

"I'd be in a major bind without your help. And I hate to have to run off, but I have to catch my flight," he said, looking at his watch, "son of a bitch…in two hours. I didn't realize how late it was. I better get going."

"I hope this job is good for you."

Trip's face softened. "I think it will. Thank you, Jane. I really am in your debt."

Jane nuzzled the pup against her cheek. She avoided looking at him. She feared her eyes would betray her hope that he would repay the debt with his heart. That was all she wanted from him. She peeked up at him as he shook his head. Before she could wonder what he was thinking, he took two steps closer and cradled her face in his hands. His thumb stroked her cheek. "You really are something else…. I have to do this…." Taking a deep breath, the pressure of his hands increased ever so slightly as he pulled her closer. Before she could imagine what he planned, he landed a quick kiss, smack on her lips. Jane experienced a flutter that left her warm and slightly weak in the legs and mind.

That was the most tantalizing peck she'd ever dreamed of.

He let go of her and stepped away. "For good luck."

Jane nodded, swallowed hard, and prayed her rubbery knees could hold up the rest of her.

Trip kept moving backward toward his car. "Wow, you have the prettiest eyes. I can't believe I never noticed them before today."

"I, uh." Jane didn't know what to say. Her cheeks felt hot as fire. She took a deep breath and tried to keep from passing out.

Trip stopped, hand suspended above his door handle. "Oh, money. He pulled out his wallet and handed Jane a card. "Here. This is my debit card."

Jane pushed his hand away. "No, no. You can't do that."

"It's the only thing I can do. You'll need money for the vet, and for food. I can't even guess how much it'll cost. You take it." He wrote on a scrap of paper. "This is my pin and my email. Maybe you could send me updates on Eve? Maybe I could even talk you into sending me pictures?"

"Of course. But to give me this?" Jan held out the debit card.

"I trust you. Besides, even if you cleaned me out, you'll only get what's in my bank account. And that kiss was worth that."

Jane shook her head. "Are you always this crazy, Trip

Coulter?"

Trip laughed. The sound echoed. "No, never. But I gotta tell ya, I feel like my life is on the verge of something really good."

"I think you are too." Jane eagerly agreed.

He tapped the tip of her nose with his index finger. "You seem to be the only one who believes in me. And you don't even know me."

Jane flushed as her heart tripped over itself. "I just think everyone's dreams should come true."

"Thank you, Jane. You are the sweetest."

As compulsively as a child who gets a gift of a lifetime, Trip grabbed her and gave her a hug, squeezing her body into his. Jane thought she might pass out from the constriction his grip put on her lungs and the dizzy feeling hope sent to her head. "I hate to go. I feel like I could talk to you all night, but I have to catch that plane. I guess I'll see you in three months?"

She nodded silently, her euphoria dampening with the reality— he was leaving.

"You will email, right?" he asked.

"Of course," Jane promised.

Jane watched dumbstruck and barely able to manage even the little wave her hand somehow produced as he climbed into his car and drove away. She took her first breath as his tail lights disappeared around the corner of the garage.

She knew it! He did long for adventure! She was right about everything. Her dreams were vindicated. But, she wouldn't tell him that right now. He'd think she bypassed crazy and headed straight for Looney Town.

She'd wait and tell him all about it on their honeymoon.

Chapter 3

She didn't walk home; she floated. Worries can't bother a brain cluttered with whimsy and musings. And as of today…none of it was just a day dream. It was reality. She had the squirming, affectionate pup to prove she was wide awake. She hadn't just talked to Mr. Perfect, AKA, Trip Coulter…she knew his name and the feel of his kiss on her lips.

It was a fact…he kissed her! The dreamiest guy in the world…kissed her.

Nothing could pop her happy bubble…not even the whole getting back to work thing. This day could hold no blemish. None whatsoever could be imagined…until she stepped off the elevator and remembered Sasha.

She forgot to ask her roommate, yet again, if she could bring home a dog. Sasha's uncle owned the apartments and allowed them to stay rent free in exchange for caring for the building and its occupants. Were it not for Sasha, Jane would be homeless, or worse. She bit her lip and nudged the wooden door open a bit, poking her head inside. Silence. She breathed a sigh of relief. Sasha wasn't home.

The tiny apartment was in the basement, wedged between the laundry and boiler room. It had the basics: a kitchenette the size of a small walk-in closet, a living room that fit a sofa and small chair, and two cubby-hole bedrooms joined by a shared bathroom.

Kissing the pup's head, she set her on the couch, then stripped off her shoes and her tunic. Back aching from the heavy bags of laundry, she plopped down on the couch, sinking deep into the sagging cushions. Pulling Eve onto her lap, she figured she would rest a minute before heading to the last floor. Frosty appeared, nosing his way onto her legs as he sniffed and checked out their new guest. Jane scratched each dog behind an ear.

Guilt over the breach of roommate courtesy dissolved with the relaxed feel of her body as she closed her eyes and remembered the feel of Trip's mouth on hers. Yesterday, she wondered if she'd ever speak to him…ever in her life. And today? She not only talked to him, she kissed him. What a precious moment…his body was so warm…lips sweet, with a hint of peppermint. A sigh escaped her and seemed to echo in the empty room.

Sasha found Jane with her sappy smile glued to her face, so engrossed in her thoughts, Jane didn't hear the door open and close. Sasha stood in front of her, hands on her hips, face as grim as a prison warden's, her voice harsh, her accent thicker than Jane's. "Oh my god. Another dog?"

Her eyes popped open, and she nearly let out a scream. Tucking Eve under her arm for protection, she mumbled, "I'm just dog sitting."

"For a resident?"

"Well, sort of."

Sasha's green eyes narrowed. She pulled her auburn hair out of its ponytail and rubbed her scalp. Sasha exhaled hard. "I hope they pay well."

"Oh, yes, he said he'd pay me."

"How much?"

"We didn't have time to discuss that, but I'm sure he'll be fair."

"For God's sake. You took on the responsibility of someone's dog for nothing?"

Well, not nothing, Jane thought. *For a kiss…and the opportunity to see him again.* She gave Sasha a weak smile.

Sasha frowned down at her and studied Jane's face for a moment. "You're as simple as a child. Does nothing I teach you open your eyes?"

Jane shrugged.

"This is pointless," Sasha said with a sigh. "My only promise was to keep you alive, not make you smart. Why didn't he put it in the pound?"

"Sash," Jane scolded. "That's mean."

"Then I am mean. And you need to learn to be mean. Your life may depend on it. What if you don't always have me? You're safe now, but what will you do if we get out of this…situation…and you can be on your own? This world will eat you alive."

"I'll be fine. You just see the world as bad because you…."

Sasha shot her a glare. "Stupid girl. You grew up sheltered and spoiled; did that save you from reality?"

Jane shook her head. Sasha resumed, "So, don't assume being an orphan changed me. This world has little justice, little mercy. Everyone's out for themselves." Sasha walked to the bar that separated the living room from the kitchen and picked up the mail, blindly flipping past envelope after envelope as she continued her lecture. "You must protect yourself, Jane. Life's to be endured, not enjoyed." Sasha tossed the letters on the counter and turned to Jane. "Your father ruined you with a soft, English mother. He should have stuck with a good Russian woman, and his life would have been easier."

Jane nodded, hardly able to argue the rightness of Sasha's theory. It was true. Her mother brought ruin to her father. She bit her lip and nodded, stiffly pulling the dogs closer for some comfort.

Sasha gave Jane a disgusted look and headed for the bathroom. She left the door open as she pulled out her make-up and began applying eye shadow. Jane followed, setting Eve on the floor by Frosty. She stood in the doorway and watched Sasha transform from beautiful to glamorous.

"Where are you going?" Jane asked, her curiosity wiping out all the guilt from Sasha's scolding.

"Out."

"A date?"

"Mmm, hmm," Sasha said as she blended the black eyeliner into the smoky gray shadow.

Sasha awed her. She was stunning. Hollywood glamorous from

the golden age. As for Jane, she was always in need of a make-up touch-up. Or her hair was either limp or would fly away. Sasha's behaved. *It probably feared her,* Jane thought with a grin.

"So, who is the lucky guy you're getting all dressed up for?"

"A fifty-year-old senator with a wallet as fat as his belly."

"That's mean…and sad." Jane frowned. "You're so pretty and intelligent, you could have any man."

"I've done my homework. This man is perfect. High profile Washington urchin. Happily married, well connected. I'm sure he'll be more than generous."

"How could he be happily married and dating you?"

Sasha's glare made Jane blush

Jane asked, "It's just that if he is happily married…."

"All right, so he's comfortably married and is looking for discreet entertainment."

"Don't you ever want to fall in love?"

"No." She wiped excess mascara on a piece of tissue as she explained, "Love is weakness. People in love do stupid things, because it mushes up the head. And you remember what your father always says?"

"A fish rots from the head," Jane answered, laying her head against the doorframe and rolling her eyes.

"And do you know what that means?"

Jane nodded, but Sasha explained anyhow, "Separate rational thought from emotion. Simple as that."

"But love can…."

"Listen," Sasha said as she twisted her hair and pinned it to the back of her head, "women make all the sacrifice, they give up everything to be shit on in the end. Take fatty. I bet his wife has spent her whole life building his family and his home… backing him as he climbed the ladder, and what does she get in return?"

Jane remained silent.

Sasha pulled a sparkling tennis bracelet from a box in the drawer and slipped it onto her slender wrist. "The bastard buys me diamonds. That's who men are. Here, England, home…they're all the same." She bent over to grab her clutch purse from the cluttered floor. Eve was chewing on its edge. Sasha gently pried it out of the dog's mouth. She shot Jane another scowl as she asked, "So, how long are we saddled with the animal?"

"Three months."

"What the hell? Where the hell did they go?"

"He never really said," Jane answered with a grimace and a blush.

"He?"

"Yes, it was a man." Jane dropped her head in attempt to hide the two large pink splotches on her pale cheeks.

"What man?"

"His name is Trip."

"No one in the building is named Trip."

"He doesn't actually live in the building. He dates the girl on four."

"Which girl on four?"

"The lawyer."

"Olivia?" Sasha said the name like Jane had told her she added a barracuda to the goldfish tank.

Jane nodded.

"Olivia?" Sasha repeated a little louder.

"Yeah." Jane turned redder. "So?"

"So, she will whip your ass. There are bitches in this world and there are beasts, and she is definitely the beast of bitches."

"Well, I'm not dating him. I'm just watching his dog."

"So why the stupid grin?"

Jane shrugged.

"Holy shit, Jane. You are truly unbelievable. She has him, and you have the dog." Sasha sighed. "Look, this man you get all pink checked over—he'll marry the bitch on the fourth floor. She has status and culture and money. She will be the picture perfect wife and you'll be the tramp cleaning shit for him."

Sasha doused Jane's good spirits with that shot of realism. Jane's shoulders sagged.

"Ah, hell. Don't."

"Don't what?"

"Look that way. Sad as the damn dog. I don't mean to hurt you. But you must be taught to think." She kissed Jane's cheek and tweaked her ear like she was a child. "Don't get involved with men who have women. It's always a heartbreak. Or scandal. And you have more to lose than most, no?"

Jane nodded and picked at her thumbnail.

"You look like shit." Sasha's tone was gentler. "Your eyes are almost black. Tough night again?"

"Yes. It was the dream again. Maybe I should see a doctor? You know, a, ah psychiatrist? To see why I keep having the dream?"

"It's stress. Drink a shot of vodka before you go to bed. That'll help."

"I tried it already. I'm beginning to think it's something more than just stress." She followed Sasha to the closet as Sasha slipped her feet into a pair of high heels. "I think, in my dream, I'm trapped in a coffin, getting buried alive. And I wonder if that could be, what do you call it? A symbol maybe. A forgotten memory?"

Sasha cursed in Russian and broke a nail as she got her thumb stuck in her shoe's strap. "Nonsense. This is nonsense. Next you will think you are having a dream of future."

Jane's eyes opened wide. "I hadn't thought of that."

"Oh, hell." Sasha rolled her eyes and pulled her long, curvy body erect. "It is a dream. You constantly worrying, trying to figure it out is what's causing you to have it over and over again."

Jane nodded slowly. Sasha was probably right.

"And get over the idea of talking to anyone. Much too dangerous."

Jane bit her cheek and nodded her agreement, though she didn't look completely convinced. Sasha stood in the doorway a moment as if she had something she wanted to say, but instead, she bent down and scooped Eve off the floor and looked her in the eye and warned, "Shit in my shoe like the other mutt and I'll make a pair of gloves out of you." She handed the pup to Jane, turned, and headed toward the door shaking her head. "Three months." Sasha turned at the door and said to Jane, "Oh, and Eddie asked if you would come work the desk for him...again.... I told him probably...you're a sucker fool."

*****

"Miss Jane," Eddie cooed. "Aren't you a lovely sight for sore eyes?"

"No butter-up needed, Eddie. Go on home."

Eddie rubbed his curly blond locks. He looked more like a California surfer than the apartment concierge. The look of leisurely slacker was deceiving. Eddie ran the front desk like a master. The residents loved him. He knew everyone in the building, and the names of their children, grandchildren, and probably where they all worked. Heck, he probably knew everybody's favorite food delivery orders. Forrester Apartments had all the luxuries of home and a five-star hotel bundled into one high-rent package, and Eddie was part of that package.

"Ah, Miss Jane. I'd thought you'd be in a glorious mood today…seeing as how you got the guy and all."

Jane's mouth dropped open.

Eddie winked. "Don't worry. Secret's safe with me."

"How did you..?"

"Brian, in security. Saw you two on the garage camera feed. Bow chicka wow wow."

She gave him a shoulder shove. "Stop it!" She spoke to him like she would an annoying brother. "I was doing him a favor," she said as she joined him behind the long desk.

"I'd say that's some favor," Eddie whistled. "Woo hoo. Probably lit the poor little nerd…."

"He's not a nerd!" Jane gave him another shove.

Eddie laughed as he gathered his coat and back pack. "He's a total nerd. But I like him. He's a cool guy and deserves a helluva lot nicer gal than that bitch he's dating. Man, she's a piece of work. Fine ass, but…."

"Go, Eddie. I don't want to talk of her. Not today."

He slapped a big, wet kiss on her cheek. "Thank you, sweetness. And Jen thanks you. She hates walking to the strip club by herself."

Jane rolled her eyes and waved him off. Jen was a waitress, but

27

Eddie liked telling people he was dating a stripper. Made the men go ooh and the ladies go eww and somehow that entertained Eddie.

He paused at the heavy glass doors and said, "Seriously, Jane. You're a great catch. Just make him see it. I speak truth, eh, Mrs. Little?"

Jane turned and smiled at the approaching elderly woman. Mrs. Little gave Eddie an affectionate smile. "You're as wise as you are handsome, Edward."

"And Mr. Little is lucky I despise home wreckers. You, Mrs. Little, know the way to a man's heart." Eddie patted his chest and then tipped them a two finger salute as he backed out into the cold.

Mrs. Little waved him off with a shake of her gray head. Jane turned her attention to the elderly lady at the front desk. Inez Little was as quiet as her husband was chatty; as thin as he was round.

Jane smiled. "Can I help you, Mrs. Little?"

"Inez. And yes, my washer won't drain, so I need to put in a work order with the super and perhaps sign up for laundry service until it's fixed."

"Of course." Jane pulled papers out of filing cabinets and laid them on the counter. "George should be in tomorrow, so why don't we see what he has to say before charging you for laundry?" Jane jotted some numbers on a piece of paper and placed it on top of the work order. "That's the code for the washer in the basement. The elevator won't go to that floor without a key, but you just tell Eddie to hit the override button from the desk if I'm not around."

"Why, thank you, Jane." Inez folded the paper neatly and tucked it in her purse. "You know, Eddie is right. You will make some lucky man perfectly ecstatic."

"Yeah, well…the one I like…sort of has a girlfriend."

Inez chuckled as she slid the purse over her shoulder. "All's fair in love and war, dear." A slow smile spread across Inez's face. "As a matter of fact, when I first met Henry, he was dating my neighbor. But all she had was big knockers, no brains. They weren't meant to be. So, when he went off to fight in the war, I," she said as she looked over her shoulder before leaning in closer and whispering, "took her letters to him out of the mailbox and burned them. And sent him letters of my own. By the time he came home, he was as hooked on me as a pup on milk."

"Why, Mrs. Little…that is…."

Inez patted Jane's hand as she pulled back. "Love. Sixty years…seven children…and twenty-three grandchildren. I don't see a thing wrong with nudging fate in the right direction."

Was she joking? Or was sweet Inez really that bold and devious? Jane didn't have time to think the thought through as a throat cleared to her left.

Jane turned to find Olivia tapping pink nails on the front desk. "I found my shirt in the hall. The public hall. You evidently dropped it. If you lost my shorts…you will pay for them. I don't pay two thousand dollars a month for you to scatter my belongings like some sloppy vulture. If you could ever keep your damned eyes off my boyfriend long enough to get your job done, maybe you could at least half-ass it. My God, it's not rocket science."

With that, she left. She didn't wait to hear Jane mumble an apology or assure her the shorts, if lost, would be replaced. Jane's cheeks blazed, and she felt sick to her stomach. She had been so happy, but reality slowly crept in…. Olivia was as evil as she was perfect. How could she compete? And seriously, was she so totally obvious in her crush on Trip that *everybody* in the building knew about it?

Inez gave her a wink. "Breaking them up would be doing him a favor, don't you think?"

Chapter 4

Jane unwrapped another chocolate and popped it in her mouth. She tucked her blanket tighter around her as she chewed. Sasha sat cross-legged beside her on the couch. Jane offered her a chocolate, so Sasha took the bag and tossed it on the coffee table.

"What are you sulking about?" Sasha asked.

Jane frowned. "I'm not sulking."

Crossing her arms over her chest, Sasha asked, "Really?"

"Really," she said with a sigh. Of course she was sulking. She cleaned Olivia's apartment today and happened to read an email from Olivia to Trip that was so sickeningly sweet and apologetic for being a bitch. Now they would get back together, or more accurately, would stay together. Dammit, Sasha was right—all she'd ever have was the dog.

Jane dropped her head against the back of the couch. "I can't beat her."

"Beat who?"

"The bitch on four. She is perfect, and I am plain and ugly."

"Seriously?"

Jane nodded.

Sasha gave her a leg a slap. "You realize, your mother, aside from being an evil, cheating bitch…was a raging beauty?"

Jane shrugged.

"And you look just like her."

"I look similar."

"No," Sasha said slowly, "just like her. Only difference is you are softer, more friendly looking."

Jane laughed. "What the hell does that mean?"

"It means Tracy Dugan knew how to be stunning; she wielded her beauty like a weapon. Men noticed because she knew she had it."

"Like you?" Jane lifted her head and looked across at Sasha.

"I am nothing like your mother." Sasha lit a cigarette and flashed her a glare.

"But you know how to be stunning."

Sasha rolled her eyes. "Thanks, I think."

"So, I want to be like that."

"No, you don't. You want to be like you. You are sweet and beautiful in a different way."

Jane grabbed the candy off the table and pulled out another piece. "I want to be stunning and get the man."

"You like him that much, hmm?"

Jane nodded as she freed a candy and popped it in her mouth. Her words were a little garbled by the chewy caramel. "I like him way more than I should. I barely know him, yet I am more depressed knowing I lost him than I was at my own mum's funeral. How sad am I?"

Sasha took the bag of candy once again, but this time secured it on her lap. "Tracy Dugan was never a mother. You're as motherless as I am…maybe even worse. Hell, at least I can pretend my mother abandoned me because she had no choice; you just have to accept that your mother is a cow."

"See? That should anger me. You're talking of my dead mum and all I can think is, I agree. Good God, Sasha, do I have a heart?"

Sasha leaned over and grabbed the ashtray from the table. "You have a heart…too big a heart. Just like Viktor. Your father could have eliminated his problems, but he didn't. He tried to live around them. He had all the power…. He should have been respected."

"Before everything happened, Nikki told me Poppa had his mother and my mother killed."

"Bernadette?" Sasha looked surprised. She tapped the ashes from her cigarette. "Why would Viktor kill Bernadette?"

"To marry my mum."

Sasha shook her head. "No, he didn't kill Bernadette, and he didn't kill Tracy either. I thought he should, but he refused."

"Sasha." Jane looked dumbstruck. "I can't believe you said that. You told Poppa to kill my mother?"

Sasha nodded, her face emotionless. "But I knew he never would, no matter that she humiliated him in the worst way. He lost respect and power because of her."

"But to kill her? Sasha that's awful."

Sasha flashed her a broad grin and smashed her cigarette in the ashtray. "Feel better? I proved you have a heart, just like Viktor."

Jane threw her ball of chocolate wrappers at Sasha. "You are bad to tease me. I thought you were serious."

Sasha shrugged. "Viktor couldn't kill either. He was a good man, and you are like him, not her."

Jane felt a swell of pride at the thought of being more her father's child than her mother's. She might look like her mother, but she had the heart of her burly father. "I miss him so much," Jane admitted, the candy in her mouth suddenly tasting like chewy saw dust. Her poor Poppa was gone. Betrayed by the people he thought he could trust, taken from this life by the hand of his best friend.

It wasn't right, but at least she avenged him.

"Look Jane, you can't sit around and pout over lost men…even lost fathers. We escaped and it's up to us to build a new life. We sure as hell don't whine or overdose on chocolate." She wrapped the bag tight and pointed with it as she spoke. "You're a Sarkhov; you know what that means?"

"It means I am the daughter of a man who built an empire from nothing. Who feared no one."

"Exactly!"

"Hmm…." Jane took a deep breath. "You're right. A Sarkhov would fight for what she wanted."

"Always."

"And all is fair in war and love?"

"Umm…sure." Sasha's words held less conviction, and she added a hesitant "Why?"

33

"I have an idea…. Come on." Jane grabbed Sasha's hand and dragged her from the apartment.

"What are you doing?"

"Fighting." Jane rode the elevator to the fourth floor and marched right to the bitch's door; Sasha followed slowly behind her.

"Have you completely and totally lost your damned mind?"

"She's not home." Jane promised as she turned the master key in the lock. "Eddie told me this morning she was going to be gone all week at some policy thing or something."

"And if Eddie's wrong? We go to jail?" Sasha actually sounded squeaky. Since when did a little breaking and entering make her so edgy?

"Eddie knows everything. Besides, all you have to do is watch the door." Jane moved through the apartment, straight to the glass and chrome desk, and pressed the power button on Olivia's computer.

"If you're so sure…why am I watching the door?"

"Variables."

"Variables?"

"Yes, things that I'm not counting on."

"Dear God. You have lost your mind. I only wanted you to stop pouting and eating enough chocolate to kill yourself. Not do this. This is completely insane."

"Turn-around is fair play." Jane's fingers flew over the keyboard. "That bitch has humiliated me for the last time, Sasha. I am a Sarkhov, no?"

"Yes, but…"

"No buts. Poppa would be ashamed that I let her walk all over me. Time and time again. He would expect me to get revenge."

"True. But this? What are you doing?"

"I spent a little time last night doing some artwork. Then it was just for fun, because I didn't have the guts to do anything with it. Now I know exactly what to do. It's like I have been given the whole plan, as if fate wants me to intervene."

Sasha abandoned her post at the door and leaned over Jane's

shoulder to view the screen. Jane had picture after picture of Olivia in bars with men. Sasha took a sharp breath. "How did you get those?"

"I made them," Jane sounded as gleeful as a four-year-old with a new finger painting.

"You what?"

"I made them. With the proper Photoshop program, everyone is an artist! And as soon as I have her password...which is...yep...legalbeauty1234."

"How the hell?"

"I'm a genius." Jane opened a drawer and held up a Betty Boop notebook. "And she was dumb enough to write down all her passwords. And hid it..."

"...in her desk drawer," Sasha finished Jane's statement.

"Exactly." Jane put the book back on the desk. "Now, to post to Facebook. Tag Mr. Coulter. And hmm," Jane said as she clicked the mouse and made her changes, "I think I should change the bitch's relationship status. Shazaam!" She closed the program. "Now, just for fun...." a few more strokes of the keys, "...we have a virus ready to crash her hard drive. As soon as she clicks on the picture, it will link her to a worm that will begin threading its evil way into her computer memory until the whole thing is locked up."

"I didn't realize you were so mean. I'm impressed."

"Hah! I might have failed algebra...and geography...and literature, but I got an A in programming."

Sasha straightened. "Okay, Ms. Gates, you can screw everything up, but can anyone track it back to being done from her own computer, while she wasn't home?"

"Nope. Virus will wipe everything"

Jane flipped through the book until she found the email account address and password. "Now, I think Miss Olivia doesn't feel like sending Trip mail."

"How are you...?"

"Reset email passwords and security questions. Won't stop her for long, but it will slow her down." Jane powered down the computer and stood. "I'm done being gum on her shoe."

"And it's all untraceable? You don't think she would suspect you first?"

"She'd never think me smart enough." Jane tucked the notebook away. "I am the stupid Russian cleaning girl with a hopeless crush on her boyfriend. To her I'm a joke, but I am not a joke. She will never know it was me, but I will know. I didn't let her disrespect me...over and over...and get away with it."

They walked to the door together, peaked around the edge and then slipped out of the apartment. She whispered more to herself than to Sasha, "We'll see who laughs loudest in the end."

*****

The first three months flew by. Jane passed the time emailing and skyping Trip...and diligently monitoring Olivia's email account from the safety of her own laptop. It took Olivia three days to get her password back under her control, but in those three days, Jane hit the jackpot. She intercepted Trip's email to Olivia with the change in his email address. Olivia, or more specifically Jane posing as Olivia, emailed him that she had the change and thank you. Then Jane deleted, feeling quite smug and happy at the thought of Olivia sending message after message to Trip's old address. Jane nearly bit her lips till they bled when she overheard Olivia tell someone on the phone that she was done sending messages to Trip.... He never answered, so the hell with him.

Jane never got to hear what she thought about her new Facebook photos. The suspense almost killed her, but satisfaction kept her going. She was content in her knowledge that Trip was also equally as frustrated with Olivia. After three of his messages went unanswered, he sent her a scathing "go to hell bitch" message. Well, that's what the message said if a girl knew how to read between the lines. His was more like: *sorry you have to take this so personally, but I think we are headed in two different directions and should just be friends.*

Let's be friends. The relationship kiss of death. Even a stupid Russian cleaning girl knew that.

But after that high, came the low. A week clicked by without contact. Then month four passed in silence and she wondered if her tech tampering and relationship tinkering had been exposed. Olivia never attacked her, so evidently not. Month five rolled around and she wondered if she understood the timeline correctly. Maybe he meant three years? As month six started, she almost convinced herself that he had forgotten all about her and poor little Eve. A rational person would give up on him, but not Jane. She might have been losing hope, but she never gave up. She still sent him an email every single day.

She had nothing to lose, everything to gain by bugging him.

Unless he was laughing at her; mocking her for her incessant presence in his inbox. She shook the thought off. Trip would never do that. Besides, she read his last email at least a million times. It was friendly, even a little flirty. She even lowered herself to asking Sasha to read it and assure her he didn't sound like he was bored with her.

No, he was probably busy with work…. He did say it was getting more intense. A message was coming any minute; she knew it—knew it so well hitting refresh on her email was her newest hobby.

Tying a knot in the bag of trash, she hauled it out into the back alley. This life of hers was more and more tedious with each passing day. Clean all morning for ungrateful people; spend afternoons at the front desk or in the laundry room or hauling garbage to the dumpster. She tossed it in and let the lid down with a crash. The boom it created was strangely satisfying.

It wasn't fair. She was the daughter of Viktor Sarkhov, a powerful man who ran a multi-million dollar business. All the stress and worry from the last few months made her think more and more of her old life and how different it was from her new one. She was raised to be a fighter, not a sad little mouse who hid behind a green tunic and a scrub brush. She was pathetic. A coward. *"Trus."* She spat the word in Russian and gave the dumpster a kick. As her foot made contact with steel, she let out a yelp. The pain infuriated her, so she kicked it again. A flurry of Russian curses rolled from her lips as fluently as the Bratva she learned them from.

She put her foot to the ground gingerly and felt the pain streak up her leg like lightning.

"Anyone with a lick of sense would've stopped after the first kick."

Her eyes were greeted by a handsome guy with short buzzed hair and shoulders as broad as a broom stick. Jane was about to tell him where he could shove his words when she recognized the eyes.

It was Trip. He came back after all.

Chapter 5

"Trip?" Jane balanced herself on one foot, the other she propped on her toes.

Trip smiled, kneeling down, he touched her ankle, gently pressing into the sinew. He moved carefully down until his thumbs pressed into the sore spot on her foot. Jane yelped and pulled her foot back.

"It's not your ankle, maybe you stoved your big toe." He sighed and looked up at her with a frown. "And here I was going to ask you to go dancing."

Her heart sank. She couldn't hide her disappointment. What horrific luck! Every day for the last six months, six whole stinking months, she had dressed with absolute care—which was totally unlike her. She put on her make-up and painstakingly did her hair, thinking she'd look pretty when he returned. And what did that get her?

Zero. Zip. Nada.

Now, here she stood. Hair a mess, make-up forgotten, self-inflicted banged up foot throbbing. She came to the only logical conclusion: God hated her. The universe hated her. Nothing in her life was ever fair. Ridiculous tears stung her eyes. Spewing more curses in her native tongue, she jerked her foot out of his hand. She planted it on the ground ignoring the volts of pain that shot up her leg. Crossing her arms over her chest, she stuck her chin in the air. She looked as defiant as an impetuous child.

Trip stood and said with a grin, "I think you'd want to meet my mother before you made such accusations."

She bit her lip. How the hell did he know Russian? Her cheeks went from warm to burning. She pressed cool hands to her cheeks and groaned. Her goal was to impress him, not curse like a street thug…and look like one too. This was nothing like she imagined his homecoming. She thought she would run to him, throw herself into his arms, and maybe get another one of those kisses. Now she felt as shy around him as the days before the fated dog day. How could she rewind and go back?

"Ah, Janie. I shouldn't tease you. You're in pain."

Before she could think another thought, he scooped her off her feet. He carried her inside the building through the back fire escape that led directly to the laundry and living quarters. Jane gave him directions, though she was feeling more than a bit befuddled by the soap-scented skin. Jane gave him her key and he opened the door. Setting her on the couch, he moved to the kitchen. Through the cut-away he asked, "Where do you keep your pain pills and stuff?"

"Top cupboard, over the sink." Jane could hear cupboards opening and closing.

Her embarrassment faded. She was too curious about his take-charge demeanor and changed appearance. What happened to the skinny guy who blushed at hello? He was rummaging through her kitchen like its master. She suddenly wished she had done yesterday's dishes. And she prayed to God he didn't need to use the bathroom. She had a tendency to pile dirty clothes in the corner until she had nothing left to wear. Now she wished she had listened to Sasha and kept the place picked up.

Her worries were interrupted as he re-appeared with a glass of water, a kitchen towel, a bag of ice, and the pain killers. He handed her the pills and the glass of water with the simple directive, "Take these." Kneeling once again at her feet, he set about unlacing her tennis shoe. He slid it and her sock off carefully. Jane's heart flip-flopped, and she nearly choked on her water.

"Sorry. Did that hurt?" His warm brown eyes settled on hers.

Jane shook her head and hugged the glass of water to her chest.

Trip laid the towel over her foot and set the ice on it. He relaxed his body on his heel as he propped her injured foot on his bent knee. His thumb stroked her ankle, his face looked concerned. "Any better?"

"Much." She prayed she didn't pass out. Her heart raced every time his thumb moved. She licked parched lips as she studied him. "You look so different.... I almost didn't recognize you."

"Different? Is that different good or different bad?"

She thought a moment. With twenty packed on pounds of pure muscle, a crew cut, and a new look of stern confidence, Trip was no longer cute, but strikingly handsome.

"I'm beginning to think it's a bad different," Trip said.

"No. No. Not bad or good. You were handsome before...you are handsome now...different, but same? No? Your glasses?"

Trip smiled. "Gone. Eye surgery was recommended for the job." His cheeks finally showed a bit of flustered color as he asked, "So, the differences? You disappointed?"

"No! Never," Jane blurted with a shake of her head.

Trip pulled himself up and sat beside her on the couch. It was so quiet in the apartment Jane could hear the fridge hum and the elevator groan as it moved from floor to floor.

Trip broke the silence. "I apologize for taking so long. I was told three months, but then things...happened."

"Oh, no worry. I, uh, barely noticed."

"Really?" Trip sounded disappointed. "Not exactly what I wanted to hear."

"Oh, no. I did miss you, but I meant Eve was no trouble. She was a good puppy...though she's not much of a puppy anymore."

"Eve! Where is she?" Trip looked around the tiny apartment.

"She's out for a walk. Sasha always takes the dogs for a walk in the afternoon."

"Really? The red-head? She never struck me as a dog person."

"Sasha is soft as pudding. She just seems cranky."

"She had me fooled." Trip grinned. He nodded toward her foot as he asked, "So, since dancing is out, how about dinner? Think you can hobble out to eat? It's the least I can do after sticking you with my dog for three extra months. I didn't realize how crazy shi— I

41

mean crap would get."

"I can go out! And Eve? She wasn't a problem at all. She was good dog. I will miss her."

Jane remembered Eve's photos. "Oh, and I...." Jane stood and hobbled to her "desk" of stacked milk crates and brought back an album. She handed it to Trip. He flipped through the pages, and Jane couldn't help but watch the muscles in his forearms move under tanned skin with each turn.

"You're too much, Jane."

Her eyes rounded as if he knew she was checking him out. He gave her leg a pat as he stopped on a recent picture and sighed. "She's beautiful. She probably won't recognize me." He closed the book and set it on the table. "This was very thoughtful. You know your emails kept me going. I wasn't able to email back because everything sent out had to be encrypted for security."

"Security?"

"The company I work for offers protection for some pretty important people, and they get weird about what information is shared."

"Protection? Like bodyguards?"

Trip shrugged. "Something like that."

"Oh. Is it safe?"

Trip hesitated before answering, "Sure, sure it is."

"It doesn't sound—"

Trip interrupted. "I will say, every time I could access the internet, I'd check my email and there would be a message from you. There were days when I was ready to quit, but you'd keep me going. I could hear you telling me not to give up on a dream."

Stunned, Jane said nothing. Was she daydreaming again? She looked at Trip, searching his face for some proof she wasn't putting wishful words in his mouth. Her heart nearly missed a beat when he lowered his head and blushed. She saw it. He *blushed.* That spoke volumes, right?

She reached out and touched the warmth of his cheek. His fresh stubble was a new and wonderful feeling against her palm. And when he looked up at her, he had that same look as in the garage

42

after he kissed her. She locked her gaze on his. His skin grew warmer to her touch. *Do it,* she willed silently. He moved closer, coming so near she could smell that soapy fragrance, feel the heat their bodies trapped between them…feel his breath against her skin. Eyes fluttered closed…

Then the door slammed. Dogs barked. Trip sat back against the sofa.

"I got a ticket for not cleaning up dog shit." Sasha waved the ticket in the air. "I thought I left communist country." She ripped the ticket into tiny pieces and threw them on the kitchen counter. Looking at Trip as she set the dogs free, she asked, "You the owner of the mutt?"

Trip nodded as he sprang from the couch. Sasha released the dogs and stepped into the kitchen to pour a glass of vodka. She lifted her glass in a mock toast. "Yay. You're back. Didn't think my day could get any better."

Eve retained her adorable puppy look from her floppy ears to her black tipped tail. Big brown eyes made contact with her master and she barreled toward him. Eve barked and whined as Trip scooped her off the floor for a hug. "Damn, she's grown." Trip rubbed her ears and spoke to the hyper-whining dog, "Yes you have. You're a big girl. Did you miss me?" Eve answered with a bark. Sasha rubbed her forehead and grimaced. Jane couldn't help but laugh. Eve was so happy. The dog-sized pup finally settled into her master's lap, content to be rubbed as she chewed on his sleeve.

"Sasha," Jane croaked, then cleared her throat. "This is Trip. Trip, this is…."

"I know who he is, Jane. He's the guy banging the lawyer on four. Right?" Sasha paused, but not long enough for either Jane or Trip to answer before she continued, "I know the type. I don't need introduction."

Sasha grabbed the bottle of vodka, her glass, and went to her room, closing her door with a bang.

Jane blushed. Trip sighed.

"Sasha is just…"

Trip interrupted. "Sasha *was* right. But not anymore. It's over between Olivia and me." He took her hand in his. "I would never have asked you out if I was dating her."

Jane smiled and nodded.

"So, will you still have dinner with me tonight?"

"Of course." Jane felt the world glow a little brighter. Even her foot felt better.

"Good." He gave her hand a squeeze and then dropped it. "So, then, I better get Eve home." At the sound of her name, the dog looked up at her master. "You ready to go home, Eve?" The dog wagged her tail. He kept her tucked in the crook of his arm as he stood and turned to Jane and asked, "I'll see you about seven?"

"Seven is good." Jane agreed and then set about gathering Eve's stuff and hooked her chain to her collar. She handed the leash to Trip, and he set the dog on the floor.

"Say good-bye to Jane, Eve."

Jane bent down and gave the dog a hug good-bye, then stood to face Trip. Eve pranced and whined, eager to go.

"She missed you. She's so excited to go."

Trip grinned as he juggled leash, toys, and food. Jane opened the door for him, and he reminded as he left, "So… tonight?"

"Tonight," she repeated.

Chapter 6

Jane dressed and redressed for her date. The pile of clothes on her bed grew as each outfit was chosen, judged, and promptly discarded. Sasha sauntered in and sat cross-legged on the pile. Jane felt her presence even though her back was to her as she dug into her closet. Jane wasn't in the mood for nay-saying so she shot Sasha a warning, "If you don't have anything nice to say, Sash…"

"What? I am just keeping company."

"You were a bitch today."

"*Da.* I s'pose I was not nice." She mumbled as she pulled a hanger out from under her and tossed it on the floor.

"You suppose?" Jane turned to face her and sputtered like a stubborn child. "You were more than not nice. You were rude. You made him feel unwelcome."

"He isn't welcome." Sasha sighed and leaned back against the wall, stretching her legs out across the bed. She pulled a pack of cigarettes from her leather jacket, tapped one free, and lit it, taking a long drag.

Jane's mouth dropped open, and her head shook. She couldn't believe Sasha was so…so comfortable with being so mean.

Sasha wriggled out of her jacket and laid it next to her. "Don't give me that look." Sasha turned away a moment, then turned her attention back again to Jane. "I am helping you. You are going to get yourself in trouble."

"Trouble? Why is my having a, uh, friend trouble? And if I want to go out on a date, why is that so bad? You date. You're not in trouble."

Sasha sighed and rubbed her forehead. "I am different from you. You are…"

"An adult? I'm not a child." Jane's face was red, but she tried to keep her voice low. She didn't want to fight with Sasha. She knew in her heart that she was only trying to protect her, but still, she had no right. With a shake of her head and a frown on her lips, Jane resumed her closet excavation.

"He *has* a girlfriend," Sasha reminded her, flicking ashes into a Diet Coke can on the night table.

"Your date has a *wife*," Jane reminded without turning from her closet.

Sasha sighed. "You willing to be the other woman?"

Jane turned and answered smugly, "I'm not the *other* woman. They broke up. He said so."

"So, now you have a pissed off ex-girlfriend to deal with. You ready for that?"

"I'm not afraid of her. Poppa taught me—"

"Your father taught you many things, but he's gone. Your very existence in this country is based on a lie that is no more solid than the phony papers it's written on."

Jane yanked a shirt off a hanger and threw the empty plastic against the wall. "Well, then the same could be said for you."

"No. It couldn't. I am not stupid enough to think I am *in love*. If things get too serious, I will get out. I'm afraid you won't be able to see so clearly. You will take chances. You will miss things because your silly heart will make you blind."

"I can take care of myself. And it's my own hide on the line, right?" Jane held the shirt in her hand under her chin while looking in the mirror. The yellowish color and Sasha's ill temper made her skin look sallow. She tossed it on the floor and pulled open a dresser drawer.

"You think?" Sasha grunted. "You think KGB will just come after you? I harbor a fugitive."

Jane slammed the drawer closed. "Fine! So, when *can* I live my life? When I'm too old to care? Even then I will still be wanted. I might as well turn myself in." Her eyes stung and her lower lip quivered.

Sasha closed her eyes and said quietly, "Don't be stupid. And for God's sake, don't start crying. I might vomit." Sasha lit another cigarette from the first. "All right. You can do this, if you promise to get out if I tell you things are trouble. And you must, I mean you must, be discreet. You can*not* be honest with him." Jane nodded, a smile twitched at the corners of her mouth.

"Stop looking so, so…eager. I need you to listen to me."

"I am. I swear."

"No matter how much you want to be honest, you can't."

"Yes. Yes. I know." Jane sat down by Sasha, closed her eyes, and took a deep breath. "I know what is at stake. And I have been…I will be quiet like a mouse."

Sasha looked her in the eye and added, "And you know what happens to the mouse when it's caught in a trap?" Sasha slammed her hands together. Jane winced but added, "I know, it wouldn't be good. I understand."

Sasha nodded and gave her an approving smile. "Good. Since you promise to be careful, I promise to be…not so insulting. But keep me posted on everything. You are still a silly girl who needs someone to watch over you."

Jane jumped up from the bed. She was free! Jane thanked Sasha for understanding. Sasha grunted and puffed a few smoke rings toward the ceiling. Jane had a crazy notion of giving her a hug, but decided she'd pushed Sasha enough for one day. Instead she asked, "So, what do you think I should wear tonight?"

Jane was dressed and ready to go forty-five minutes before her date, but at t-minus twenty, she had cold feet about her outfit and ducked back into her closet for another quick change. Then another. And yet another. She was still examining herself in her full length mirror when she heard the knock on the door. Sasha opened it, ushering Trip in with a wave of her vodka glass.

Trip stood near the door, quietly shifting from one foot to the other. When Jane emerged, his smile was broad and glowing. Jane wasn't certain if he was glad to see her or glad to be saved from

Sasha. Either way, she was just pleased he looked so radiant. Her final outfit change was into a pair of dark denim pants that sat low on her tiny waist topped with a red silk camisole. She added a black velvet jacket and gold hoop earrings. Her hair was pulled back in a sloppy twist at the nape of her neck.

Jane breathed a sigh of relief that she had taken the time to change out of her appropriate- for-burgers-and-fries outfit and into something a wee bit dressier. Trip wore a suit jacket and khakis. He handed her a small bouquet of flowers and gave her a light kiss on the cheek. Jane hugged the flowers to her chest and inhaled their sweet scent, though truly the strongest scent was the tissue paper they were wrapped in, but to Jane they were the sweetest smelling flowers her nose ever encountered.

Sasha shook her head and drained her glass with a grimace. Jane hesitated between taking her flowers to the kitchen and staying by Trip's side. She took a stutter step, then stopped and looked back at Trip. Sasha sighed and held out her hand. "Give them to me. I can put them into water." Sasha yanked the flowers from Jane's hands plucking out a white rose as she walked into the kitchen. She stuffed the flower down the garbage disposal and ground it to nothing. She made a sign of the cross before dropping the remaining flowers in a tall glass, holding them up to Jane as if to prove they were safe. She then turned back into the kitchen, banging cupboard doors and cursing.

Jane grabbed Trip by the hand and whisked him out the door. He looked over his shoulder as if he expected Sasha to appear with a butcher knife and chop him to bits and pieces. Jane bit her lip and explained. "Sasha believes it is bad luck to have even number of flowers. She is very superstitious. She doesn't believe in God, but still, she fears Him." Jane's laugh was a little nervous.

"Someone told me once not to shake hands over the threshold, or to put my feet on the table in Russia. The flower one is new to me." He pushed the elevator call button.

"It is no big deal. Sasha is just…Sasha." The elevator doors opened. They stepped in among the people and were silent as they rode it to the parking garage. As they walked to the car, Jane changed the topic. "So, where are we going?"

"I, well, umm. I made reservations at the Evergreen."

"I have never been there. Have you?"

"No, I never have. To be honest, a friend of mine made the reservation," he said as he unlocked the car door.

Jane waited until he slipped into his seat before she asked, "A friend? So, you were busy?"

Trip started the car and as he backed out and headed on their way. He admitted with a flush, "No. Nothing like that. I just wanted to pick the right place, and my friend has better taste than I do. I mean I probably would have taken you to McDonald's."

Jane laughed, her head tipped back against the leather seat. "McDonald's? That was my first thought, so I threw on jeans and a sweater, then I got this feeling of...I don't know, scaredness, that you would be planning something else so I hurried up and changed."

"Well, you look...beautiful." Trip gripped the steering wheel and glanced nervously her way.

"Thank you." Her cheeks turned scarlet and her heart raced. She wished she was more like Sasha. Sasha would have accepted the compliment with finesse. She was quiet a few moments until her nerves finally settled. "You know, Trip, McDonald's would have been fine by me. I mean, you didn't have to do anything special."

As Trip slowed the car to a stop at a red light, his voice held a bit of a nervous croak, "Yes, it did have to be special."

She smiled at him and gave his arm a gentle squeeze. Trip pulled the car into the valet parking, handed off the keys, and then hurried to Jane's side as she stepped out of the car.

The restaurant was in the east wing of a hotel built before the Civil War. The high domed ceilings were washed in baby blue with gilded ornamental moldings and high arched doorways. The red carpet under foot was thick and luxuriant. From the winding stairwell to the hand-carved crown molding and cherub statues, the place had the look and feel of history. She imagined women swishing past in hoop skirts and corsets as she craned her neck from left to right to take in all the oil paintings of the capital before it was a metro area.

Trip led her to the dining room with a satisfied smile on his face. "You like?"

"I love. I can feel the history. I like reading about history and how it explains the culture. Like Russians: Russians are tough because for years and years they have had a history that promises them hardship and minimum. But Russians also know they will endure. The homeland has been scarred by war, by dictators, and by communism. They survived it all. There is a strength that comes from hardship.... And may also explain why Russians think Americans are soft."

"That explain Sasha's hostility?"

She laughed. "She's not even Russian. She is from Chechnya. My father, um, adopted her. But yes. She has a, um, distaste not just for Americans, but for most people."

"And you?"

"Certainly not. I am thrilled by the idea of getting a good life. Of not living a hard, roundabout life."

"Roundabout?"

"Yes." Jane nodded. "In Russia, the best way to get things done is round about. Like college. You can go to college for free, if you are smart enough or if you have enough money and connections to go round the rules. It's round about. If you have no money, no connections, no high scores? Then no college. In America, that is different."

"But not for Sasha?"

She shook her head. "No. She still lives round about." Jane thought of her rich "date" and sighed. "Sasha knows how to survive. She doesn't know how to dream."

Trip opened his mouth, but closed it as the maitre d' asked for their reservation name, then escorted them to their table. Trip pulled Jane's seat out for her, and she sat, her smiling face tipped to his. Then she gasped as she turned her attention to the menu.

"Trip, this is too much."

"It's no big deal."

"All for watching a dog?"

"Not just for the dog. But also because," he said as he unfurled his napkin. He stared down at the white linen, and continued with just a bit of sweat breaking out on his brow, "I wanted to impress you."

"Really? " Jane toyed with her silverware. "How do you know? I mean, how do you know I am even worth impressing?"

"Because I do." Trip looked up at her and relaxed as he looked into her eyes. They were a liquid blue, the color of the deepest sea. They seemed to sparkle when she teased like sun reflecting on water. He leaned across the table. "As a matter of fact, I remember the first time I ever saw you."

"When would that be?" Jane couldn't hide her pleasure. Her smile was relentless, her heart beat with such anticipation and hope that she thought she might burst into a happy dance right where she sat and scare the absolute hell out of him. She adopted a look of calm, hands pressed together, bottom firmly glued to her chair.

"The first time I came into your building you were on the elevator talking to Mr. Little. He was telling you one of his many WWII stories…which, I must point out, was so full of holes if it was a ship it would sink like a rock." Trip's head shook as his hands went palm up. "I mean the guy was storming the beaches of Normandy and being held captive in the Pacific. I wondered if you knew he was full of crap. Then you looked up at me and gave me a grin and the tiniest wink. I thought, she knows he's full of it, but is kind enough to play along."

"It was *quite* a story." Jane shrugged. "An elderly man's fantasy. An attempt to be…." Jane thought a moment, "Relevant?"

"I figured." Trip smiled at her. "It's sweet that you even take the time to listen to him. You're good people, Jane. As my Grams would say, 'Beautiful inside and out.'"

Sprouting a blush as red and warm as fire, she didn't know what to say. She had never been told she was beautiful by a man, except her father.

Fortunately for her, the waiter arrived and she quickly turned her attention to ordering dinner. Concentrating on the menu was difficult. She could see Trip watching her over the top of his menu. Flipping the gold hoop in her ear, she couldn't make a decision, so she closed the menu and looked to the waiter for help. "What would you suggest?"

"We have the best Asian salad with blackened chicken. The chef makes a peanut sauce that is amazing."

"Is it very spicy?" Jane asked scrunching her nose.

"Just a hint."

"Just a hint…hmm…okay." She handed him the menu. "I will take your words on it."

He took the menu. "Trust me. You'll love it." The waiter leaned closer and whispered, "I'm honestly jealous I won't be joining you for dinner."

Jane smiled up at him, then looked across the table at a scowling Trip. The waiter cleared his throat. Jane noticed he had sweat on his brow. She didn't think it was present a moment ago.

"And, uh, how about you, sir?"

"I'll have what the lady is having. Add a bottle of Chenin Blanc?"

"Excellent choice. You know your wine, sir." The waiter gave a slight bow, grabbed the menus and scooted.

As the waiter backed away, Trip mumbled, "Suck up freaking flirt."

"Pardon?" Jane asked.

"Nothing," Trip said as he sat up straighter in his seat. "Just thinking out loud."

"Oh. I don't do that." Jane thought of her wild imaginings and what people would say if they knew what she was thinking. Her laugh was soft, almost inaudible as she said, "Thankfully, or I'd always be in trouble."

Trip's brow shot up, but he never asked what thoughts were too bad to share because the hasty waiter returned, the bottle of wine open and breathing. He poured them each a glass, then exited with a small nod of his head.

Jane took a sip of hers and enjoyed the much needed relaxation it brought her. Leaning her body forward, she decided to reach for the moon. "So," she asked absentmindedly tracing her finger across the base of her wine glass, "if you thought such good things, when you first saw me…why did you never speak to me?"

"I figured you were too young…and there was…."

Olivia. Crap. Jane didn't want him thinking of her, not now. She quickly interrupted his sentence, "Forget I asked. Stupid question." She needed a follow-up question. Fast. "So, your muscles? Work related or were you bored while you were away?" Hearing the question as it rolled off her lips made her cringe a little.

"A little of both. A certain degree of physical fitness goes with the job. I did it more than I needed, probably, as you said, out of boredom." Trip straightened the utensils on his napkin until the bottoms of each one was in a perfect line. "Though I did have your emails. They were the highlight of my day. I wanted to write and ask you if you'd go out with me when I got home, but I could never work up the courage. Fortunately for me, you crippled yourself and gave me the perfect opportunity to feel like a hero and get up my nerve."

"Courage? To ask out me?" Jane laughed. "I'm not scary."

Trip shook his head in disagreement. "You are to me. I've spent my whole life as a techno geek. I have my mother to blame for setting me up with Olivia—she was my mother's intern her first year in congress." Trip frowned. "No, a guy like me doesn't approach girls like you."

"I think you are filling my head with that sugar talk again."

"Not sugar talk. It's all truth."

"Really? Well then, Mr. Coulter, this may not be a wise thing to say, but…." Jane leaned across the table and whispered, "I'm not one to invite competition, but every lady in this place…and I think that man back in the corner…took notice of you."

"You think?" Trip leaned back in his seat and scanned the room. "Well, let's see…now that I have options…."

Jane kicked him under the table.

Trip laughed. "I'm content right here." His grin was broad. "Though that guy…he looks like he'd be a big spender."

Jane couldn't help but giggle. "You are bad. A bad, bad man." She took another sip of wine as she thought of something else to talk about. "So, what is this new job?"

Trip drained his glass and poured himself another. Rubbing a hand across his chin, he said with a shrug, "I sort of do security for people, mostly cyber stuff. I, you know, help people who have problems with, um, security."

"So, you hunt down people who break into other people's computers?"

He shrugged. "Something like that."

Jane picked up her own glass, drained it, and poured herself another.

Chapter 7

Dinner finished, they strolled out of the restaurant and were greeted by an unseasonably warm winter evening. The lights of the city twinkled as buildings were slowly draped in Christmas trim, and the air smelled not of exhaust and concrete, but of crisp air and freshly cut pine.

"It's so nice tonight." Jane paused on the sidewalk. "Eddie says it's not usually this warm in December?"

"No, usually below freezing by now, but the cold will get here. Real soon."

"Simply perfect." Breathing deeply, she asked, "Walk with me?"

"What about your foot?"

She shrugged. "It's fine."

"If you're sure...."

Jane didn't answer. Instead, she gave his arm a tug and off they went.

Without thinking or contriving, she wrapped her hand around the crook of his arm. It wasn't until after she did it that she questioned her action. Her apprehension was short-lived when he smiled at her, giving her hand a squeeze and allowing his fingers to linger on hers.

Strolling along together, they shared stories, and before she realized it, they had gone several blocks and were standing within a hundred feet of the iron fence of the White House. Car traffic slowed as the night wore on and the foot traffic was sparse compared to the bustle of the day. The park across the street was nearly empty, so they had no trouble finding a bench to settle on. It faced the glow of the white-columned edifice of freedom.

"Amazing, isn't it?" Trip asked.

"It's beautiful. You know it was first called the Presidential Palace? I like White House much better. I don't know why, but I don't like palace."

"Too regal for a nation of mutts?"

"Mutts?" Jane laughed.

"Yeah, I'm English with a bit of Irish and German…a mutt. A mixed breed."

"I'm a mutt, too. English and Russian."

"See?" He gave her hand a pat. "Now you're in America— where mutts belong."

Jane laid her head against his arm. "You ever wonder what's going on in there…right now?"

"Every time I go by the place, I wonder that. Imagine the decisions, the power…while out here, life just goes on. Ordinary people with ordinary lives. It's like two different worlds."

"Yes, out here it is just ordinary people's secrets, lies, and mischief. Inside, there is the chaos of extraordinary secrets, lies, and mischief," she said with a grin.

"Am I seeing a jaded side to you, sweet Jane?" Trip teased.

"No," Jane laughed. "I'm just saying everyone hides something." Jane lifted her head from his shoulder so she could look him in the eyes. "Wouldn't you agree?"

Trip shrugged and gave a half nod as he looked down at her. The street lights lit her face but left shadows. It made her look mysterious. He whispered, "Can't imagine you having anything to hide."

"Everyone has something," Jane answered.

"So, what are your secrets?"

"They wouldn't be secrets if I told." Besides, Sasha would have her hide if she shared.

Trip grinned and tweaked her nose. "One day, little lady, I will know everything about you."

Jane swallowed hard. She started this conversation, like a fool. Why couldn't she think straight with him near? Laughing to lighten her words, she added, "Pretty confident for a guy who was afraid to speak with me."

"Touché, Jane, touché." Trip's laugh broke the still of the night. "So, take pity on me. Tell me one—just one—secret about yourself. Something no one else knows."

Jane considered the request with narrowed eyes. She opened her mouth to speak, then closed it again.

"Come on," Trip teased, lowering his nose till his nearly touched hers. "Just one."

"Like what?"

"Like anything."

Jane's head began to spin. She was suddenly certain the CIA or Mi6 didn't have as effective interrogation strategies as Trip Coulter. Scooting away from him on the bench, she fanned herself and said with a sigh, "You're too close for me to think straight."

"Why's that?" In a single motion, he closed the gap she put between them. His leg pressed close enough to hers that she could feel the heat and solidity of his thigh.

"It's because...." Jane began, but then stopped, mesmerized by the feel of him, the feel of his breath warm against her cheek as he dipped his head toward hers. She closed her eyes, and her heart squeezed in her chest. He was so close. Without thinking any further, she heard her breathless self say, "One secret I have is how long I have dreamed of this moment."

His fingers traced the sensitive skin along her chin. "Of a starry night alone in a park with a man?"

Jane giggled. "No, not just any man...just one."

His fingers remained on her flesh. Her throat went dry. She managed to admit, "No one knew I was dying with envy. That woman had you, and I hated her for it. The day you two fought I wanted to yell, 'I'm the one you should be with!'" Jane's laugh sounded nervous and tinny, even to her own ears. She rubbed her hands down the top of her pants. "What kind of fool would you have thought I was if I said that?"

"If you'd just screamed that? Out of the blue?"

"No warning. Just grabbed you by the hand that day and yelled it."

"Oh, well, I'd have been shocked." He whispered in a hoarse voice, lowering his forehead until it rested gently against hers. "But I'd have thought you were the bravest, most beautiful, most perfect crazy lady around. And I would have tripped over my own tongue because I already had the biggest, hugest, got-to-ignore-the-feeling crushes on you."

"Then why ignore me?"

Trip leaned back in the seat, but wrapped an arm across her shoulder as he answered. "First, I figured you were too young, no more than nineteen."

"That's not too young!"

"Um, yes it is. And I figured if, in the odd chance you were over twenty-one and old enough to date, then you probably had a boyfriend. I couldn't imagine a girl like you not having a guy in the palm of your hand. And there was…"

Jane interrupted. "No boyfriend. I never had a boyfriend. Never had a man here." She held out her hand and pointed to her palm. "You think I could fit one here…like my toy? Even a man like you?"

He took her hand and kissed the upturned palm. "Especially, a man like me."

Jane stomach did a flip-flop. She thought of all the times she watched him and loved him. How certain she was that he was the man for her, that he would love her. She was right; he *was* created for her. Leaning in, she kissed him. Quick and sweet, just to prove to herself she could. That she had the right. As her lips brushed against his, she relished in her victory. He pulled her tight, his hand wrapped at the base of her neck, warm fingers sliding into her hair as his mouth pressed against hers, demanding more. She gripped his shoulders, holding on tight as her mind whirled and spun. He kissed her long and deep…cleansing her mind of everything, including Sasha's warnings.

Chapter 8

Jane cleaned her block of apartments with a rejuvenated spirit. Her movements were quick and effortless as she hummed a merry tune while loading bag after bag of laundry onto her cart. Her good humor might have been the leftover glow of a magnificent week of perfect dates, or it might have been that she is finally sleeping at night. No bad dreams, no worry of bad dreams…just thoughts of Trip.

She shoved the cart off the elevator into the laundry room. She turned on her iPod, put in her ear buds, and cranked up the volume. She swiveled her hips to Pink, more certain than ever that she, too, was a rock star. The beat coursed through her ears to her veins. She moved down the row of washers with the grace of a belly dancer, closing the lids as she passed and setting the machines to wash. While she waited, she danced, hips gyrating, fingers snapping. She sang the words she knew; hummed the ones she didn't.

It felt good to feel this good. She thought of her evening with Trip. Pure glee bubbled in her spirit, making her feel light and free, invulnerable to trouble or harm. She played their conversations over and over in her mind until she could hear his voice in her ear. Heard her name on his lips.

Jane.

It was so beautiful when he said it. It sounded so real.

She heard it again, only closer…then something grabbed her shoulder. She spun, yanking the ear buds from her ears, fists balled, ready to strike.

"Whoa, Jane." He put his hands in the air. "I'm unarmed."

"Trip." She smiled, her shoulders relaxed and fists unclenched.

"I called your name, but you couldn't hear me."

She blushed. "How long were you there?"

"Long enough."

"Long enough for what?"

"Long enough to know you could make a fool of me on the dance floor."

She covered her mouth with her hand. "So embarrassing."

"Why? You're quite good." He grabbed her and wrapped her in muscular arms. "Dance with me, Jane."

"No." She giggled, blushing several shades of red. A washer beeped and stopped. She backed away from him and headed to the slowing machine. "I have work to do."

Trip was close behind her and stepped in and pulled clothes out of one of the washers from over her shoulder. She paused, a single pair of slacks dangling cold and wet in her hands. Work suddenly forgotten, she ogled his tan skin as it rippled and flexed as he pulled shirt after shirt out of the washer and dumped them in the rolling laundry basket.

Washer emptied, he took the pants from her and tossed them with the rest and asked, "So, other than dancing your way through your work, what have you got planned for today?"

"Aren't you a funny guy." She pulled the cart to a dryer and started shoving clothes in. She shook her head as she explained, "I have to dry these, then fold, and bag them, then return them to the owners."

"So when we get that done...then what?"

"We?"

"I've got time off, so I thought I'd spend it with you. And if you're working, then I'm helping."

"You are?" She shut the dryer and leaned against it, her arms crossed over her chest.

"Yep. Just tell me what I'm to do. And when we're done...I was thinking...have you been outside today?"

"Not since 6:00 A.M. when Frosty went to do his, ah,

business."

"Well, it's still beautiful outside. Skies are blue, sixty-three degrees. Perfect day for a picnic."

She grinned at him. "That sounds fun."

"Good. And," he said, taking her hand and playing with her fingers, "I want to invite you to come with me to my brother's. They want to meet you…see for themselves if you're as good as I say."

"When? I thought you said they lived…"

"Down south? Yes, they do. But, my oldest brother, Tres, he invited us to his house for the weekend, and if you're coming, Craig says he'll be up for sure. Says he has to…well, let's just say…he'd like to meet you."

"What? Why?" Jane nudged him with her shoulder.

Trip squeezed his eyes closed and rubbed his head with his free hand. "Craig hated Olivia…."

"I like him," Jane said with a laugh.

"Yeah. He didn't like her at all. And I was telling him about you and he is further convinced I have impaired judgment."

"Oh." Jane's spirit hit the floor.

"It's my fault. I never should have told him what I was thinking, about you being special."

"Oh?" Jane's spirits found their way back to the ceiling

"Well, you are. And yes, we've only been going out for a week, but I feel like I've known you a lot longer than that. But Craig doesn't get it." Trip took her hand and held it. "But after he meets you, he will understand."

"I don't know. They don't sound like they approve."

"They just want to meet you. It's either we go there, or I assure you, they will come here."

"But an entire weekend? That would leave Sasha with all the work. I can't do that."

"I could hire someone. Aren't there cleaning crews you can hire by the hour?"

Jane shook her head. "No…well, I'm sure there are, but not just anyone can clean. The people trust that their stuff is safe." A blush heated her cheeks as she thought of her amateur hacking, but she shrugged the guilt away as she reminded herself that all was fair in the love war.

"Please? I'll help you clean as much as you need. See?" He held up a pair of neatly folded track pants and said, "I do good work."

"I don't know...."

"Yes, you do. You want to go with me."

"Of course I do. I just don't know how I can."

"How about this? We leave Friday, after work, and I get you home Sunday night. You will only miss Saturday. That's workable, right?"

"It is far, no?"

"I can make it work. Will you go with me?"

"I don't...."

He put a finger over her lips. "No, no. Don't say no. Say yes." Moving closer, his lips hovered close to hers. "Yes is the only answer I'll accept. A weekend, with me...at the beach. Tres lives on the Outer Banks. I think you'll like it there. Besides, you can't break my heart and say no."

Jane chewed on her lower lip. Sasha was going to kill her, but— "I will think about it. Best I can say for now."

He planted a kiss on her that made her heart skip a beat, and then he smiled as if he'd already won her agreement.

"You really shouldn't have, Jane," Trip argued as they walked out of McDonald's and into the glorious December sunshine.

"Of course I should. You helped me finish my work. Me buying lunch is completely fair."

"Well, thank you."

She carried the paper bag with the burgers and fries. He carried the sodas. They settled on a park bench and ate as they watched the water sparkle off the duck pond. The brown grass and barren trees seemed so much less gray and ugly with the glitter of diamonds on the water.

"It is a nice day. Thank you for getting me out."

"You're welcome."

"So...." He took a drink, then asked, "Why did you come to

America?"

Jane thought a moment. She didn't need to lie to answer this question. "It was Sasha's idea. Her uncle needed someone to run the building."

"Thank God for Sasha," Trip said looking to the blue sky. He turned to Jane and said, "Never thought I'd find cause to say that."

Jane giggled. "Sasha is more than a good friend. She's family."

"You got a lot of family?"

"No," Jane said simply. "You?"

"Mmm, hmmm." He swallowed his bite of food. "We used to be a small family, but then my brothers and my mother got married and wow, now there's a bunch of us."

"How many brothers?"

"Two. No sisters. I have my mother, and a new stepfather. I have two nieces and three nephews, and of course there's Grams. Can't forget the lady who practically raised me."

"You weren't raised by your mum?"

"Well, she was there, technically. But when my dad died she had to go to work and was always busy. Grams moved in and took care of me. My brothers were teenagers and out doing their own thing…getting in trouble…making my mother miserable…but that's a whole different story."

"I'm sorry about your poppa."

"It's funny. My brothers," he said as he looked at Jane and smiled, "they remember life with my dad. I know he died of a heart attack when I was eight. I remember the funeral, sort of. But the times I spent with him? I don't really remember much. I just remember we were happy. So weird. I can't recall details, just the feeling." He looked at Jane and sighed, taking a slow bite of his burger before he continued. "My brothers remember the family being rowdy and close. I remember a family of bitter adults and fights between my mom and my brothers. This whole new big family, this new crazy group with all these little kids? I have to admit…it's pretty freakin' great. I feel like everything is finally falling into place."

She leaned over and brushed a kiss across his cheek. "It is sweet that you have big family. I also had a poppa that I loved. He was the only family I was really close to."

"I'm sorry."

Jane shook her head. "It's fine…he was enough."

"Is he still in Russia?"

"He is," Jane said and looked to the pond oasis, "gone."

"I'm sorry." He wrapped an arm around her shoulder and kissed her temple.

"Thank you. I'm doing fine. Poppa taught me to be strong. And I am strong." Jane tossed some fries to a duck waddling past. He honked for more, so she threw him another. She turned to Trip and shrugged. "But you already know…. You lost your poppa, too."

"But I was too young to know what I lost."

Tilting her head as the memories of her father played through her head, Jane admitted, "I wouldn't give up a single memory of him, even it if it eased the pain of losing him." She turned to Trip. "No, I am the lucky one."

He tucked a strand of hair behind her ear. "You're a special lady, Jane Mitchell."

She beamed. "I think the same of you. Though, not that I think you are a woman, but that you are a special person."

Trip chuckled. "Good thing. I'd sure hate to be in this alone."

The duck honked again. Trip threw his fries as far as his aim could reach. "Dang. You think he's on Sasha's payroll?"

Jane laughed. The duck waddled off, but she knew he'd be back. "No, I created that nuisance."

"Well, I was trying to create a moment. One where you feel the magic they talk about in books and you come under my spell and do as I ask."

"A spell?" She made big eyes at him. "Sounds serious."

"It is. I really want you to come with me…to meet my family."

"It's not that I don't want to…."

"Please? I swear, it won't kill you."

Chapter 9

Jane gripped the armrest. Air travel always made her nervous. It wasn't natural. People weren't meant to flap around in the clouds. The cabin shook, and she had to bite her lip to keep from screaming for the pilot to let her off the plane.

Trip gripped her hand. "Sorry, the ride on a puddle jumper is always a bit rougher than a big plane. I'd have gotten the jet, but I didn't want my mom to know I'm sneaking you to the island."

Her belly gave her a different sort of pain. "You don't? Why?"

When Jane told Sasha her plans for the weekend, she had flat out told Jane she was insane…that no good would come of it. Her dismal prophesy had taken some of the fun out of the escapade, and now this? First, the plane ride from hell, now he admits he doesn't want his mother to know about her? Couldn't be a good sign….

"My mother can be a load. I'd rather you judge me by my brothers. Then when I have you in my web, I'll let you meet her. Sure as hell don't want to let her scare you off."

"You're sure that's all?" *Please don't let me vomit*, she prayed.

He placed a hand on her shoulders and rubbed her back. "I swear. Can I get you anything? How about a Sprite? Or ginger ale? Grams swears by ginger ale when you're nauseated."

Jane shook her head. "I'll be fine." The plane hit another bump. "How long until we land?"

"Soon."

"And then what?"

"I think Tres is meeting us at the airport, and he'll take us to

65

his house."

"In a car?"

Trip chuckled. "Yes. In a car."

"Good." Jane rested her head against his shoulder and closed her eyes.

"It's only about an hour drive to the island. My brother lives down in Buxton. The Cape Hatteras Lighthouse is down there. I'll take you to see it." She couldn't make small talk while her stomach tried to figure out what altitude it was at, so she nodded.

"It's a beautiful place. Have you been there?"

She shook her head against his shoulder.

"If we had more time, I'd take you to the Lost Colony and the Wright Brothers. You enjoy history, right?"

"Mmm, hmm."

A smile spread across his face, and he pulled her tighter, kissing the top of her head. "We'll come back some time. There's shipwrecks and pirates…so much to see."

The pilot announced their descent. Trip reached across and buckled Jane's lap belt, giving her leg a pat before settling his hand in hers.

*****

Trip stepped out first, then turned and took Jane's hand, leading her down the air-stairs. She looked pale as hell and more than a little nervous. Last step cleared, he wrapped an arm across her shoulders and tucked her close.

He spotted Craig first. His second older brother was the tallest of the three of them, so he stood out no matter the crowd, which in this private little airfield was nearly non-existent. Only the family boarding a Piper and a crew working on a Cessna moved between them. Craig spotted him and gave him a head nod hello. Up popped Tres, his oldest brother, with a little guy on his hip. Sammy, his nephew, offered a two-handed wave and yelled, "Uncle Trip! Did you fly on the plane?" The sandy-haired fella lifted a toy plane in the air. "Look, I got a plane."

Normally, Trip would run to the kid and give him a helicopter spin, but he was afraid to let go of Jane. She might pass out. He figured he better get her some food or something, so she didn't look so green.

As he came closer, Jane pulled away a bit, straightened her back, and smiled. Trip wanted to hug her. He knew she felt like hell, but she evidently wasn't about to let on to his brothers.

"Tres, Craig…this is Jane." He turned to Jane and said, "Jane, these are my brothers and my rotten nephew, Sammy." He tickled Sammy's ribs. The little boy squealed and wiggled.

"Give me a piggy ride, Uncle Trip!"

Trip hesitated a moment, but Jane shoved away gently, nodding to the child as she said, "Yes, Uncle Trip, give him a piggy ride."

Before Trip could say yes or no, the boy climbed on his back. Sammy planted a pair of airplane clad sneakers in his uncle's ribs as he yelled, "Giddy-up!"

"Whoa, sport, we better not run through an airport. Security might think we're escaping bank robbers and take a shot at us."

"Really?" the boy asked.

"Yep," Trip answered.

Sammy's voice was serious. "We don't want that. Huh?"

Trip shook his head and followed the group to the car. Tres and Craig made small talk with Jane about the warm weather in DC. It had been warmer up north than in the South. As they passed a soda machine, Craig stopped and bought a Sprite. He handed it to Jane. "Here you go. My wife was green around the gills most of her pregnancy."

"It's from the plane. It kept hitting turbos and was bumpy. Up and down the whole way."

Both of his brothers grinned, neither corrected her by explaining she had hit turbulence. She was nervous. Her English went to crap when she was nervous, and he loved that she took meeting his family so seriously. Trip wanted to stop where they were, grab her, and kiss her.

On the drive, Jane and Trip sat in the back seat, with young Sammy sandwiched between them in his car seat. As Trip strapped him into the seat, Sammy gave Jane the essential information. "I have a little brother. And I have a big brother. My big brother is

Tanner, and he lives at college now, but I'm not going to college. Mommy says that's fine; I can do whatever I want. My little brother's name is Chas, and he's trouble. He eats your toys."

Jane gasped. "Oh my, I'm glad I didn't bring mine with me."

"You didn't?"

Jane shook her head no and offered an exaggerated frown.

"Well, I can let you borrow mine." Sammy offered up his plane. Trip settled himself in his seat as Tres put the car in gear and started the engine of his Ford Excursion.

"Why thank you, sir. That's mighty generous of you." Jane gave him a broad smile.

"You're welcome." Sammy smiled at her then added, "You talk funny, like the lady at the grocery store. Do you work at the grocery store?"

Tres shook his head and said, "Sammy, Jane is from Russia. She doesn't talk funny. She speaks another language." Tres made eyes contact with Jane in the rearview mirror as he explained, "Tonja is here on a work visa from Poland. She gives the boys gum, so they love her."

"I see." Jane smiled and nodded.

"How many languages can you talk?" Sammy asked.

"Just two. Russian and English."

Sammy nodded. "How do you say plane?"

"Samolet."

"Wow, so Sammy is plane in Russian! Did you hear that Dad? Sammy is plane is Russian." He pointed to the plane in Jane's hand. "See this? It's the Blackbird. It's the fastest plane in the world."

"The fastest, wow! That is really cool." Jane held the plane up, turning it from side to side as if inspecting it from top to bottom before handing it back. "I think this is a magnificent plane."

Sammy listed all the major parts, like the wings and wheels, while Jane listened. As the car turned off on the two lane road that led to the island, the boy yawned and tucked the gray plastic craft into his chest like it was a teddy bear as his heavy eyes dropped closed.

Jane tipped the plane so the nose didn't bite into his chin and smoothed the hair across his forehead. She winked at Trip. "He's adorable. Never thought I'd think a guy was cuter than you."

Trip chuckled. "You hear that, Tres? Your kid stole my girl."

Tres laughed, flipping on windshield wipers as a soft drizzle hit. Craig said nothing, but turned and looked at his little brother, then to Jane, then back to Trip. Trip could guess what he was thinking. Knew his brother would never call a girl *his*, well not until Mollie. Craig would be the tougher sell. If he liked Jane, then Trip would know he had a good one. And if his brother didn't like her? Trip glanced at Jane and decided…it really didn't matter.

*****

They arrived at the house a little past nine. Bombarded at the door, Jane was greeted by Trip's sisters-in-law. First up, the shorter and more talkative of the two, Mollie, with her soft, brown curls and girl-next-door smile was her usual, warm self. Jane was barely in the door before Mollie wrapped her in a hug.

Mollie saved Trip the awkward introductions as she kept Jane tucked in her arm and said, "I'm Mollie. Craig's wife." She pointed to Craig. "The tall guy with the tendency to look grumpy." Mollie winked at Craig before adding, "And this is Jenna, Tres's wife." The tall blonde looked more like a thirty-something Coppertone model than someone's wife. "I see you've met Sammy." Mollie grinned at the little boy who wiggled from his dad's grip to get Jane by the hand.

"Miss Jane wants to play with me," Sammy contended.

"I think Miss Jane wants to be with the grown-ups," his mother said gently as she tried to pull the boy away.

"No!" Sammy stomped a foot. "She wants to play with me, to see the rest of my planes."

"I see someone is up way past bedtime," Jenna said dropping to a knee and adjusting the boy's hair.

"I did tell him I would see his planes. If it is all right?" Jane said softly.

"Oh, well, of course." Jenna rose and smiled at Jane before looking down at the boy. "You can show her your planes, but you only have ten minutes, then bedtime. No arguing, no fussing…understood?"

"No brushing?" Sammy asked.

"No, you still have to brush your teeth."

"And Jane can read me a story?"

"Well," Jenna blushed and looked to Jane, who nodded. "I suppose."

"Good. Come on, Miss Jane." He led her from the room, probably stealing her heart forever as he observed, "You're a lots better than Old Livia."

Mollie slapped a hand over her mouth, but the giggles still escaped. Jenna covered her eyes, but said nothing.

Tres muttered as he gathered Jane and Trip's overnight bags, "Out of the mouths of babes…guess I better get these to your rooms."

Jenna shoved a hand in her husband's back pocket and slowed his escape. "I better go with you. Show you where they go. Trip, I assume you know how to make yourself at home?"

Mollie, righting herself, said, "I'm sorry, Trip. I know you liked her, and I suppose she wasn't all bad…."

"Who? Olivia? That's over."

Mollie's eyes were bright as she grabbed his hand and squeezed it. "So, how did you meet Jane?"

"She watched my dog while I was overseas."

"You told us that…. I mean, how did you meet her? Does she run a kennel?"

"No. She manages a hotel," Trip said.

They found their way to the living room as they talked and settled onto comfortable overstuffed couches. Mollie curled up on her husband's lap as her interrogation of Trip continued. "So you placed an ad?"

"No. Honestly? She got caught in the middle of a fight between Olivia and me; Olivia was extremely freaking rude to her, and I grabbed her at the elevator to apologize. And we hit it off."

"Really?"

"Yeah, while we were talking, I mentioned I needed someone to watch Eve, so Jane volunteered."

"Wow. And she didn't even know you? Is she a saint?"

Trip felt his heart do a flip-flop. "She's something all right."

"Why aren't you telling Mom?" Craig asked as he traced lazy circles on Mollie's arm.

"I don't want Mom screwing things up. I've only known Jane a few months; only gone out with her a few times."

"Hard to believe she barely knew you and still offered to watch your dog. You sure she's not a gold digger?"

"She has no clue what our family is worth."

"That's what they all say," Craig said.

"Craig!" His cynicism got him a shoulder slap from his wife. "That's an awful thing to assume."

"Someone has to use their head. If Tres and I hadn't talked sense into him, we might have gotten stuck with Olivia for a lifetime." He turned to Trip. "You do realize, little brother, Olivia loved Mom's connections more than she ever loved you."

"Craig, that's horrible." Mollie turned to Trip. "He didn't mean that."

"Yes, I did," Craig said.

Mollie's mouth dropped open.

"It's okay, Mollie. Craig's right. I should have seen it myself. But," Trip leaned forward in his chair, "Jane is different. But I won't tell you. You'll see for yourself. She's sweet, she's funny and thoughtful. I—"

"Don't say it," Craig ordered.

"Say what?" Trip asked.

"Don't say love. You're not allowed to use that word this early."

"You only knew me…." Mollie started, but Craig interrupted, "That's different. I wasn't fresh from a, good lord, how long did you date that bitch?"

"Two years."

"So, spare me. You're not to be trusted."

"That's why I brought her here," Trip answered.

"Brought who?" Tanner asked as he sauntered in.

"A, um, lady friend," Mollie answered.

The now twenty-year-old offspring of Tres and Jenna planted himself by his Uncle Trip. They both had the same blond good looks, unlike Tres and Craig who were both dark haired. "Check 'em out, Tripster. Bet you ain't got guns like these." Tanner flexed an arm.

Trip laughed as he struck his own pose. "Boo ya, nephew, I've got you beat."

"Holy shi…" Tanner looked over his shoulder with a nervous jerk of his head. "Crap. I mean holy crap. You doing steroids?"

"No. Just trained and worked out."

"Bull. The governments, probably sneaking them in your food," Tanner said with a punch to his uncle's shoulder.

"I work for a private company," Trip said.

"As what? A science experiment?" Tanner asked.

"You realize, Mom is pissed you did that, right?" Craig asked.

"Trust me, she's told me. Another reason I didn't want to bring Jane around her yet."

"Hell, now is perfect. She can't get any madder at you." Craig laughed. "To think you were the perfect one. Way to make Tres and me look good, little man."

"Careful with the little man stuff, sweetie. I think Trip might be able to take you," Mollie said.

Craig gave her a playful squeeze. "You'll pay for that, woman."

Mollie buried her face in under his chin. "You know I'm just teasing. No one could beat my big, strong, manly…"

"Mollie. Baby alert," Tres said from the doorway. "One was crying. I still can't tell which is which."

Both Mollie and Craig hurried from the room. Their twin girls, Hope and Grace, were approaching the six-month mark, but their parents were still amazed at the wonder of them. Mollie's bout with childhood cancer left the prospect of children to fate, and fortunately for them, fate smiled on them.

Tres gave Tanner a shoulder punch as he passed. "You made it. Better tell your mom. She was worried about you driving so late."

Tanner shook his head and rolled his eyes.

"Your mom loves you, humor her," Tres said. "Go tell her

you're home safe."

Tanner turned to Trip and asked, "Up for some Call of Duty? Or is your girlfriend here to lecture us about…what does she call it?" Tanner thought a minute before answering, "Brain-numbing futility?"

"Olivia isn't here," Trip said.

"Seriously? How did you sneak out of town without her? Didn't you just get back this week?"

"Yeah. Uh, we broke up," Trip said.

Tanner gave an approving nod, but quickly added, "Sorry though…sort of."

"It's all right," Trip assured.

Tanner bumped into Jane as she and Jenna came into the room. "Excuse me, pretty lady." His apology dripped with all the cockiness and smoothness of self-assured youth

"This is your uncle's girlfriend, Jane. Jane…my son, Tanner. He's the kind of guy smart girls avoid," Jenna answered dryly as she gave her son a hug. "But he's my baby, and I love him anyhow." She let go, rubbing his arms with her hands. "Did you just get here?"

"Yeah, I did." He gave his mom a kiss on the cheek.

"You hungry?" Jenna asked.

"Nanny back from her cruise?"

"No, they won't be back until next weekend."

"Sooo, you cooked?" Tanner sounded skeptical.

"Yes."

"Then no, I'm not hungry."

Jenna rolled her eyes. "Your Aunt Mollie helped."

"Well, in that case…." Tanner had his arms ready to block his mother's punch. "I'll grab a bite while the old farts decide if it's too late and Trip decides if he's too whipped to play some COD." Tanner wandered off toward the kitchen. Jenna turned to Jane and sighed. "I'm afraid my kids will want to steal all of Trip's attention. He's their buddy. Well, all but Sammy—you seem to be his new obsession."

"He is adorable. All of your boys are handsome. You are a lucky woman."

"I am blessed. Truly blessed." Jenna smiled. "How about you? Are you hungry? I'm not nearly the horrible cook my son says."

"No, I'm fine. The flight left me queasy, so food is the last thing on my mind."

"How about some lemonade? I bet that would help. When I had morning sickness, lemon was the best cure."

"That actually sounds good."

"If you'd like, you can join Trip and I'll bring you a glass."

Jane nodded, but hesitated, then said, "Your son, the older one…he is home from university?"

"Yes, he came home to see Trip, why?"

"Then I should tell Trip to play with him, then help you make lemonade? If you don't mind?"

"Oh, of course. Why don't I get Mollie, and we'll make some vodka lemonades and hit the hot tub? Well, Mollie can't drink. Breast feeding, but she can be our designated swimmer."

"That sounds like fun," Jane agreed. "I will tell Trip."

"And I'll get Mollie." Jenna sounded pleased by the change of plans.

Jane nodded and headed for the living room.

Jenna headed back down the long hall, spotting Craig and Mollie slipping out of the bedroom they were staying in, closing the door very gently.

"Mollie!" Jenna whispered. "Jane and I are going to make vodka lemonades and hit the hot tub. You game for some girl time?"

Craig gave Jenna a wink as he said, "Smart girl, Jenna. Get her drunk…then pump her for information."

Chapter 10

Tanner set up the videogame and handed out the controllers. "Trip and I on a team?" he asked as he curled up on the couch, grabbing a bag of chips and a two-liter of soda from the floor and bracing it beside him.

"My ass," Craig answered. "The two biggest nerds in the family aren't allowed on the same team."

"You two are just getting old. Bifocals probably aren't up to speed," Trip squawked.

"Screw you. We're not old," Tres said.

"Then you guys against us," Trip challenged.

"Fine," Tres said.

"You nuts?" Craig asked. "We're about to get slaughtered. It's going to be freaking Desert Storm all over again, and we're Iraq."

"We can take them," Tres predicted.

"Yeah, right," Craig answered.

Seconds into the video game, Tanner's avatar leaped from a burned-out building and snuck up behind his dad's player and knifed him.

Craig's went down seconds later. Also stabbed in the back. As the game respawned their characters, Craig took the opportunity to point out to Tres, "I told you this would be a slaughter."

"You need to cover me! Warn me when the little shit is sneaking up behind me."

No sooner than the game offered him up another life, Tres took two steps forward and went down again. This time it was Trip, who got a good laugh and offered his gaming partner and nephew a knuckle bump.

"Where the hell did you come from?" Tres asked.

"Told ya you needed those bifocals," Trip said as he sliced him yet again. He turned to Tanner and said, "I'm not even wasting my bullets on these two. That'd be like shooting fish in a barrel."

"Haha, you little asshole." Craig got in a sniper shot from a bombed out window.

"Wanya play that way, huh?" Tanner took out his dad and then called in an airstrike.

Tres shook his head. "Un-freaking-believable. How do we get an airstrike?"

"Earn the points…by killing someone," Tanner laughed.

Tres rounded a corner in the game and bumped into Trip. He tried to aim before Trip could stab him, so he yelled, "Tanner was hitting on your girlfriend. Maybe if you weren't grabbing girls from kindergarten, you wouldn't have to compete with your nephew."

Trip turned to Tanner. "Huh? You hit on Jane?"

Tanner turned red. "I just said hello. I was being friendly."

"Your hello or a normal guy hello?" Trip asked.

"Normal. I guess. Hey, I thought she was a nanny or something. Not your girlfriend. Don't worry. Won't happen again."

"I wasn't worried," Trip assured. "I trust Jane."

"What the hell?" Tanner yelled.

"Watch your mouth. Your mother will have my ass. Blames me for your potty mouth," Tres said.

"Uncle Craig, you're humping my character? Your own nephew?"

Craig laughed, head tipped back to the ceiling. "Who's the old man now, bitch?"

"Check it out," Tres said. Trip, who had been lost in thoughts of Jane, looked up. Craig's player was dancing on his player's corpse. Trip grabbed a throw pillow and beamed it at his brother's head.

"Chill, Trippy," Craig caught the pillow mid-flight. Craig looked at Tres and whispered as loud as he could, "Roid rage. His penis is probably back to two inches like when he was a baby."

"Screw you," Trip said.

Craig grimaced and said, "Irrational anger is a side effect."

"I'm not on steroids. I swear."

"Out of curiosity…why does doing tech security require you to look like mini-hulk?" Craig asked.

"It doesn't. I just didn't have anything better to do between jobs."

Craig laid his controller in his lap. "Seriously, what the hell have you gotten yourself into?"

"Security," Trip said flatly. His player walked up to Craig's. "You wanya even try to defend yourself?"

Tres snuck up behind Trip's guy and pistol whipped him. Trip's player dropped to the virtual dirt.

"You wanya tell us the truth?" Tres asked.

Trip also dropped his controller. "All right. Fine. It's a little more than tech security.'"

"Cool. What is it?" Tanner asked.

"Go get your homework done."

"I'm in college. I don't have homework." Tanner settled his feet on the coffee table and ripped open his chips.

"Somehow that doesn't sound right, but I guess you are an adult. So, whatever is said here doesn't get repeated, understood?" Tres warned.

"Of course," Tanner said around a mouthful of food.

Tres seemed satisfied with his son's promised silence, so he turned to Trip. "So, what are you into?"

"You know I was already working for National Security, right?"

"Yeah, in an office," Tres said.

"Yeah, and that office got stuffy. Then, I met a guy at the agency. We talked and his job sounded like more fun than mine, so I asked how I could get a job, and he hooked me up."

"What guy?" Craig asked, his voice a little more harsh than Tres's.

"Frankie," Trip explained.

"Holy shit, kid," Craig said as he ran a hand through his hair. "That's merc shit."

"You're a mercenary?" Tanner sounded impressed.

"No, it's not like that. We do jobs for a fee. Like this one…we went into Pakistan and got some guy's daughter out. Pakistan is an *ally,* so the government couldn't just send a rescue team in, but she was being held, so we got paid to go get her."

"And if you had gotten caught, no one would have claimed you ever existed, so there would be no international fuss," Craig offered.

"Exactly!" Trip was glad his brother understood.

"That's a freaking merc," Tanner said.

"No, mercs are paid to fight. We do rescues, security envoys, some surveillance."

"What the hell, Trip?" Tres stood and paced the room. "Are you insane?"

"No, I'm just doing what I want to do. I like what I do," Trip said.

"This is what caused the fight between you and Olivia?" Craig asked.

"Yes, she didn't want me to do it."

"What does Jane say?" Tres asked.

"She told me I should do what I want."

"Holy shit. Never thought I'd say this, but maybe you should reconsider Olivia," Craig said with a frown.

Trip shook his head. "Screw you. That's never going to happen. I like Jane. She understands me; she encourages me to do what I want to do."

"She knows you're a merc?" Tanner asked.

"I'm not a freakin' merc! It's security. She knows I work in security."

"But does she know it could get you killed?" Tres asked, returning to his seat.

"It won't get me killed. I have a good team." Trip stood and shut the game down. "You guys should come to Mom's. They're all coming to my welcome back party next weekend."

"Next weekend? 'Cause you lied to Mom about when you'd be

back, right?" Tres said with a sigh.

Trip shrugged. "I don't need Mom in my business right now. It's my life. I thought you guys, of all people, would appreciate that."

Tres ran a hand across his face and said, "None of this is like the little brother I know. What's gotten into you?" Tres looked tired and worried, his voice dropped to a near whisper as he asked, "Hell, little brother, do I even know you anymore?"

Chapter 11

Trip tossed his controller on the table. "Come on. I didn't give you guys hell over your choices. I backed you all the way."

Craig rested his elbows in his knees as he pointed out. "But none of our choices were stupid."

"Seriously?" Trip's voice rose. "You married Mollie, and you only knew her a few months."

"Mollie wasn't going to get me killed," Craig reminded in a volume that matched his brother's.

"He's right, Trip. We don't want to lose you. This is dangerous way to thrill seek," Tres spoke calmly, his words steady.

"I'm not thrill seeking. I've made changes. Changes that I think are positive. I thought, of all people, you guys would understand." Trip stood to leave. He'd go find Jane. She'd understand. Turning toward the door, he didn't have to look far to find her. There she was, fresh from the hot tub, wrapped in a terry cloth robe. Tears sparkled in her eyes. "Jane," he said as he moved toward her.

With a shake of her head, she ran from the room.

"What the hell?" Trip asked as he followed behind her. She ducked into the bedroom Jenna had taken her to earlier. Jane tried to shut the door, but Trip shoved against it.

"What's wrong?"

"I think it is best I go home."

"No," Trip's words were firm.

"You will hold me hostage?"

"If I have to." Trip folded his fingers inside the door, she'd have to crush them to get him to let go. "Let me in and talk to me."

"I don't want to talk to you."

"Yes, you do. Now step back, so I don't hit your toes."

She pushed with both hands against the door. "No!"

"Jane," he said quietly as he increased the pressure. She turned and put her back against the door to stop him, but the shift in her weight left her off balance, and the door swung open. It took her several stutter steps to get her balance. Righting herself, she tucked the robe tighter around her waist.

He pulled her close and held her. Her body was stiff and uncooperative, but he had no intention of letting her go. He wasn't going to let a misunderstanding about his job piss her off at him too. Tipping her chin until she had no option but to look at him, he explained, "It's just a job. No more dangerous than being a police officer."

Confusion clouded her blue eyes. "What job?"

"The job Tres and Craig were giving me hell over."

"They were mad about your job?"

"Yes, they think I'm just thrill seeking."

Her body relaxed a little. "Oh."

His fingers teased damp curls at her neck. "What were you thinking they were yelling about?"

Jane shrugged and laid her cheek on his chest. Resting there a few minutes she whispered, "Me."

"You?" Trip laughed. "How the hell could you be dangerous?"

Jane played with the collar on his shirt. "I wasn't sure, but I guessed they didn't like me."

"No, it's the job, not you."

She nodded; her body trembled.

"You cold?" he asked.

"No. Nervous I guess."

"Why be nervous?" he asked with a grin.

"I suppose it means a lot that they like me."

"Listen," he held her by the shoulders and said, "I'm sure they like you, but whether or not they do doesn't matter. I like you. I want you with me, and that's what's important."

Jane felt the hot sting in her eyes, but she nodded and attempted a happy smile.

"Ah, Janie. Don't cry." He brushed the hair from her face as he bent to kiss her. She tasted so sweet and felt so right, he couldn't pull her close enough or kiss her deep enough. As he pulled back, she let out a little sigh that warmed his cheek and melted his heart. She felt so small and vulnerable, alone in a strange world. Scooping her off her feet, he settled himself on the edge of the bed with her cradled on his lap. Her robe slipped open, widening the V where the fabric met. He couldn't resist helping gravity, tracing a finger down the space between her breasts.

She was better than he imagined. Olivia was all hard lines and sinewy; Jane was soft curves and smooth skin as pale as a china doll. And her breasts. Nothing about them was firm. They were full and warm, pliable and tempting against his chest. He shouldn't have peaked. He thought she'd be wearing a suit, not the flimsy wet lace of her bra. His brain kept nudging him to slip a hand in her robe, between the damp cloth and warm flesh.

He coughed as he shook his head. *Get a grip*, he told himself. Groping her would only send her running. Closing his eyes, he willed his body to calm the hell down.

Wrapping cool arms around his neck, she played with the hair at the base of his skull. "You all right?"

Trip had to clear his throat or he'd sound like a croaking teen. "I'm fine. I just was thinking I should let you get into some clothes." Or out of them. That thought made sweat bead up on his forehead. "You're probably cold."

"I'm all right," she said as she nuzzled his neck with warm lips.

One move and you have her on her back. Trip shook off the thought. She wasn't some tramp.

"Why were they mad about your job, Trip?" she whispered

He paused, mustered a few brain cells, and answered, "They think it's dangerous."

"Is it dangerous?" Cool fingers slid down the corded muscle along his throat.

He felt so hot, and she felt so cool, it was natural that he'd consider taking a dip in…*dear God, Trip! Get control.*

Her touch, so slight against his skin, only paused to frame his face as she forced him to look her in the eyes. "Promise me you are safe. I've lost everything; I can't lose you too."

All thoughts of relationship strategy lost, he pulled her close, then leaned her body back into the soft mattress. A single bare leg wrapped around him for support; her arms tightened around his neck. He kissed her. Sex was no longer a thought. He was driven by something more, something closer to spiritual than sensual. It was a need to know every inch of her, to get so close he was lost.

She didn't know how long he kissed her before she felt the heat of his hand slip inside her robe. The feel of his hand against such sensitive flesh made her head spin, but not so fast that she couldn't hear the creaking of floorboards in the hallway and the good night call from Tanner to his parents. She couldn't do this here. No matter how tempting, she wouldn't want his family to think poorly of her.

Pulling back, she placed a finger over his lips. "Trip?"

"Hmm," he answered without opening his eyes.

"You need to go to bed."

His eyes popped open. "Why? I'm thoroughly," he said as he ducked her finger and trailed kisses across her collar bone, "enjoying this."

"Your brother has little kids. It will look bad."

"Tanner's old enough to understand, and Sammy and Chas aren't. Perfect ages."

She giggled as she squirmed out from under him.

"Where are you going?" Trip asked.

"To bed," she said as she dropped her feet to the floor.

"You were in bed." He grabbed her hand and tried to pull her back to him.

"I'm going to sleep. As are you."

He rolled onto his back and grinned up at her.

"Alone," she said as she tugged her robe together and tightened the belt.

"Spoil sport." Trip rolled off and stood in front of her. He traced her jawline as he promised, "You'd sleep better with me here."

"I'm certain I will have to make do."

He kissed her lightly. "Sure?" he asked.

"Positive." She offered him light kisses as she backed him out of her room.

Pausing at the threshold, he leaned his head against the door casing and frowned. "You're breaking my heart. You know that, right?"

"I…no…I just…."

A huge grin spread across his face. "I'm teasing you, Jane. You're so sweet. I can't believe you ever thought people would think you were dangerous."

Jane's smile was weak as the thought filtered through her head…*oh, if he only knew*. But he couldn't.

Chapter 12

The flight home was much less traumatic. The skies were clear, and the plane didn't hop and jump every few minutes. Jane looked out her window and waved bye to Sammy. The little boy almost cried when she left. He was her beach buddy on Saturday. They walked up and down the sand, accumulating treasure. Jane had a purse full of tiny shells. Sammy said they were made for girls. The big ones were made for boys.

As the plane lifted off the ground, she turned to Trip and said, "I really enjoyed the weekend. I am glad you talked me into it."

He took her hand in his and lifted it for a kiss. "My only regret is you kept running me off at night."

Jane blushed and shook her head at him.

"They loved you, Jane. Even Hope and Grace loved you. Were you pinching them before handing them to me?"

"Of course not!" She gave him a punch. "I wouldn't pinch babies. They did cry when you held them."

"And never for you."

"I just got lucky," Jane assured him.

"You have a gentle spirit. That's what Jenna and Mollie said. They liked you."

"I liked them too. They are so nice. And informative. They told me stories of your girlfriend."

"My girlfriend?" Trip acted shocked. "I don't have a girlfriend. Just this hot little Russian tamale who won't let me snuggle with her at night."

"A Russian tamale? What's a tamale?" Jane laughed.

"It's Mexican food. Bad analogy. I couldn't think of a Russian food."

"Boiled cabbage," Jane offered.

"Oh, God no! Let's just go with a Russian sweet."

Jane leaned across his seat and gave him a kiss on the cheek. "That works for me."

He gave her hand a squeeze. "Good."

"So, did you want to know what they told me?" Jane asked.

Trip rolled his head against the back of the seat. "I'm not sure. Is it going to get me in trouble? Make me look bad? I'm trying hard to impress you, ya know."

Jane rolled her eyes and spilled the beans. "Well, it seems Old Livia."

"Old Livia, eh?"

"Yes. Sammy said that was her name. Who am I to argue?"

Trip laughed.

"Anyhow, Old Livia told Jenna she should never use motherhood as an excuse for being soft in the middle. And she told Mollie that she was smart to leave teaching to stay home with the girls, because teaching wasn't really much of a profession anyhow."

"She said that crap to them?" Trip looked shocked. "Why didn't they ever mention it to me?"

Jane shrugged. "I guess they didn't say anything to your brothers either. They just did prayer vigils that you'd get smart."

He caressed her cheek with his thumb. "Oh, I got smart all right."

Jane's smile was thin, but her eyes shined bright as she said, "I'm glad you got smart, too."

Departing the plane, Trip's phone rang. He grimaced and answered.

"Hello." He placed a hand on Jane's back as he escorted her down the air steps. "I'm stepping off the plane now." Trip cradled the phone against his ear as he grabbed their luggage off the cart. "Just landed, I swear." They walked together toward the car. "No, I'm not lying. No, I haven't forgotten. I already said I'd be there."

He dropped the luggage on the ground and dug into his pocket for his keys. "Love you, too."

He hung up the phone and slid it in his pocket. As he dropped the luggage in the trunk, he said, "Still want to meet my mother?"

Chapter 13

Jane hovered over Sasha in the kitchen, peeping over her shoulder, waiting for the right moment to ask a favor.

Sasha slowly mixed herself a cup of hot cocoa, oblivious to the agitated shadow of her friend. She licked clean the cocoa spoon, rinsed it, dried it, then carefully placed it neatly on a napkin on the counter. She cast a glance over her shoulder at Jane and finally asked, "You wanting cocoa?"

Jane shook her head. Sasha frowned. She tucked her satin robe tighter to her body with a sigh as she picked up her mug and slid past Jane, muttering something as she passed from the kitchen to the couch. Jane was pretty certain her grumbling was a creative mix of curse words selected from the three languages Sasha was most fluent in.

Jane assumed she was being avoided, but undeterred, she followed.

She and Trip had gone out every night this week. And ever since she returned from the weekend at the beach, every date and mention of Trip left Sasha with a permanent scowl. The mere mention of a date detail sent Sasha into narrow-eyed, tight-lipped irritation. Talk to her of dogs, work, even politics and she was friendly. Well, as friendly as Sasha could be.

Jane cleared her throat and licked her dry lips. She felt like she was facing a dragon rather than a friend. "Sasha?"

Sasha didn't acknowledge; she flipped on the TV and tossed the remote on the table.

Jane traced the plaid pattern on the couch. "Can I ask a favor?"

Sasha gripped her cocoa and grimaced.

"Please, don't say no until you hear me out."

Sasha set her mug on the table and turned her attention to Jane.

Jane jumped in. "Trip invited me to his coming home party tomorrow night."

"He's been home for two weeks."

"I know, but his mother is just getting around to it."

"So, how does that concern me?"

"Well, for beginners, I don't have anything to wear. Trip said it will be formal."

"Not that I care, but how formal?"

Jane shrugged.

"Black tie? Business suit?"

"I don't know. That's why I'm asking you. He just said it was formal, that his mother likes to do things fancy."

"That figures." Sasha rubbed her forehead, then she looked at Jane. Sasha suddenly looked tired. "Jane, you know you are playing with fire."

"It's just a party."

"With his family. You should avoid that kind of personal involvement."

"I'll be smart. I've been smart."

"No. No, you're not. You have been with him every day. You go too fast. At that speed, you will not think right." She tapped her head with her finger. "You need to understand...." Sasha took a deep breath and shook her head. "You can't fall in love. You can't be honest with him. Ever. Don't you get that?"

Jane nodded and gave Sasha her best puppy dog eyes. "Please? He makes me happy. That's all. I've never truly had a proper relationship. I just want to be normal, for just a bit. I am very careful.... I swear."

Sasha rolled her eyes.

"I never even got to go to a dance as a student."

Sasha frowned. "Poor baby. Having a rich daddy and servants not enough?"

"I'm talking boyfriends. I never had one. Never went to a movie with a boy. Or had a romantic dinner. Or…"

"Good God, just stop. Fine. Fine." She agreed, though her tone was annoyed. "I will show you what to wear."

Jane took a suck of air. Easy favor down. Tough one on deck. "There is one more favor."

Sasha shook her head and dropped her chin toward her chest.

"Will you please, please, please come with me to the party?"

Sasha offered her a rare look of astonishment. "You're joking, right?"

"No. I don't want to go alone because, like you said, Trip's mom and her friends will be there. I won't know anybody, and I've been to more boxing matches than I have parties. I mean I can't even think of a party I have attended. Well, my birthday, but Poppa brought in circus bears and clowns, and that was not fancy. A party for adults? I won't know what to do."

Sasha didn't budge.

"Please? Poppa always told me you would be the one to teach me to be a lady. Please? Come, Sash, for Poppa?"

Sasha's eyes narrowed as she took a sip of her cocoa. "Using your father against me….is cruel. Maybe I will go, but only to keep a better eye on you."

"Yes. Yes, you're right."

"Da," Sasha said. "Now leave me alone." She leaned over and grabbed her mug. "My cocoa is getting cold and I am missing *Jersey Shore."*

Jane grabbed her and wrapped her arms around her for a big hug. Sasha accepted the hug stiff as a board, but without complaint.

"Let's pick out clothes," Jane sang.

"Now? Party is not till tomorrow. Why now? I am in pajamas, with my cocoa. I am relaxed."

Jane looked as pathetic as a kicked pup. Sasha sighed and stood up. She started toward her room, then turned to Jane, who was still on the couch, and asked, "Well? Aren't you coming?"

"Really? Thank you. Thank you. I want to look beautiful. I want them to not think Trip is dating a peasant, no? Too bad I don't have any money. I could go buy something brand new."

"I have money. You can—"

Jane shook her head. *"Niet."* She held up a hand to Sasha. "I just talk foolish. The money we save is for a good reason. Not for this. But dreaming is fun, yes?"

Sasha shrugged. "I don't like to dream. I am better suited for reality." She opened the closet door and ruffled through her dresses. "Besides you dream enough for the both of us. That's what scares me most. What kind of dreams have you hatched for the clueless Mr. Trip?"

"I haven't even thought—"

"Really?" Sasha asked as she pulled cocktail dresses from her closet and tossed them on her bed.

Jane sorted through them with youthful vigor, telling Sasha, "This is so much fun. Better than dress-up! We'll have a good time, and I swear, I will always remain rash."

"I pray you mean rational…but I fear you speak truth without realizing."

"Yes, rational. I'm excited…silly mistake."

"Mmm, hmmm." Sasha groaned as she dug deeper into the closet. She pulled out a gauzy blue dress. "This one." She held it up to Jane. "It will be beautiful on you. You have pretty eyes. They catch attention with their blue."

"Really?" She held it to herself and looked herself over in the mirror. "Trip says he loves my eyes too." She giggled and spun back to face a grim-looking Sasha. Jane sighed. "Please, Sash. Don't be grumpy. We are having fun."

"Sorry. I can't help but worry. You are going to get hurt. You dream too much. And dreams are useless. And reality sucks. That's the truth of life. You can't live happily ever after with Prince Charming. You can't ever marry him, can't have children with him. I know hurt is coming for you."

"Not necessarily…one day…."

"No day. Everything takes fingerprints and ID. The fake crap we have wouldn't protect us from anything more than a traffic violation."

"They fingerprint…even to have babies?"

"Of course, Jane. They do it for security. To keep people from stealing them and to keep sloppy nurses from mixing them up in nursery."

"I never really thought about it."

"Well, you better start. Especially as fast as you move."

"But I've never…Trip has not really…even…you know."

Sasha held up her hand. "But he will. Sex is always on men's minds. I promise you. And sex is one thing, but I fear not enough for you. You will want *love.*" Sasha seemed to gag on the word. "You won't be able to separate yourself from emotion and you will be hurt." Sasha sighed and slammed the closet door closed and then turned to Jane. "I cleaned Miss Bitch's apartment for you this morning…she still has his picture by her bed."

Jane shrugged, nonplussed. "That's not Trip's fault."

"Unless he never broke up."

"He wouldn't lie to me."

"Really?" Sasha quipped.

"Really. He's a good man. And I am smart. Smarter than you think."

"I know you're smart, but you're also stubborn. How do I make a stubborn girl listen?"

Jane's defense of her relationship and Sasha's question were totally forgotten when her cell phone messenger went off. She pulled it out of her pocket and read the message from Trip. He was across the street at the private park next to the building. Without even saying good-bye to Sasha, she threw on her shoes and coat, grabbed Frosty and his leash and bolted. She nearly ran across the street, Frosty cradled under her arm as she dodged honking cars. Trip leaned against a swing set, standing straight and waving at her once he spotted her.

"I thought you were to spend the day with your friends?" Jane asked, breathless, as she approached.

"I know I said I couldn't come, but I doubt I could sleep tonight without seeing you. And Eve wanted to go for a walk."

"So you drove her to the park downtown?" Jane asked as she

bent over to give Eve a pat.

Jane put Frosty on the ground and wrapped herself in Trip's arms. She squeezed her body against his. Sasha was partly right about things moving toward a more intimate relationship. Jane didn't know if Trip was thinking about it, but she knew she was plagued with curiosity. No matter how much she tried to ignore thinking about *it,* the thoughts were there. And when she was close to him, she didn't know exactly what it was she wanted, but she knew she wanted much more. Jane closed her eyes and relished the feel of cool air on her warming face.

Sasha's words rang in her memory. Could she simply have sex with him? Would it be enough? The idea depressed her. And how could she have any sort of relationship when most everything she shared with him was lies and partial truths? If she told him the truth, she could lose him. If she didn't tell him, she would never truly have him as her own. And if he somehow found out she was lying to him, then what? Could he ever forgive her? Trust her? She laid her cheek against his chest. Why couldn't her life just be normal? He kissed the top of her head and rubbed her back, a satisfied sigh eased from his body as he held her in the brisk night.

She looked up at him. She tried to brush aside her worries, but she couldn't. She smiled and hoped he didn't notice. Trip's eyes narrowed. His thumb brushed across her cheek. "What's wrong, Janie?"

She sighed and her shoulders sagged. "Oh, I...I have just missed you." She buried her face back into his chest. "I guess I was lonely today and fell into stupid Russian thinking that bad luck always follows good."

"Are you sure that's all?"

She nodded against his chest.

"You seem sad."

"I-I-I...." Jane stammered. "I suppose I miss my poppa. I thought of him today. I thought... Poppa will like Trip.... Then I remember Poppa will never meet you. It made me sad. It made me miss life like it was before he died. And the holidays come soon....and...."

Trip brushed her hair back from her cheeks. "I understand. I still miss my own father on holidays, and it's been years since mine passed on. But...." He kissed her temple. "This year we'll be together. I want you to come stay with me. We'll get a tree. I'll make you dinner. You won't have time to be blue."

A giggle bubbled out from behind unshed tears. Only he could make her feel this happy with all that was wrong in her life. "You're too good for me."

"Shh, don't say that. You're exactly what I need. With you in my life, I have everything I could ever want.... Well, at least I would if you would kiss me."

She gave his waist a squeeze, but offered no kiss.

Trip shook his head. "Come on...kiss me."

"Hmm, I guess, bossy American."

He laughed and pulled her tight. She burrowed her arms deeper into his coat wrapping her arms around his waist. She wished they weren't standing in a park, in the middle of winter, heavy clothes separating them. She didn't know where the desire came from, but she wanted to feel his flesh, bared and vulnerable. She knew he felt the same. His hands gripped the back of her neck, pulling her tighter until she could feel his quickened breath. All rational thoughts melted away, leaving only desire. She wanted to feel him closer, was about to tell him, beg him for more, but cold fate, or more precisely, the cold winds of November interrupted.

Frosty whined, then started to yap. Jane couldn't ignore the little dog's pleas. His thin, white coat of curls was no match for the chill. She looked down at him, and his body trembled and shivered. "Oh, poor *pebohok*." She stepped away from Trip and picked the dog up and stuffed him in her coat.

"How is it the dog gets to be where I want to be?"

Jane grinned and gave Trip a quick kiss. "I have to get him inside. Sorry?"

"He's the one who should apologize. Rotten mutt. Eve's taking it, old boy. Jane," he looked serious, "your dog is a wuss."

Jane laughed. "A what?"

"Wuss. Pansy. Momma's boy."

"No." She laughed, kissing the dog's ear. "He just has so little hair. You leave him alone."

Trip grumbled good naturedly about the dog all the way to her door. He kissed her forehead. "You work early tomorrow?"

She nodded. "6:00 A.M."

"Then get some rest. Dream good dreams?"

"Of course."

"Good." He kissed her again. "So, I suppose I better go."

"I would invite you in, but...."

"Sasha might eat me?"

"No, she likes you."

Trip raised an eyebrow at her.

Jane laughed. "Okay, so she maybe doesn't. But I do. Isn't that all that matters?"

"For now?" he asked. "Yes. I will be content that you *like* me."

She grinned at him. "I like you way much more than just *like*."

"Good. 'Cause I'd hate to be *in like* all by myself."

She started to walk away, but his hand held onto hers. He looked seriously immersed in thought. She took a step closer, gave him a light kiss and asked, "What are you thinking? You look a little grumpy."

"Not grumpy. Just thinking how badly I don't want to say goodnight and let you go."

"How else do you say goodnight?"

His jaw clenched, and his brow dipped slightly, almost imperceptible.

His meaning washed over her. "Oh," was all she said. She was ecstatic that he felt that way about her, yet couldn't shake the total disappointment of the reality Sasha so clearly painted for her. No marriage. No babies. No happily ever after, because nothing erased truth. And the truth was she was a murderer.

Chapter 14

The two women arrived at the party ten minutes early. Jane tugged at the hem of her teal satin dress, but it wouldn't budge lower than mid-thigh. She checked and rechecked her hair and make-up in the rearview mirror of the car. Was her hair formal enough in its simple twist? Was her dress too short for meeting Trip's mother? Was her eye-liner too heavy, or maybe not heavy enough?

She snuck a look at Sasha, who stood outside the car blowing smoke rings into the icy air. Whether Sasha was nervous or not was a mystery. She looked as cool and calm as ever. Sasha dropped the cigarette butt on the ground and twisted it into the concrete with a turn of her stiletto. She reapplied her red lipstick using the window as a mirror and rapped on it with the case when she was done. "Hurry up, Jane. I am freezing my tits off out here." Dropping the lipstick into her purse, she pulled the gauzy shawl tighter across her shoulders. "I swear," she said to Jane as she emerged from the car, "if I die of pneumonia, I will haunt you."

Jane's dress was a satin sheath covered in chiffon. The gossamer fabric revealed well-shaped arms and shoulders without exposing too much flesh. It was simple and elegant. Her blond hair was parted down the side and swept back in a French knot. She traded in her usual dangling earrings for simple faux pearls. Sasha was dressed in a curve-hugging red dress that fell to mid-thigh and plunged daringly between shapely D-cups. Sasha's ears were adorned with long diamond-encrusted earrings. Her red hair was a riot of curls, lifted off her neck, and spilling over the pins that secured them.

Sasha put the keys in her handbag and snapped it closed. "This is it. Are you sure we want to do this?"

"Of course," Jane insisted, heading toward the door of the brownstone building. As she mounted the steps, her pace slowed. By the time she reached the top, she came to a complete stop. She turned to Sasha. "You go first?"

Sasha shook her head. "This is your party." Reaching around her, Sasha rang the doorbell, then quickly retreated to the rear position, leaving Jane without as much as a moment to fortify her nerve. Before Jane could mumble a single word, the door swung open and a middle-aged man in the crispest suit Jane ever saw answered with a simple, "Hello."

"Hi, I'm Jane. Um, Jane Mitchell. Trip invited me?" She bet Sasha was rolling her eyes. Jane's throat went dry, wind and embarrassment made her eyes water.

"Of course, Ms. Mitchell. Mr. Trip told me to notify him immediately when you arrived. Step inside?"

He escorted them to a room with a grand piano, a couple of sumptuous brown leather couches, and walls covered with art from ceiling to mid-wall. He said as he backed out of the room, closing the door as he went, "Please, make yourselves comfortable."

With the door closed and the man safely out of earshot, Jane turned to Sasha and asked, "Real or fakes?"

"Real or fake what?"

"The paintings. Have you ever seen so many in one small space?"

"What makes you think I know?"

"I heard one of Poppa's men say once that you could be an art appraiser…if you ever needed a legitimate job."

Sasha sneered. "Stupid thing to say. My work for Viktor was legit." Sasha crossed her arms over her chest as she walked around the room, slowly moving from one gilded frame to the next. She turned to Jane and let out a whistle. "All real. If I was still a thief I could live for a lifetime by scoring just a few of these."

"Really?"

Sasha nodded. "What is it that Trip's mother does?"

"She's a senator."

Sasha's mouth dropped open and her head shook slowly as she said, "What are you thinking? We must go."

"We can't leave now, it would be rude. Besides…"

Jane's words were interrupted by the opening door. "Jane!" Trip was in the room and gathering Jane for a hug before she could calm Sasha.

"Sasha, I'm surprised Jane talked you into coming. My work crew is here. I'm betting the sight of you will brighten their night."

"Why, Trip, is that a compliment?" Sasha asked adjusting the purse on her arm.

"Yes. And since I'm being nice, would you do me the favor of not devouring any of my friends? They're all good, defenseless men."

"Pah," she spat. "Defenseless and men can't be used in the same sentence. But, for you…I will try to leave them whole."

"Much appreciated." Trip put a hand across Jane's back. "This way, ladies."

He guided them from the study to a huge room with high ceilings, twin fireplaces, and clusters of antique furniture where people gathered in pockets of conversation.

He led them slowly across the room, pausing to make small talk as he moved, to a bored looking group tucked in a corner. "These guys have become like family. I can't wait for you to meet them," Trip said to Jane.

Jane nodded and looked over her shoulder to assure herself Sasha was following. Instant anxiety formed in her belly like a wave that begins its swell way off shore. She clutched her bag to hide shaking hands and at least to fake calm, but it was useless. Her hands began to shake, and before Trip could make a single introduction, Jane seriously thought she might pass out. She took a deep breath.

Trip propelled her with a hand on the small of her back. "Jane, this ragtag group of shit…I mean miscreants, are my new co-workers." Trip nodded to a handsome man with a neck as thick as a tree trunk. "This is Shane Cucculo and his wife, Faith. Faith's grandfather married my mom, so that makes her my niece. Though, come to think of it, not once, Faith, have you called me Uncle Trip." The group laughed. Faith, a tiny dark-haired beauty, shook her head at him, though her face radiated pleasure from his teasing.

Next was a tall strawberry blond with a smooth, friendly nature. He was first to step forward and introduce himself. His British accent took Jane by surprise. "I must express my sincere pleasure, ladies." He took Jane's hand and gave it a kiss. "Lieutenant Bruce Armstrong, Royal Air Force…. Retired, of course."

"Back off, Bruce, she's with me." Trip warned with a grin as Bruce looked over Trip's shoulder, his gaze falling on Sasha. Sasha sneered, pressed her hands together behind her back and looked away. Bruce smiled and backed up. He motioned to the people in the corner and said to Jane, "Any friend of Trip's is, of course, a friend of ours. And his tales of your beauty were not, as we shamelessly suspected, at all exaggerated."

"Oh buggers, Bruce. It's bad manners to cozy up to another man's girl in his presence. I thought Mum taught you better than that."

"Oh, and the harpie? That's my little sister, Cammie, and her unfortunate husband, Trevor Jimme."

"It's a pleasure." Cammie stood. She was a tall woman, probably as tall as her husband. She looked sturdy and down-to-earth. She gave Jane a hug. "Forgive my brother, I fear he loses his mind when he sees a skirt."

Bruce turned to Trip. "All lies, brother, all lies. I would never tread in another man's territory."

"I'd have to hurt you if you did." Trip's grip on her waist tightened as he said, "I'm keeping this one for myself."

Jane's heart fluttered. *He called me his!* But before she could digest the sweet sentiment, he was making more introductions. Next was Gunny, an ageless man with a trim, muscular body. Last there was Frankie Bonmarito. Frankie's hair was as dark as his eyes, and Jane bet he was once a very handsome man, but now his face was covered in scars, and his frown lines ran so deep they looked like they were chiseled into his face. His arms were folded over his chest, and he didn't even bother to nod a hello, his gaze scanned her briefly and then settled on Sasha.

Jane followed his gaze back to her friend and noted with some amusement that for once in her life, Sasha appeared to be blushing. She stepped nervously from one foot to the other and chewed on the side of her cheek. Sasha's eyes dropped to the floor as if she was intentionally trying to not make eye-contact with Frankie. But like a magnet pulling on a shard of steel, she did. Jane thought she saw fear flash across Sasha's face for a moment; the briefest fluctuation in color and a flash of wide-eyes. But then as smoothly as honey being poured from a spoon, Sasha's seductive smile appeared and her body relaxed. She stepped from behind Jane and approached these new "friends" with handshakes and clever compliments.

Frankie's eyes stayed glued on Sasha. It was a brash perusal that made Jane's stomach tighten, but she ignored the feeling. Told herself Sasha could handle anything and allowed herself to be lured from the room by Trip. Sasha's eyes bore into her as she exited. She felt a tad guilty, but she couldn't refuse Trip's request to meet his mother. He led her through a back hallway, stopping a moment to give her a kiss, his hands gripping her arms gently. He smiled down at her and twisted a tendril of hair by her ear around his finger. "Thank you for coming."

Jane didn't speak, her eyes were still closed, and her body felt warmed by his closeness. What she wouldn't give to stay like this forever.

"You only have to meet my mom. My stepfather couldn't make it. But maybe you can meet him New Year's Eve. We usually go to Tres's. I know they'd love for you to come back."

Jane nodded, but that little voice in her head that spoke hard truths, reminded her that she couldn't really make any plans for the future.

"You all right? My mother's not that scary."

Jane looked up at him and smiled. "A little nervous. But now that I've gotten a hug...I'm ready."

"Then come with me, my lady." Trip did his best Lt. Armstrong impersonation as he opened the door revealing his mother's office. The walls were lined with book shelves that went from the floor to the ceiling, and yet books and papers were stacked on the desk and on the floor. It seemed a wreck, but further examination proved that the stacks were meticulously organized but too voluminous to be contained in the massive cherry desk. A tiny woman sat behind it in a red leather swivel chair. Bifocal glasses perched on the end of her nose, she sat clicking away at her laptop without bothering to look up when the door opened and closed.

"Mom?"

She slowly shifted her gaze from screen to son. "Ahh, Rowan." His mom shoved her desk chair away from the desk and stood, arms outstretched to her son. Trip moved immediately to his mother and gave her a hug that lifted her feet from the floor. His mother laughed as she ordered, "Put me down. I'm a senator for cripes sakes, not a rag doll."

"You need to put on some weight, old girl. Good thing you got all that hot air to hold you up while facing congress."

Barbara Coulter shook her head at her son. "Where's your respect?"

"I respect my mother."

"Ha." Barbara laughed and rubbed her son's shoulder. Her good humor quieted as her eyes landed on Jane. Trip's eyes followed his mother's, and he cleared his throat. "Mom, I'd like for you to meet Jane. Jane, this is my mother, Barbara Coulter O'Leary."

Jane said hi, though it was barely audible.

Barbara looked her son over, finally asking, voice crisp as frozen linen, "So, who is Jane?"

Trip flinched. He took Jane's hand and pulled her closer to him. "I should have said something to you sooner, but I know how busy you've been and…." He took a deep breath and said, "Jane is a friend of mine."

"Really."

Jane's body shook, and she gripped Trip's arm tighter, nearly cutting off circulation. Barbara removed her glasses and looked

Jane over like a stock animal. "So, Jane, what sort of education do you have?"

Jane's voice stammered as she said, "I don't have a degree. I studied at Oxford, but never finished."

Barbara frowned. "Your accent? Not completely British?"

"Well, I have been in America for a year and before that I spent several years with my father in Russia."

"So, your father is Russian?"

"Yes, ma'am."

"Well, that's very interesting. Does he have business in America?"

"I'm afraid he passed away."

Barbara touched her hand to her chest. "I'm so sorry. Trip lost his father when he was a young boy. I know first-hand what that does to a child. Your mother?"

"Also gone," Jane said barely above a whisper.

"Oh." Barbara reddened. "Again, my apologies."

Jane took a breath, played the part of orphan and looked at the floor.

"Well, I hope you enjoy the party. It was nice meeting you." She turned to Trip. "Darling, might I have a word with you? It is a private matter. A…business matter."

"Of course." He turned to Jane. "Excuse me just a minute?"

Jane stepped out into the hall and waited.

Barbara closed the door and leaned close to Trip. "What's going on with you and Olivia?"

"We broke up."

Barbara glared at her son and grumbled, "Seems you're making changes to your life right and left without speaking to your mother first."

"That's because I know you won't agree with my decisions."

"You never give me the chance to agree or disagree."

"So, if I had asked, you would have supported my career change?" Trip asked, crossing his arms over his chest.

"Of course not. Damned dangerous foolishness you're getting yourself involved in."

"National security isn't foolishness."

"Leave it to the experts."

"But I am an expert. I'm fully trained. I have skills few others have."

She shook her head and said with more than a little disgust, "Save the recruitment poster lingo for some other schmuck. You're my son."

"So what? Leave the scary stuff to other people's children?"

"Don't lecture me on duty," her voice rose a moment, then quickly returned to normal. "If this was simply a call to serve, I might understand. But this…this is nothing more than you grasping for some adventure."

"Is looking for adventure a bad thing?"

"Go skydiving. Go mountain climbing. Joining those men? My God, did Tres and Craig knock you over the head during that fishing trip?"

"No, but they made me realize they're happy and I wasn't."

Barbara massaged the bridge of her nose and asked, almost in a groan, "So, what is the lure of the girl? Is she dangerous also? Let me guess? Russian mafia?"

"Hardly. She, uh, manages an apartment building. I met her by chance."

"Oh Trip! You're telling me you're trading in a well-respected lawyer for a college drop-out? That makes sense. Is it because she's cute?" Trip started to answer, but Barbara interrupted, "Son, that only keeps a man's interest for so long. Or is that part of the new 'you', too? A James Bond with a new flavor each week? Or…"

"Mother." Trip's tone was sharp. "Do I get to answer a single question?"

"Of course…why have you gone insane?"

"Come on, you know I don't do anything on impulse. You know me better than that."

"Do I? You are turning your life upside down with nary a word to me until it is all fate accompli."

"I've only been dating Jane for a little while, so you're in on the ground floor."

Barbara thought a moment, then nodded. "I see." She moved back to her desk and shuffled some papers. "You really hurt my feelings joining Shane and his cronies without even talking to me."

"You would've blocked me."

"I would never involve myself in the lives of my sons."

Trip laughed. "Seriously? Should I call Tres and Craig in on this? I'm sure they'll tell a different tale."

Barbara shrugged and snorted. "Try to help your children, and they...."

"Just relax." He rounded her desk and gave her a hug. "You have to trust me.... This life I'm building... it's what I want. You owe me the benefit of the doubt." He smiled down at her, not recalling her being so little before. "I was the one who supported your marriage to Max. If it weren't for me, my two big brothers would still be sulking over the memory of dad."

"Yes, darling. You were a champion getting your brothers to accept the change."

He sat on the edge of her desk and stretched his legs out in front of him. "Because I realized that life is better if it's lived happily than if it's just lived by rules. And now? Look at how well all of this has turned out? You have a husband and a step-granddaughter who loves you."

"Hmmph. Faith is a dear, but it was probably Shane who put these ideas into your head. He did, didn't he?"

"I approached him. Shane told me no several times because he knew you would eventually blame him."

"You just don't know how much it scares me to think of anything...."

"Nothing will happen to me. I'm still just a geek. All I do is break encryptions and leap firewalls."

"You could do that working in the State department!"

"Plus, I also get to play with guns."

"Oh, lord. Men are such children." She rolled her eyes and laughed a little before becoming serious again. "This girl? She seems rather wretched. No mother...no father. You're not playing games, are you, darling? I would never expect that sort of thing out of you."

"No. I like her. A lot. There's something about her that just makes me… well, let's just say, the idea of leaving her makes me wish I hadn't joined up with Shane. If I had met her before I enlisted, well…who knows. "

"Oh? Well, in that case, shall I book a church?" Barbara laughed, then sobered and said, "Seriously, though. I thought the situation with Olivia was beyond friendship, so you will forgive me when I tell you I invited her tonight."

"Olivia?" Trip asked. Barbara nodded with a grimace.

"Oh shit."

"It may do well to take Jane home before they come face to face."

"But how do I explain that? She just got here."

"Tell her the truth. Men are so dense. This whole party has been nothing but a disaster. Had I known your brothers would bow out, I'd have skipped the whole thing. Hope and Grace got colds and Craig acts like they need intensive care."

"He gets nervous."

"I know, I know. Max and I are going to head down there after I get all of this," she threw her hands up in the air, "under control. Craig keeps calling, thinks the girls need to be in the hospital."

"Do they?"

"No, I spoke with Jenna, she went up to help them out. Sniffles and coughs. First parent jitters, nothing more. As for, Jane…was that her name?"

Trip nodded.

"Bring her by in a few days so I can get to know her? Until then, as horrible as this sounds… you must get her out of here before there's a scene."

Trip sighed and ran a hand across his shorn hair "You're right, and I don't want Olivia hurt. I just can't help how I feel about Jane."

"Good boy." Barbara kissed her son's cheek.

Trip left his mother's office, closing the door quietly behind him. Jane was leaning against the wall waiting for him. He took her hand and pulled her in for a hug. He kissed her temple and sighed.

"Now you've met my mom. Still interested?"

Jane laughed. "Of course." Jane felt shy, but had to ask, "Does she hate me?"

"Of course not. Why would you say that?"

Jane shrugged and chewed on her lip. Trip hugged her tighter.

"I have to be honest with you though. There is a…situation I need to deal with. And as much as I hate to say it…I need to send you home because…."

Before he could finish, a door opened. The sounds of small talk and Vivaldi filled the hallway, and then quieted as the door settled back into place. Replacing it was the sound of high heels on marble floors moving at an unimaginable speed. Both Jane and Trip turned toward the sound. Sasha barreled down the hallway, her shawl picking up wind and blowing off her shoulder. She grabbed Jane by the arm and hissed, "We have to leave. Now."

Elizabeth Seckman

Chapter 15

Trip escorted them to the car, apologizing to Jane the whole way for the turn of events. Sasha cursed and grumbled in her native tongue. Jane cringed as she made out "dirty bastard" from the mumblings. Jane turned to Trip and said, a bit too loudly, "I will see you later. It's best that we go home anyhow. Sasha appears to be in a foul mood."

Trip sighed and pulled Jane's wrap closer to her body. "I'll be over as soon as I can get things worked out."

Jane nodded and shivered against her will. She tried her best to ignore the chill, but the temperature was dropping and the air was growing heavy with mist. Trip kissed her forehead. "Now, you get out of the cold before you get sick. We have a holiday to prepare for, right?"

Jane smiled. For the first time in a long time, she felt a thrill. She was celebrating an American holiday properly. And getting a Christmas tree? Why she felt as flighty as the twelve-year-old Jane who last celebrated the occasion with her Aunt Tilley. Her father, a child of Stalin's Soviet Union, never celebrated the holiday. Jane had tried to introduce it to him, but she could always tell, that he, like Sasha, just never got it.

She stood on tip-toe and kissed his cold cheek. Her smile was bright, but her teeth chattered. She gave him a quick hug and reminded, "Until later."

"Later. As soon as I, uh, deal with…things."

"Secret job with secret emergencies," Jane whispered in his ear as he leaned forward to open the door for her.

Trip's laugh held a nervous edge. Glancing across the car at Sasha, he said slowly, "I'll explain it all later."

He guided her toward her seat. She said good-bye as he stepped up onto the curb and waved. Sasha gunned the gas and pulled out in front of a passing car. Tires squealed and a horn blew, which prompted Sasha to roll down her window and flip the perturbed driver the bird.

Sasha sped past stop signs and ran more than one red light. She flew onto the interstate on- ramp with barely a glance over her shoulder. She drove at break-neck speeds, shifting the gears of the compact car in jerking, engine grinding haste. "You trying to kill us or just get a ticket and get us locked in the gulag?"

Sasha glared at Jane, but slowed down. Sasha chewed at her cheek, her shoulders were tense, and her hands gripped the steering wheel.

"Did something happen?" Jane asked.

Sasha said nothing. She reached onto the floorboards and flipped open her handbag fumbling through the contents until she found her pack of cigarettes. She lit one and took a long drag. She trapped the smoke in her lungs until she had to exhale for a breath of air.

"What is it?" Jane asked cracking her window.

"Roll up the window. It's cold."

"Those stink."

"This whole mess you've gotten us into stinks," Sasha hissed.

"What did I do? What's going on? Your driving is insane. And why were you calling Trip names? He understands Russian, probably even Chechen."

"And you've never wondered why that is? How many freakin' Americans speak Russian?"

Jane shrugged. "He's smart."

"And you're an idiot."

"*Sukin syn!* What is your problem? Good God, you act like I kicked your dog."

"I only wished you had *just* kicked my dog. For God's sakes,

Jane, you've kicked open a whole bag of *der'mo*."

"Me? How did I?" Jane didn't get to finish before Sasha interrupted.

"That room was so thick with CIA, I'm surprised we made it out alive. If any of them recognize us..." She looked across at Jane, Sasha's face was paler than milk. "We'll be screwed."

"I think you're just..."

"I'm not 'just' anything. I know. I can spot them. I can tell by the way they scan a room constantly. They come out of the field, but the skills are always working. A 'hello how are you' is analyzed with those eyes that look through you, never just at you. And the tattoos, Jane. Didn't you recognize the tattoos?"

"No," Jane answered, her voice rising, "I didn't notice any tattoos."

"All different, but the same. Each and every tattoo was for special forces—but each from a different branch," Sasha explained, lighting another cigarette.

"So, that's not so uncommon. Old military stick together."

"Army befriends Army, Navy with Navy, Marine with Marine. What the hell brings together a grunt, a jar head, and a sailor?"

Jane shrugged. Sasha whipped the car onto the off ramp so quickly, Jane had to grip the door handle to stay upright. Sash slowed as the car skidded around a sharp turn. "The CIA. The NSA. Or whatever in hell black ops are being called at the moment. That's what brings together different branches to become one tight little group of blood sucking friends. Oh, and the Brit. Where the hell did they pick up Captain Bruce of the Royal Air Force? I'm telling you, Jane, we're in trouble."

Jane took a deep breath. "Okay, so let's say they are who you say they are. Why would they be suspicious of us?"

Sasha bit her lip. It was several long seconds before she shrugged.

"You've been to state dinners *with congressmen* and no one has ever gotten suspicious."

"Politicians are blinded by ego. Soldiers are...just different. This will be bad." Sasha sucked so hard on her cigarette that it crackled and flared.

"But still," Jane theorized, "why would they suspect us? Because we're Russian? There's thousands of us in America after the fall. And besides…you are the coolest of the cool. And I wasn't even in the room but a moment before Trip whisked me away."

"That is true," Sasha grudgingly agreed, but then added, worry still evident on her face. "But that one guy, the one in the corner, with the deep pockmarks. I didn't like the way he looked at me."

"The really big guy? That's Trip's aunt's husband or something…."

"No. Not him. The guy who didn't say hello."

"Who didn't say hello?"

"The guy in the corner," Sasha said gripping the wheel and rubbing it nervously against her palms. "He just stared."

"Oh…the smoker?" Jane asked with a snap of her fingers.

"Yes, the smoker in the corner."

"I remember him now. Well, he just didn't look happy to be there at all. I don't think we had anything to do with it."

Sasha looked at Jane with narrowed eyes as she considered Jane's explanation. Her head nodded slowly as if logic told her it was a possible explanation, but instinct might not concur.

"And the Brit?" Jane reasoned, kicking off her heels and tucking her feet under her. "The tall one, not the blond, but the dark-haired one? The tall, dark-haired woman, with the freckles? That's her brother, and she's married to the guy they called Jimme something. That's how he got in the mix."

"I wish I could believe these guys were together by coincidence."

"Oh, seriously, Sash. Trip doesn't exactly fit the description of a secret agent."

Sasha's head moved side to side. Jane could hear it crack as she rolled it from shoulder to shoulder. "Another thing that bugs me…." She glanced at Jane. "Trip made a complete change in six short months. What exactly is this new job? I mean, he went from computer geek to Adonis. Sure did wake up that bitch he was dating."

"Olivia?"

"Yeah." Sasha shook out another cigarette from the pack and pushed in the console lighter; then she pulled it out before it popped and impatiently puffed hard against the incomplete glow. It slowly ignited, and she returned it to its place and turned her attention back to Jane. "She was working the room like she was the Mrs."

"Olivia was there?" Jane's heart slid toward her toes, leaving her chest hollow and achy.

"I knew you didn't know!" Sasha sighed. "She came in shortly after Trip dragged you off. I managed best I could to avoid her. I don't think she saw me. And as soon as she wasn't between me and the door, I scooted. Last thing we need is her scratching your eyes out and the police being called. Damn it." Sasha banged the wheel with the heel of her hand. "That bitch could be a problem. We can't survive exposure, do you understand that? I just thank…well, I am happy you didn't argue with me about leaving."

Jane nodded, but it was a slow, mechanical motion. She averted her gaze to the window. The tears she didn't want Sasha to see burned her eyes. Olivia was the reason Trip shuffled her out the back door. Tears silently dropped from her eyes. Jane wiped them away and blotted at her nose so she didn't make a sniffle.

"Oh hell," Sasha spat. "You didn't leave because I asked you to, did you?" Sasha asked sounding almost empathetic.

Jane shook her head no. She couldn't speak right now. If she did, she'd turn into a blubbering mess.

Sasha offered her a cigarette. Jane shook her head again then leaned her forehead against the window on the door. Clouds blocked the moon and an icy mist speckled the glass. She heard Sasha click on the wipers, toss another cigarette out the window, and then immediately dig out another. Sasha spoke around the cigarette clenched in her teeth, "*Durachit.*"

Jane wasn't sure if it was her or Trip Sasha was calling a fool. She supposed it applied equally to them both.

Elizabeth Seckman

Chapter 16

Jane slipped out of her dress and tossed it to the floor. Tomorrow she'd take the thing to the incinerator. She never wanted to wear it again. It was tainted; ruined by bad memory. This was the worst night of her life, she decided as she plopped herself, half-naked, on her bed. Well, okay, hardly the worst. The loss of a guy she now realized she barely knew wasn't like losing her family, but the pain it caused felt as sharp as if all the losses were fresh. A tear slid down her cheek and dropped onto her hand. She watched the first roll off as another dropped. One tear replaced by another, then another.

As the drops started to turn black from her mascara, she wiped her hand on her bedspread. Sniffing, she rubbed the wetness from her cheeks and took a breath. She wasn't going to sit and cry over nothing. She didn't really *lose* anything. How do you lose something, or more precisely, someone you never had? Never really could have?

She stood, forcing heavy legs to carry her away from her bed; a bed which lured her to crawl in, pull the blankets over her head, and allow pity to lull her to sleep. She rummaged through a laundry basket for her favorites: plaid pajama pants and her most cherished, faded and worn to its last few threads, sweatshirt. She pulled them on and hugged herself. It was his loss, anyway. Her eyes burned, and she felt a fury deep within her breast. With nowhere to vent, she kicked the laundry basket against the wall on her way out of the door.

In the bathroom, she washed away the smeared mascara and unpinned her hair, ruthlessly brushing it out and securing it with a highly unfashionable, yet practical scrunchie. She closed her eyes at her image. She didn't need to stare at splotchy red skin, dark circled eyes, and lips that were still just a little fuller, a little plumper from Trip's kiss good night. He'd held her so tightly, almost like he didn't want to let her go; his lips so urgent against her own.

She could have sworn he felt something for her. But then again, she had thought her father was invulnerable and her life unchangeable. She was horribly wrong on all accounts.

Stepping from the bathroom to the kitchenette, she smiled pitifully at Sasha, who had changed into her robe and was busy in the kitchen making a bag of popcorn. "Want to watch a movie?" Sasha asked as Jane approached.

At least she still had Sasha. In less than a year she had gone from family employee to best friend.

"Maybe in a bit. Right now, I need chocolate. Good Russian chocolate. I'm tired of America. Tired of Americans." Jane rummaged through cabinets and drawers as she bitched. "Nothing like Russian chocolate."

Sasha twisted the cap off a bottle of Russian Standard. "Since when is Russia known for chocolate? Now vodka. Vodka is what Russians do best. It is comfort food."

"Vodka isn't a food," Jane pointed out with a half-hearted laugh.

"You sure?" Sasha looked at the bottle as if she was shocked by the revelation before setting it on the counter with a sigh. "Ah, good Russian vodka. Nothing in the world quite like it." Sasha pulled a glass out of the cupboard and filled it. "I always wonder when I pour myself a glass…." She looked at the clear liquid in her hand and said, "If this might be from Sarkhov stock."

"Poppa never let me drink it, so I don't know if it tastes like ours or not."

Sasha took a swallow. "This is good. It could be. Funny. All the vodka I drank with your poppa was still blue."

"I think he preferred it blue." Jane leaned against the counter.

"Reminded him that his empire was built by his brain. It was his understanding of chemistry that passed vodka off as washer fluid. It was a testament to his outsmarting and beating a corrupt system." Jane picked up the bottle and traced the red and silver letters with her thumb. "Funny, he would never tell me how he did it. Do you know?" Jane asked as she set the bottle on the counter. "Do you know how he removed the blue color?"

"I have no idea. He never told me either."

Jane sighed. America sucked. She wished she could go home. "Talk about lost family recipes."

Sasha sipped her drink and shrugged. "Don't worry over it. You'll know one day."

"How? Poppa's gone."

Sasha's cheeks flushed. "Oh, I figure Nikki knows."

"I seriously doubt that. Poppa didn't trust Nikki at all."

Sasha choked on her drink. Her eyes turned red as she gasped and slapped her chest. Jane patted her on the back. "You all right?"

"Fine. Fine." Sasha waved off her concern. "Went down wrong. Not Sarkhov. Sarkhov vodka goes down smooth." Sasha's laugh sounded fake, and her eyes narrowed. Sasha cleared her throat and asked Jane quietly, "How do you know Viktor doesn't trust Nikki? Did he say something?"

"No. He never said, 'I don't trust your brother.' Didn't you ever notice how he'd end his business when Nikki came in the room? I mean I'd sit in his office while he talked to his associates; he would tell them how to fill the drums; how to add the dye; even who in customs was friendly and who to avoid. I mean he just talked business, you know?"

Sasha nodded.

"And if Nikki would enter the room, everyone would shut up. Dead silent."

Sasha nodded slowly and said, "I know your father's men hated Nikki after what happened with your mother. But I wasn't sure if Viktor held it against him. Viktor never said a bad word about his son in front of me."

Jane shrugged. "No, he never did to me either. I believe he tried to forgive Nikki, but the best he could do was be polite. Formal. Poppa and Nikki's interactions were very…fake, friendly, and stiff, don't you think?"

"Definitely. But, dear God, Nikki is just so bizarre…who could get along with him? No matter how nice he acted to me, I could never bring myself to trust him. I think he could be dangerous, don't you?"

Jane paused. She didn't trust him either, but he was still her brother. Unpredictable and angry—a complete spoiled brat, but he shared the same blood as her. But it was Sasha who smuggled her out of Russia. Sasha who found her a place to live and work; got the fake ID she needed to keep herself out of prison. She owed Sasha a greater faithfulness than a brother who could barely stand her.

"Yes, I believe he could be dangerous. He thinks of no one but himself. And no, I don't trust him. I know in my gut that he hates me." She looked to Sasha a moment to see if she seemed shocked by her words, but she wasn't. "And Nikki hated Poppa." Jane leaned her back against the counter and crossed her arms over her chest. "I don't think he ever saw me as his sister, but as Poppa's daughter…does that make sense?"

Sasha nodded slowly. "I heard some of the guards say he attacked you?"

Jane grabbed a glass from the cupboard, poured herself a shot, and swallowed it with an eye-popping head shake and a throaty, "Wow. Definitely warms the blood." Jane wiped her mouth with the back of her hand. Thoughts of her brother on the night of their father's death added to the loss of Trip felt like her heart was being squeezed even tighter.

"Did he hurt you, Jane?" Sasha whispered the words.

"Not really. He slapped me and grabbed me by the throat, but guards arrived before he could do any harm."

"Why? Why did he do that?"

"He was distraught over my mother's death. Carried on and on about it being murder."

"She died of a drug overdose!" Sasha's voice echoed off the kitchen walls. "In London. How is that Viktor's fault?"

Jane shook her head. "That's what I told him. But you know Nikki. Remember, I told you he blamed Poppa for Bernadette's car wreck too?"

Sasha sighed and rolled her eyes. "Yes, I remember. Though if Nikki had half a brain, he'd realize that if Bernadette hadn't died in that wreck, Viktor would never have met Tracy Dugan.... Therefore, Nikki wouldn't have known her either. Then he'd been robbed of the love of his life," Sasha said with a blend of sarcasm and repulsion.

Jane thought a minute. "You know, I wonder...if Nikki's theory was true...which it isn't, but *if* Poppa killed his mum to marry mine, why did he never blame her? Seems the woman who marries your father right after your mother's death would be high on the hate list, but he never saw the bad in her."

"That is true." Sasha took a swig of her drink. "But Tracy was having sex with him. That softens a man up."

"Seems silly, but I suppose." Jane polished off the rest of her drink and shivered.

Sasha laughed. "You're so naïve it's cute. Darling, a woman can make a man do insane things...forgive insane things. There is power in the...relationship."

"I'll take your word for it." Jane set her glass on the counter and gave it a shove toward the sink.

Sasha flashed her a sly grin and a wink before pouring herself another drink and returning to the original subject. "So, this fight between you and Nikki? What started it?"

"He told me Poppa was a killer. That Poppa ordered people to have Tracy, uh, Mum...killed. I told him he was insane. He kept going on and on about it until I finally told him: *if* Poppa was a murderer, then him *and* his whore wife would have been dead long before now."

Sasha nodded. "True."

Jane nodded. "It's only reasonable...*if* Poppa was the killing type. But he wasn't. Mum and Nikki made him look like a weak fool. He was cuckolded by his own son. Anyone else of Poppa's generation wouldn't have just sent them away. They'd been sleeping in the Volga River."

"Exactly. Viktor was too kind. It was the ultimate shame. Makes me want to puke." Sasha pulled a cigarette from the pack lying on the counter. She explained as she lit up, "I honestly believe," her nostrils flared as she exhaled like a dragon, "looking like a fool is what got Viktor in trouble. People thought he was weak. He lost respect. I would bet all my money, and the bracelet from fatty, it was through that weakness...is how the KGB snuck into the family. Rats no longer feared him."

Jane stood up straight. "And that's why I will never forgive Nikki...or her."

"Can't say I blame you."

The grip on her glass tightened as Jane spoke. "I know she married Poppa for his money...that I understand. I don't like it, but what's new about that? Women do it all the time. What I don't and never will understand is why she ran away when she found out she was pregnant with me...gave birth, then ditched me on Aunt Tilley."

Sasha lifted her glass. "How about a toast to Mums who ditch their kids...though mine chose to leave me in the lobby of a hostel." Sasha's laugh was hard, the smile she offered Jane was bitter.

"I wish she had dumped me and never turned back." Jane looked her friend in the eyes. "I hate her. She will probably haunt me, but I can't pretend because she's dead that I loved her or miss her one bit." Jane was quiet a minute as she chewed on her lip. Staring into the glass, swirling the clear liquid around the sides, she said quietly, "I've never even told Aunt Tilley this, but when I was a little girl, I asked Mum once who my father was...." Jane paused and polished off her drink. With a shake of her head and a grimace, she admitted, "She told me she was raped outside a pub. How mean is that? What kind of bitch says that? To a little girl?"

Sasha closed her eyes and scowled, but offered no other response.

"Then one day, I was about twelve...she shows up...on her yearly *I'm a good mother visits*...and says, 'Darling, I have a great surprise for you!' Off we go to lunch, and there I met Poppa."

"Any idea what made her decide to tell him?"

"Money. She was still tossing the sheets with Nikki, and when Poppa found out, he cut him off. Well, Mum never had a job, only men for support, so a poor Nikki was almost useless…but then Mum must have figured she was holding the golden goose—she could sell her daughter to Viktor."

"What a bitch. Did Viktor tell you this?"

"Oh, no. Poppa never spoke of Mum or Nikki. Aunt Tilley told me. She always thought Poppa was a good man, and she didn't want Mum's lies to cloud my judgment toward him." Jane took a sharp breath, exhaled it with a near moan, "Oh, poor Aunt Tilley. She knows I'm a murderer. That has to break her heart."

"Yes, it is sad, but can't be changed. Don't get weak. You cannot contact her or tell her the truth."

"I know. I know." Jane threw her hands in the air.

"Seriously, Jane. I assure you, her every line…phone, internet…has extra ears and eyes."

"I said I know."

"No matter how lonely, or how bad you feel…"

"Stop it! I know! I won't do anything stupid. Trust me. I don't want to go to jail. And," she rubbed her eyes, "I would never do that to you."

"Well, uh, I appreciate that."

Jane's eyes clouded with unshed tears. Everything was crap. Slowly she moved away from the counter.

Sasha touched her arm lightly, said quietly, "We will get evidence one day to clear your name. To prove it was self-defense."

"How? How will we ever do that in hiding?"

"My uncle is on it. He has many connections."

"I don't think my life will ever be good again, especially after tonight."

"Nonsense," Sasha sighed. "Tonight was nerve wracking. I think we should get sleep." Sasha rinsed her glass and set it upside down on the counter.

"It was quite a night," Jane agreed; then said, "Thank you. I owe you much. I know you didn't want to go to the party, but you did, and it means a lot to me. I don't really have anyone left but."

"Pah, just stop. Have another drink. Get sleep. Tomorrow we work." Sasha toyed with the cap on the vodka bottle as she assured, "We'll survive."

"If he starts dating her again, how will I face them? I can't do it. You should get me a new identity; then I could disappear. Then if I get caught, you won't be in trouble." Jane stared at her stocking feet. "Maybe I could go to Mexico, where it is warm. I'm sick of cold places."

"You are a Sarkhov. And you are Viktor's daughter. You will wake tomorrow ready for the fight. You will not be like *sookie* and run in fear."

"Running makes sense sometimes, ya know?"

Sasha shook her head and poured Jane another half cup.

Jane continued, "I wish Poppa would have run. He had to know the KGB was closing in. Why did he stay? Why didn't he get out of the country?"

"Not Viktor's style."

Jane nodded, but the image of her father's last minutes haunted her. She closed her mind to the memory and downed her vodka. She let out a fiery whoop and set her glass on the counter. Sasha started to refill it, but Jane put her hand over the top to stop her. Sasha screwed the cap on the bottle and put it in the cupboard.

"You're a good friend, a true comrade," Jane admitted solemnly.

Sasha wiped away a tear which seemed to cause her a great deal of embarrassment. "Oh, shit. For God's sake go to bed. We will think on this tomorrow."

Jane shook her head. "I'm too anxious, and you know how I sleep when I'm nervous. I have had a week without the bad dream. I refuse to have it tonight. I'm going to the machine and get my damn chocolate. You go ahead and go to bed." Jane overturned the catch-all basket on the counter looking for loose change. She tossed the pennies toward the trash some hitting, some pinging onto the floor, as she complained, "Why do they even make pennies? Who uses them?" She dug out a handful of change and cupped it in her hand. She turned to Sasha with a tight laugh. "No one likes them. No one needs them. And what do we have? A whole basket of them. What is the luck?"

"I hear pennies are good luck. And we may need it, especially if we just spent an evening in a room loaded with covert agents," Sasha said, her hands shaking a little.

"That really has you spooked, doesn't it?"

"With everything that has gone wrong this year?" Sasha asked with an eyebrow arched so high it disappeared under her bangs.

Jane sighed. "True. With our luck, they're all agents and we're probably headed to the gulag, but before they shackle me and carry me off, I'm getting some friggin' chocolate."

Sasha snickered and lit another cigarette as Jane stepped out the door to the elevator.

Jane pushed the button and leaned against the cold block wall to wait. The elevator dinged and she rolled toward the door. When it opened, she only took one step before her path was blocked by five-feet-eight inches of blonde perfection.

Olivia.

Chapter 17

Jane's head moved side to side slowly as if bored with the constant suckiness of her life. Jane remained quiet, but took a step to her right trying to dodge Olivia without acknowledging she was there.

Olivia would have none of it.

She took a step to the left, thereby blocking Jane's exit. Jane sighed and took a step left. Olivia followed. Jane planted her hands on her hips and glared at Olivia. "Excuse me?" Jane asked.

Olivia advanced and poked Jane in the chest. Jane stumbled backward a step or two before regaining her balance. Olivia took advantage of Jane's confusion and made a hasty approach.

Before Jane's brain even had time to register it was an attack, Olivia was almost nose to nose with her. Olivia's blue eyes were wide with fury. "Stay the hell away from my boyfriend, or I swear to God, I will have you fired. Someone who steals things from people can't be trusted."

Jane took a deep breath and said slowly, "You'd be wise to back off."

"Don't tell me what to do, you ignorant Russian slut. You need to understand who you are dealing with." She poked Jane again, punctuating her words with the action. Olivia must have thought she had Jane intimidated, cowering under her verbal attack, and too afraid to utter a word of defense. Jane's silence seemed to make her bolder, her pokes to her chest coming with more force.

Olivia probably thought she was winning until a right hook—

that she obviously never saw coming—landed square on her nose. Olivia dropped like a pile of bricks to her knees.

Her torrent of abuse was replaced instantly with cries of pain. Olivia squealed and brought her fingers to her nose. She let out a scream when she saw the blood.

Jane's hand hurt a bit, but she felt good. She side-stepped Olivia's wailing form and pushed the button yet again. When it arrived with a happy sounding *ding,* Jane turned to her and said, "Maybe *you* should know who you are dealing with, bitch." The elevator doors closed and so did Jane's interest. The woman bleeding in the hallway could go to hell, and she could take Trip with her.

The elevator stopped in the lobby, and she stepped off. Turning to the right, she bumped into a body. "Excuse me," she offered as she walked onward, head bent, eyes on the ground. She was startled when that *body* grabbed hold of her arm and tugged her back. Alarm was replaced with a strange mix of satisfaction and annoyance. She recognized the smell of him, the curve of his throat.

"Trip." She stumbled and fell into his chest. She tried to right herself quickly, tried to craft her reaction to appearing cool, calm, and indifferent. Instead, she stood, face to face, bodies so near she could feel the heat of his on hers.

Punch him too, her mind screamed, *bloody his nose. Then he and his girlfriend can cry together!* Instead she did nothing. She mumbled something, not really a hello, something that sounded more like uh, oh, um rather than words. Her cheeks flamed red as she tried to pull away. This was *not* the posture she wanted to take.

"I'm in a hurry," Jane muttered. Trip still held her arm and didn't seem inclined to let go.

"Where you headed?"

"Please, Trip." She was about to cry. She could feel it. It was coming from somewhere deep inside, and it wasn't going to be pretty. She yanked on her arm and bolted.

He was right behind her, calling her name. She ignored him as she ran blindly, not sure which way she needed to go to get away. He caught up with her in no time and grabbed her arm, pulling her back to him. His grip was like iron. She was shocked by the fierceness of his hold. He held her close, his hands gripping her to him as he asked, "What's wrong?"

She shook her head. She couldn't answer. Couldn't hold back the tears. Trip brushed them away with his thumb and pressed her head to his chest. He kissed the top of her head. "What is it? What happened?"

"My father is sick, and I have to go home. I'm leaving in the morning."

Trip took a step back and looked down at her as if she lost her mind. She took advantage of the separation and dashed toward the fire escape. She realized it wasn't the bravest way to deal with her situation, but she didn't care at the moment. She hit the metal door with a thud, shoving it open, escaping into the cool hollow stairwell. She was only two steps down when Trip caught up with her and grabbed her by the waist and swung her up into his arms where he held her eye to eye.

For a quiet guy, his voice echoed off the concrete walls and rang in her ears, making her flinch. He was mad at her. Her initial shock and twinge of fear faded as she felt her spine stiffen at his audacity to man-handle her. She stood up straight and tried to wiggle free. He squeezed tighter. "What's going on, Jane? You told me your father died. Why are you lying to me?"

"*Me,* lying to *you*? You pig." She hit him in the chest. "Let go of me! You have no right." He ignored her, his arms tightened around her. "I said, let me go!" She tried to wiggle free, but she couldn't get loose, so she swung at him with her free hand and slapped his cheek. "I am sick of you. Go away!" She stuck her chin out at him and glared. Her nostrils flared as she hit him again and again in the shoulder and arm. He didn't even flinch or try to stop her. "My father is dead. And you're lucky for that or he'd bust your nose like your girlfriend's."

"What the hell? Jane, you make no sense."

"I make no sense?" she shrieked. "Me? Let's talk about you. Let's talk of how much sense your stories make. Why did you make me leave the party? Tell me of your *important* business...."

Trip sighed, he closed his eyes for a moment, and then opened them and frowned. "Olivia. Olivia was my business."

Jane's mouth dropped open for a moment, then closed with a snap. "So. Well, then go to hell…," she tried again to jerk away, "and take the bitch with you…I don't want you here."

"No." He loosened his grip on her, but not enough for her to get away. "I'm not leaving you. I love you, Jane. You." He tried to talk as she tried to pull away. "Are you going to listen to me?" He grabbed her by the hair and pulled her head back until she was looking up at him. Her mouth dropped open. He wasn't hurting her, but if she moved, it tugged, and if she tried to go either too far left, right, or back, it hurt. She was shocked speechless. She supposed she would hear his lies, get herself free, and then bloody his nose. He eased his grip as she calmed. "You will hear me out, Jane. I won't lose you because of a misunderstanding, do you hear me?"

Lose her? He was throwing her away. But he sounded scared, desperate. None of it made sense. She finally looked up at him, and she saw the man… the man she loved even if he had just lied to her. She loved the soft brown of his eyes, the firm jaw.

But she couldn't let love interfere with honor. A tear rolled down her cheek. Trip closed his eyes, and his words sounded pained as he said, "Baby, don't cry. I can explain everything." He pulled her into him and hugged her, rubbing his cheek against hers. He took a step back and took a breath. "Olivia was at the party."

"Why did you lie to me? I knew she was your reason for making me leave! And you could have told me the truth, but you lied." Her body stiffened. "The only reason to lie is to hide things. If you want to be with her, then be with her. Don't shuffle me out the back door, her in through the front. I am not a whore who is okay with being the other woman." She shoved hard against his shoulder, trying to get free. "You can't have it both ways!" She finished her words through clenched teeth. Her cheeks were red, and her hand stung. "I am not a fool, Trip. I may be a lot of things, but I am not a fool."

"Jane." He cradled her face in his hands. "I never thought you were a fool." The muscle in his jaw twitched. "And you're certainly not a whore."

"Well, you didn't have to lie to me. I knew there was nothing between us. You could have just said that Olivia was back, good-bye."

He shook his head. "I have no intention of saying good-bye to you, because you are wrong. Dead wrong. There is most certainly something between us."

Jane rolled her eyes, but warmth spread through her limbs. She supposed it was relief, but she had to be smart. He was probably still telling her lies. She looked away. She couldn't look at him and not believe him.

"Look at me, Jane."

"No," she whispered.

He moved his face until he was in front of her and looking eye to eye. "Baby, I need you, and I definitely want you in my life." Jane closed her eyes. She wouldn't cry…or believe him just because he said pretty things. His tone was more intense, almost urgent. "You make me feel like, for the first time, everything in this crazy universe is connected. When I'm with you, more of the world makes sense, and the things that don't make sense? Hell, they don't seem to matter anymore." A fat tear rolled down her cheek as she decided he was reading her mind and telling her exactly what she wanted to hear. She squeezed her eyes closed as he explained. "I don't want you to be my friend. I definitely don't want you to walk away, and I sure as hell don't want you to leave me." That said; he let her go.

Jane wiped away the tears and stepped back. She looked into his eyes and read for herself whether or not he was telling the truth. He seemed sincere, but then things could seem one way and turn out another. She knew that far too well. "So why did you…?"

Trip took a deep breath. "My mother didn't know I was bringing you to the party. I wanted to surprise her. Before I left six months ago, Olivia and I had our differences, but we were still a couple…so to speak. But it wasn't working….you know that. You saw one of the fights firsthand. And when I left, Olivia ignored me. Didn't respond to a single email."

Jane bit her lip and nodded.

Trip shrugged. "I figured the silence spoke volumes. That 'we' didn't work. But evidently what I considered a breakup, she considered a…hell, I don't know what Olivia thought. She kept up the ruse of us being a couple to all our friends, and when my mother planned this party, she naturally invited Olivia, thinking we were still together." Trip reached out for her hand, but Jane pulled away. He sighed. "I swear. I had no idea she would be there. And since she was, I felt like I had to talk to her and make myself perfectly clear." He grabbed her arm and held it gently. "But I also didn't want to embarrass her in front of all those people, and I didn't want her to see you and make a scene." Jane nodded, as if agreeing was against her will. Trip took a step closer. "I should have explained to you right then, but when Sasha was so hell bent on getting out of the house, I guess I just rolled with it."

Jane swallowed; tears blurred her vision. "So, why are you here?"

"I said I was coming. And, of course, I missed you." He pulled her close, this time holding her gently, her head resting on his chest. Trip brushed dampened hair away from her cheek as he explained, "I planned on spending my whole evening with you. I missed you…and…" He kissed her forehead. "I was disappointed…robbed of my time with you. So, I came here for my Jane fix, so I can sleep tonight."

Jane relaxed against him, rubbing her cheek against his shirt to dry her tears. She enjoyed the warmth of his chest, relished the beat of his heart. After all that had happened, after her worst fears were confronted, he was here, holding her, not Olivia.

Jane pictured Olivia clutching her bloody nose in the hallway. A shiver of fear ran down her spine. Trip will find out; he might run back to his ex and blame Jane for hurting her. Jane squeezed her eyes closed. Trip's arms closed tighter around her as if he felt her worry. Jane took a breath and admitted, "I uh, ran into Olivia on the elevator and we argued."

"Are you all right?" Trip tipped her chin up till he could see her.

"I punched her," Jane said lifting her hand; the one that

delivered the leveling blow. It was bleeding. Blood trickled down her wrist like thin streaks of paint.

"What the hell?" Trip grabbed her hand and gently pried it open. The coins had cut into the soft flesh. Trip emptied her hand and wiped at the blood with his thumb. "We need to get this clean."

"It's fine," Jane assured him. She bit the side of her cheek and whispered. "I punched her in the nose."

"You should never punch someone with your hand full. The force of the blow drives any object into your hand, dammit."

Jane shrugged. "That's not what Poppa taught me."

She saw the shock on Trip's face, but she ignored it. He mumbled something, but she chose not to ask what. He took her by the hand and led her down the steps without any more conversation. She was grateful. She didn't want to explain to him what kind of father teaches his daughter to fight dirty in street brawls, to hold a roll of coins in her fist to strengthen the blow. It wasn't very lady-like, or very humanitarian. Guilt washed over her, and without thinking, she said, "I suppose you should go check on Olivia."

Then she frowned. Why would she suggest that?

Chapter 18

Jane sat on the closed toilet while Trip gently washed the blood from her hand. Sasha leaned against the doorframe, watching over Trip's shoulder from her peripheral view. "So, you knocked her a good one, hmm? Damn, I wish I'd been there."

Sasha laughed, a low, throaty growl. She lit a cigarette, bracing the lighter against her glass of vodka. She took a long draw, then exhaled, chin tilted back, laughter still purring from her lips. "In the future, Jane, use a roll of quarters…not a handful of change."

Trip glanced over his shoulder at Sasha. Jane scowled at her.

"Just trying to teach you the things Viktor would want you to know."

Trip said nothing as he wiped the crescent shaped wounds with antibacterial ointment. "You had a tetanus shot lately?"

"A what?" Jane asked.

"Tetanus shot," he repeated without looking up from his work.

Jane's heart missed a beat, but her brain didn't. "Of course, updated all my shots to get my work visa."

"Good."

Sasha sniffed and blew smoke across the little room. "So, cowboy, why are you here? Any plans to go bandage up the evident loser in this little boxing match? Or are you keeping your next house call a secret?"

"Sash!" Jane snapped.

"I deserved that," Trip said, his voice even, eyes steady on his nursing job. "I explained to Jane that I did ask her to leave because

Olivia was there." He looked over his shoulder at Sasha, then returned to his work. "I needed to speak with Olivia to explain it was over. I wasn't trying to double deal, I just didn't want to embarrass anyone or cause a scene."

"Well, shit. Why did you want that? Oh my. A fight like that could have been a treasured memory. To have gotten to see Jane knock her out in front of everyone. In her dress, legs sprawled, uppity little ass out cold on the floor. Oh, that would have been priceless."

"It would have made an impression all right," Jane answered, cheeks reddening with embarrassment. "I'm not proud of what I did, Sasha. I don't like it when I lose my temper."

"Give yourself a pat on the back," Sasha offered. "Your father would be proud."

Jane shook her head and dropped her glance to her hand.

Trip's warm eyes bore the question good manners would not allow him to ask. Jane breathed a sigh of relief as he opened a box of gauze and silently wound it around her hand.

Jane felt guilty for telling him so little after giving him hell about secrets, so she said cautiously, "My poppa. . ." Jane thought of ways to describe her father, but couldn't. She simply summed him up with, "Was a different fellow."

"You said he taught you to punch," Trip said as he gathered up his trash and tossed it in the bin. "Was he a boxer?"

Jane shrugged. "No. He was a businessman."

"But before that he was a street fighter," Sasha offered, adding, "And he never really left that in the past. You're lucky he's gone, cowboy. He'd have taken a ball bat to your head for making his baby cry."

"Not sure I know what to say to that," Trip said.

"He wouldn't have," Jane responded hastily. "He was a bear of a man. And he seemed scary, but he was as sweet as a puppy." Jane sighed.

Trip nodded. "Sounds a bit like my mother, though I'd say she's a cross between a hell cat and mama bear. She's the one in my family people fear." Trip laughed as he washed his hands and dried

136

them on the towel hanging from the rack.

"But she's tiny. I might be able to take her." Jane grinned.

Trip laughed. He presented her cleaned and bandaged hand with a kiss. "You know what they say about mama bears and threatened cubs. Besides," he said as he pinched Jane's nose, "you're not so big yourself, little Ali."

"At least go for a featherweight. Mohammad Ali was a big bastard," Sasha said.

Jane smiled at him. "Don't worry. I never…well usually never," she looked at her hand, "resort to violence. I'm still a little shocked with myself."

"Olivia brings out the best in people," Trip offered and then added, "Kind of like your friend. Right, Sasha?"

Sasha's brow arched, but she grinned as she flipped him the finger.

"Maybe I can fix you up with Frankie from the party, Sasha. He has a caustic, abrasive personality." Trip leaned against the bathroom wall. "You'd be perfect for each other."

Jane laughed; Sasha sneered.

"I'm serious. I think you caught his eye." Sasha stood up straight. Her jaw hardened, but Trip didn't seem to notice. He continued, "He wanted to know everything about you. I've never known Frankie to be so interested in a woman. And I know he may not be much to look at, but he's a great guy."

"Sasha doesn't care about looks. You ought to see fatty."

"I think I'll stick with my fat little shit. Tell your friend to mind his business, not mine." Sasha downed her vodka, turned and headed for the couch.

Trip looked at his watch. "It's getting late. But, I did want to ask you what you are doing tomorrow?"

"Tomorrow?" Jane thought a moment, "Well, I will be working."

"You're working tomorrow?"

"Yes."

"But tomorrow is Sunday."

"Oh. Is that an important day or something?"

"Of course." He took her hands in his. "God said to rest. You going to defy him?"

Jane answered slowly, "Um, no?"

"Of course not! You'll spend the day with me."

"I would like that."

"How 'bout you, Sasha," he yelled toward the couch, "want to come for dinner?"

"Hell no," Sasha answered quickly. "I'll celebrate my celestial rest order with a bottle of vodka and a fresh pack of smokes."

Jane giggled and whispered, "I don't think she gets it."

Trip pulled her close, arms wrapped tight around her waist. "That's okay. You're the only one I want anyhow. I was just being polite."

Jane laughed and gave him a kiss. "So, will you check on Olivia?"

Trip shook his head. "Not unless you want me to. I've been honest with her, Jane. I've tried to be respectful. I don't need to listen to any more ass chewing from her. I figure she ran her mouth pretty good to get you so angry." He brushed her hair behind her ear and kissed her forehead. "You're all that matters."

She played with the button on his shirt and tried not to seem so pleased, but she was. He didn't care that she had punched her. He really did like her. She grinned. When he kissed her, she relaxed against him, her body warm and pliable.

She accompanied him to the lobby where she gave him one last kiss before saying good-night. She was so happy she offered a, "Hello, Eddie!" as she passed the front desk to the elevator.

"Way to reel him in, Miss Jane. Get that boy to put out and he'll be eating out of the palm of your hand."

Jane waved him off like she had no interest, but turned from the elevator and leaned across the desk and whispered, "What do you mean 'put out'?"

Eddie laughed and turned several deep shades of red. "I shoulda known better than say that to you. You leave no question unasked."

"You were right. I like him. A lot. I want him eating from my hand. Tell me how."

"Oh trust me, the boy is thinking it. You won't have to make it happen." Eddie sorted mail into slots, not looking Jane in the eye.

"Make what happen?"

"It." Eddie dropped the mail and leaned close as he said softly. "The nasty? The horizontal tango?"

"I can't dance."

"Oh dear God, I am regretting this. Jen always says I talk too much." He leaned even closer, his mouth inches from her ear. "Sex, Jane. I'm talking about sex."

"Ahh. I see." Jane chewed her lip as she thought. Trip was always a gentleman. It could be forever before she had him eating from her hand. "Is there a way to make him do this…sooner?"

Eddie shook his head. "Relax, Jane. He's thinking it. Don't worry about it. I was just pulling your leg."

Jane nodded, but her face remained serious as the wheels started turning. How could she seduce Trip Coulter? Silently, she walked to the elevator and pressed the button. It dinged and opened. She reached for the lanyard she usually wore around her neck with the key that sent the elevator to the basement level. She'd forgotten it again. She turned to a red, chuckling Eddie and asked, "Buzz me down, Eddie. I forgot my key."

"Sure thing, Jane. Sleep tight, sweetness."

Chapter 19

Jane's mind was a frenzy of half-hatched plans for seduction as she rode along with Trip to his home. As they passed out of the city to the surrounding wintery grey suburbs, her daydreams dissolved into worry. Turning from a four-lane to a less-traveled two-lane, then up a gravel road, tension tightened her shoulders. So, she expected him, a single man, to live in an apartment in the city. It was no big deal that she was evidently totally wrong. There wasn't a law that said he had to fit her every stereotype.

The steep private drive led them to a rustic log home. Jane chewed on her lower lip as she stared at the house. She never pegged Trip as the earthy type. As he opened his car door, he asked, "Well, what do you think?"

"It's not what I expected." Jane looked around as she mounted the wide front steps. The porch was empty. No chairs, no decorations. A single pair of muddy boots next to a welcome mat was the only decoration on the narrow, railing-wrapped structure.

"I bought it about a year ago. It was a mess, that's how I got it so cheap. At first I wasn't crazy about the cabin style, but it's grown on me. You'll have to see it in the spring. Once the trees are in full foliage, the place kind of blends in. It's very peaceful; very relaxing." Trip unlocked the front door as he explained, "Tres, he's a contractor and an amateur carpenter extraordinaire—well, you saw his house—he does good work. He did the tough stuff. Surprised me with a livable home when I got back from training. I still have all of the upstairs to finish, but I'll get to it eventually."

"I guess I'm shocked that you don't live inside the city," Jane said quietly. Woods on every side unnerved her a little. Like a bear was going to wander out of the trees and eat her.

"Ha," Trip said as he swung the door open. "I grew up on a farm—well, sort of a farm. It was in the country. No neighbors, no traffic to break up the peace. Mom's place in the city? That's where I was staying, but I hated it. I feel confined there." He spread his arms to the open space around the house. "This is where I can breathe."

"I have lived in one city or another my whole life. This is new to me." Jane took slow steps toward the door. "This much space, so close to the city. It must have cost you a fortune."

Trip shrugged. "Like I said, it was in horrible shape. And it's small. Downstairs is a small living room, a den…which is supposed to be a bedroom, and the kitchen. Upstairs is really just an unfinished attic, but I'm going to make it into a master suite…someday."

Jane grinned. He seemed so proud. That kind of pride couldn't be faked, so even if this place didn't seem to fit his personality, it had to be his. The crazy notion that this could be a ruse house, or a front for him to operate from, was completely ridiculous. She smiled up at him as she ordered her mind to relax.

Two steps beyond the foyer and her smile froze, then disappeared. She stood, paralyzed in the living room. It was decorated to near showroom perfection, nothing personal, save for the feminine touches in the paintings that hung on the walls and the flowers on the tables. Jane felt her heart begin to pound, then pound harder…and harder.

All of Sasha's warning bells rang in her head. Someone else decorated this place. No man thinks of table runners and fresh flowers. She ruled out Olivia. Olivia's taste ran to the modern. Straight lines and faceless statues were her style. Maybe he had another woman in his life? For all she knew, he could have several. That was a possibility; one that made more sense than him being a spy. But the possibility of him having an ulterior motive couldn't be ignored. Maybe meeting her wasn't an accident? Maybe he knew who she was and was playing with her?

Jane backed up instinctively, bumping into Trip as she moved toward the door. He stopped her, wrapping his arms around her from behind, resting his chin on her shoulder. His hands stroked her forearms. "What do you think? You like it?"

No dog. No dog met them at the door. Maybe Eve was a borrowed dog used to get close to her? One more look around the formal room made her throat dry. "You know...I really shouldn't have left Sasha with all the work."

Trip turned her around to face him. "Seriously?"

Jane nodded, her stomach clenched. She felt like she might faint. Sasha was right. His whole persona could be a sham. His home? His family? Even his cute little damn dog. All decoys. Her suspicions took on a life of their own as she imagined him being paid to target her. Paid to get to know her. He was out to trap her— to get close enough to her for information on her family.

It was a spy who killed her father. Demetry made himself part of their family—fooling them all for years. He sat at their dinner table, shared the personal side of their lives, as well as the family business. Her father trusted him enough to make him Jane's head of security when she went to Oxford. They trusted him.

Well, until they caught him sneaking information to the KGB. When her father confronted him, they argued. It was a loud, roof raising argument that grabbed Jane's attention. She followed the sounds of men screaming, stepping into the office just as Demetry pulled a revolver from his jacket and fired on her father.

Jane squeezed her eyes closed, trying to block the memory of her father's body jerking, arms flailing backward as the bullet slammed into his chest. Fearing he'd fire again, Jane leaped at Demetry, knocking him off kilter, and the two of them tumbled backward, crashing through the picture window in her father's office. Demetry crushed her body to his chest so tightly she thought he might suffocate her. Glass showered down on them as they hit the ground. She stood, her legs a little wobbly. She tried to run back to the house, but without warning, everything went dark.

Jane never saw her father or her home again.

When she woke, she was on a train, sneaking out of Russia with Sasha. Sasha explained she was wanted for Demetry's murder by the KGB and Interpol. No one would care that she was defending her father, who died of his bullet wounds. All anyone would care about was that a good KGB agent was dead. And the daughter of a notorious crime boss was to blame.

That was the beginning of this nightmare. One that, if she wasn't careful, would end with her dying in a Gulag. And Sasha too.

Would Trip do that to her? She could hardly believe that, but then there was a time in her life when she would have made a confident bet that Demetry would have died to protect her. She learned betrayal could hurt as much as any other loss. Hot tears filled her eyes, and her nose started to tingle. She couldn't cry! How would she explain why she was ready to break into tears? She had to think fast. But she couldn't. Nothing…not a single lie or excuse came to her spinning mind. Then a tear spilled down her cheek.

"Hey…" Trip wiped away the tear and pulled her close. "What is it? This isn't about Sasha. Is it something in the house? Tell me, I'll change it. Hell, I didn't do any of it, so it wouldn't break my heart to undo whatever bugs you."

Jane pulled back until she could see into his eyes. "What do you mean?"

"I mean," he kissed her forehead, "my mother and Jenna decorated the place. I just left them the key and some money, and they did the work. It's funny because Mom and Jen are total opposites, so my house has this kind of schizophrenic feel to it." Trip shook his head and indicated to the room around them with his hand. "Like in here, there are my mother's antiques and the useless crap on the tables. And then the room Jenna did—she's responsible for the den—is totally different. Though neither are really my taste. Shall I show you?"

Jane nodded and followed. His mother. Of course it was his mother. Paranoia was driving her insane.

The den had a big stone fireplace, soft leather furniture with hand stitched quilts suspended from the walls. The rugs that covered the hardwood floor were plush and colorful. The room felt comfortable, livable. It was very homey, just like the house they had visited over the weekend. It was the kind of place where a person could snuggle on the couch, eat some popcorn, and watch movies all day.

Jane was drawn to the large oil painting over the fireplace. The picture was of a sunny day on the beach, the blue of the waves was so real. Jane imagined if she touched it, her fingertips would get wet. The sun danced off the sparkling surf as it splashed up the beach. A man was swinging a little boy, while another little guy waited, arms outstretched for a turn. Jane smiled and turned to Trip. "This is beautiful."

"Jenna did it. She's an artist."

"She mentioned that…though how she does it with the kids is a miracle…busy lady." Jane turned again to the painting. "She's good. It looks like a snapshot."

"I guess in a way it is. Don't you recognize the studly man in the painting?"

Jane did, but she wasn't giving him the satisfaction. "Hmm…your brother?"

"Ah come on, they both have dark hair…."

Jane stepped closer and squinted her eyes as if studying the painting. "Oh yes! I know that handsome guy!"

Trip's smile was smug.

"That's my buddy, Sammy, and that must be little Chas. Now that hot guy…is he a lifeguard? Can you introduce me?"

Trip let out a growl. "You are rotten."

"No, not me," Jane laughed.

Trip took a step closer, hooking his fingers in the belt loops of her jeans. His face was so close to hers, his nose grazed hers. "You are something else." He spoke the words against her lips.

"Hmm," was the only word she could manage as her feet moved toward him closing the gap between them. When he kissed her, nothing else in the world mattered. As he pulled away, his thumb caressed the soft skin of her hip. "I've wanted you all to myself for so long. It feels good, doesn't it? To have no one here but you and me."

Jane's cheeks felt warm. Her throat went dry. Prying herself from his arms, she walked away. Looking around the room, she looked for some sign of a dog. A bed, a toy...hair on the couch...anything. The place was spotless. He probably thought she was a fool. She'd been on edge since she came here—ready to bolt through every door. She turned and looked into his eyes. His warm gaze held nothing but concern.

"Something wrong?" Trip asked.

"I'm sorry, Trip. I'm just nervous. I have never done this."

"Done what?"

Jane walked slowly to the window, not able to look at him and speak without stammering. The skies were darkening as a winter wind blew in and bent the branches on the trees. Taking a deep breath, she explained, "I've never dated. My father was very protective, and at school I had Demetry." She nearly choked on his name; it felt foul on her tongue.

"Demetry? Was he a boyfriend?"

"No! No, nothing like that." Jane stepped away from the window as she explained, "He was my bodyguard. And he was scary. You'd have not asked me on a date. He was a big man," she said, raising her arm above her head, then spread them wide to show how tall and broad her once beloved care-taker had been. "And he wasn't just huge; he had a long scar that went from his eye to his chin. He was a scary man."

"Good thing you lost him before coming to the states. I was intimidated enough. I didn't need a brute Russian to make me even more nervous. Thank God for Evie. If it weren't for her, I'd have never found the courage."

A-ha, Eve *was* his bridge to her. Jane asked, her brow cocked a little, "Where is Eve?"

"Getting spayed. Vet is going to keep her overnight. The place is lonely without her...but fortunately, I have you to keep me company."

Jane stepped closer, and like magnet to steel, he pulled her in the rest of the way.

"She take her blanket with her? She loved that ratty old thing while she stayed with me."

"Yeah, I made them let her keep it. I'm sure the lady at the vet thought I was nuts." Trip turned and opened the bottom door on television stand. "Check it out." Dog toys spilled out on the floor. Evidently Trip had *cleaned* by stuffing the cabinet with all the dog stuff, the sport's magazines, and even a few pairs of rolled up dirty socks. Trip shoved everything back in the cabinet—everything but a huge raw hide dog bone. He handed the two-pound monstrosity to Jane and grinned. "I got her this for when she comes home. Whaddya think?"

Jane laughed. "I don't even think she'll be able to lift it."

"Yeah," he said with a grin. "That's what I thought." Trip took it and leaned it against the cabinet. "Poor girl. She deserves something. Leave her for six months, come home and send her away to get cut up. I don't want her to hate me."

Jane squeezed his arm. "She loves you. She is a lucky dog."

"She might be. Ever since I found her, she has brought me nothing but luck."

Jane gave him a hug, wrapping her arms around his waist and pressing her cheek to his chest. She couldn't believe she doubted him. Stress-induced insanity…that had to be the cause. He was everything she ever dreamed he was. All of her suspicions and fears were wiped away, replaced by her need to be more than his friend.

She was going to do *it*. The thought passed through her mind as the most commonsensical, unsophisticated thought. As large, firm hands circled her waist, the heat from his body seeped into hers and she realized she had everything she needed to be content within her grasp. He pulled her closer; making her wonder if he could read her mind.

She kissed him—a bold kiss that made his heart race against the palm of her hand.

He pushed back with a shake of his head. "Wow."

Peeling himself away, he stepped backward. His cheeks were flushed, and it took him two deep breaths before he explained, "I promised you food. And I do deliver on my promises."

Jane followed, not thinking of food, but wondering—how do you make a man, what did Eddie call it? Put out?

Chapter 20

Leading her to the kitchen, where white walls and steel appliances gave it a professional look, he pulled out an apron. "For you, my dear," he offered with a bit of flare.

He wrapped the fabric around her. Suiting her up for work in the kitchen brought his body within inches of hers. As he reached behind her to cinch the strings, her pulse quickened, releasing the flowery scent of her perfume. She breathed deep, closed her eyes, and committed to memory the beauty of his scent mingled with hers. As instinctually as a dizzy traveler grabs a railing, she braced herself by latching onto to his forearms. Muscle twitched and flexed under her hands. Final loop finished, he didn't let go. He pulled her in. Slow hands spanned the curve of her back, holding her body against his. "I can't believe I have you all alone. Not in a restaurant. Or a park. And no Sasha to fear."

A smile flitted across her lips and a blush rose to her cheeks as she thought of the possibilities. She guessed they shared the same thoughts. She closed the last few inches between them, stood on tip-toe and kissed him. "Just us. What could be more perfect?"

He grinned. His fingers traced the smooth skin of her cheek. "Damn, but if you aren't a distraction."

She didn't have time to ask if that was a good thing or bad thing before he crushed her to him and kissed her until she was breathless. Then as suddenly as the kiss began, it stopped. With a brisk shake of his head, he spun her body toward the kitchen and gave her a little nudge. "Stop distracting me, wench. A man needs food."

"You started it," Jane said as she made herself comfortable on a bar stool.

"You're not helping?"

"I'm a guest. You cook for me. If I invited you to dinner, I would cook for you. If I knew how to cook."

He laughed as he opened cabinets and pulled out bowls and cutting boards. "You can't cook?"

Jane shook her head and leaned on her arms on the cool granite counter top.

"Well, fortunately for us, I am a fantastic cook. My only rule is, if I cook, you clean up."

"Nope."

"No?"

"No. I never mix business with pleasure and since my business is cleaning…well…."

Trip's laugh filled the room. "In that case, my lady, you just rest and let me take care of it all."

He threw a dollop of butter in the skillet and it sizzled and melted straight away. He hummed as he stirred and chopped; the white apron he tied around his own thick neck a sharp contrast to his tanned skin. He commented as he worked as if being filmed for a cooking show. "And we'll sauté those onions until they are slightly browned on the edges. It will release the sugars and the sweetness. Ah yes, onions can be sweet…much like my lazy kitchen mate." He winked at Jane and shivers ran from her heart to her toes. One word explained it all. Love.

She loved him. The "for real" him. This was way more than the crush she developed a year ago. A second thought crept in to her mind—why was she surprised? He was perfect. And he was hers, sort of.

He poured them each a glass of wine, then poured the rest over a dish of red potatoes. He set hers in front of her with a little bow and said, "For the lady." She grabbed it and knocked it back like a dusty cowhand with his first shot of whiskey. As the alcohol moved from her empty stomach to her veins, she felt warm. Trip looked so happy, so trusting. From out of the blue, a twinge of guilt hit her.

He had no clue she was lying to him about almost every part of her life.

Jane imagined telling him the truth, in its entirety, but she eschewed the thought as quickly as it was formed. She had to keep her senses about her. To have sex with him was one thing; to be honest was another.

His words jolted her from her musings. "I don't know why my mom always acted like cooking a bird was such a chore." He unwrapped the chicken and ran it under water in the sink before sticking it in a pan and pouring oil on his hands. "Oil it, salt it, and stick it in the oven. What's so complicated about that?"

Jane shrugged. She hadn't a clue and didn't really care. He could be roasting bologna and she would be on cloud nine.

"Bird's in the oven," he said as he washed his hands. "Potatoes are in the roaster. Why don't we," he grabbed her hand and pulled her from her stool, "go relax in the den while it cooks?"

Jane nodded. He grabbed their glasses, another bottle of wine, and pointed her to the door.

He uncorked the wine and filled their empty glasses before turning his attention to the fireplace. He stacked wood on the grate, lit the kindling, and gently blew on the growing flame.

Jane let out a contented sigh and picked up her glass of wine. She took a sip and nearly choked. Grimacing, she looked at her full glass with a frown. She had never had anything so bitter and dry. It nearly sucked the breath from her lungs. Trip's back was turned as he poked at the logs on the fire, so she took a deep breath and chugged. She didn't want to hurt his feelings. He was working so hard to make everything perfect.

She tucked her feet under her on the leather couch and leaned her body against the arm. It was so cozy in this room. The fire blazed. The snap and crackle of the wood relaxed her every muscle. Her skin tingled.

Trip joined her on the couch. "You out? Want me to get you more?"

"Oh, no. I'm…I was thirsty."

"What did you think?" he asked as he swirled the red liquid in

151

his glass.

"It was nice."

"Frankie picked it out." Trip took a swig and coughed. "That's awful. You liked it?"

"No," Jane laughed. "It was bad."

Trip set his glass on the table. "Good lord, Frankie must not have any taste buds."

Jane took his hand and settled it on her lap. "I like you, Trip Coulter. I like that you care about making me happy, but I want you to know that you make me happiest by just being you."

Trip grinned and gave the wine glass a little shove with his foot. "You're the one who drank the cat urine wine, lady."

"I held my nose and chugged...like taking medicine."

Trip's eyes were soft as he looked her over. Tucking a stray piece of hair behind her ear, his voice was low, husky. "Crazy girl. You could have said it was horrible."

Her cheeks warmed and she shrugged. "I didn't want to hurt your feelings."

His chuckle was low, sexy. As if by instinct, she snuggled closer to him. He wrapped an arm around her shoulders and tucked her body tight to him. "You're as perfect as a girl could get, Miss Jane. Hell, you watched my dog and barely knew me. You're beautiful. I swear, your eyes sparkle. It's probably all the orneriness in you, but it's still beautiful. And that smile of yours? Oh hell, it just makes me weak."

"This smile?" Jane flashed a cheesy, exaggerated smile.

Trip laughed. "Um, sure."

A fit of giggles caught hold of her. She tried to get serious, but she couldn't control her laughter.

Trip cupped her cheek in his hand. "There it is. That smile. Damn lady, but I'd gladly do backflips just to make you happy...just to see that."

Jane looked up at him. "You can do backflips?"

Laughter rumbled in his chest. "I didn't mean the physical kind exactly."

"Oh, so you can't actually...." Jane made flipping motions with her hand.

"Well, I've never actually tried…but if you want…."

He started to get up. Jane grabbed his arm and pulled him back. "No, no. You don't have to prove anything. Besides, you might hurt yourself if you fail."

"Me? Rock solid, baby. Nothing can hurt this." He gave his chest a slap.

"Oh, okay. I see. But still, you don't have to do backflips to impress me. I like you very much just the way you are too."

"I've grown on you, huh?"

Jane rested her head against his arm. "Like mold."

Trip's laugh filled the room. "I'm mold. How perfect. I tell you how beautiful you are, and I get called mold."

Jane rubbed her cheek against his arm. "Oh fine…," her voice was teasing, "you have a sexy smile."

"Me? Sexy smile? That's pretty good…though I did have to fish awfully hard for it."

Jane hugged his bicep. "You know I liked you for forever…that I thought you were handsome…."

"Thought?"

"Think," Jane corrected. "I think you're handsome."

"Yeah, 'cause I worked on my guns." He flexed the muscle under her cheek.

Jane laughed and rolled her head against his arm. "You were beautiful before, too."

"Handsome."

"Oops, handsome. I daydreamed of you all the time—wanted you for myself. When you said you needed help, I jumped at the chance! I knew I just needed a chance and I'd win you for myself."

"Smart girl." He kissed her forehead, looked down at her and smiled. "Beautiful. Sweet. Conniving. Ferocious right hook. No wonder I love you."

"Really? You *love* me?" She choked out the words.

Trip nodded. "It might sound crazy, but I do."

"So, what about tomorrow and the next day?" Jane's words were quiet.

"I'll love you each and every day until you are old and gray."

Trip kissed her again. His lips lingered on her warm skin.

Jane's spirits soared, then reality brought her back down to earth. She felt nauseous. She didn't know what to say—didn't know what to do. The truth sat on the tip of her tongue. She could explain everything to him—that she tried to protect her father. But in Russia, the word of a criminal's daughter versus the body of a dead KGB agent, would get her jailed or killed for certain. And Sasha harbored her.

Thoughts of Sasha assured her silence. She took a breath. "I, ah, I have to use the bathroom." She leaped from the seat and looked around the room.

Trip stood slowly. A frown and a clenched jaw made him look much too serious. He probably wondered how she went from happily cuddling to freaked out quicker than a Siberian freeze.

He sighed. "It's back here." Jane almost ran, slipping inside and locking the door. She tried not to cry, but tears sprang to her eyes and rolled down her cheeks. *Oh, Trip, Trip, Trip…what do I do?* She sat down on the floor and hugged her knees to her chest, her head resting on top of them. *Why did you have to die, Poppa? You could help me.* She choked on a sob, the sound echoed in the tile-filled room. She covered her mouth with her hands. Confusion and indecision made her head hurt. Why couldn't she just be happy with right now? Why did she have to keep thinking of the future? What was wrong with her? He said he loved her; he didn't ask her to marry him! Burying her face in her hands, the harder she tried to manage her tears, the more they flowed. Her old life was gone and she was on the run…maybe forever. It wasn't fair. Not fair at all.

"Jane." Trip spoke through the door. His voice was so close he had to be leaning against it. "I'm sorry. I shouldn't have said that. I knew you were nervous and it was stupid of me…."

Hiccup. "I'm fine."

"I can hear you crying. Please, open the door and talk to me."

Jane sniffed, took a deep breath and stretched an arm up to the lock. He swung the door open and stepped into the little room, sliding down the vanity to sit on the floor beside her.

Jane wiped her eyes and looked at him. His eyes glistened with unshed tears. He took a sharp breath and cleared his throat. Jane's heart sank to her toes, making her stomach feel ill as it passed by. A smart girl would end this here and now.

He touched her cheek gently, wiping a tear away with his fingertips.

She ran the words through her head like a trial balloon. *Yes, this is too fast. I don't love you. I really should go. We could be friends....* Then she could walk away and never see him again. She couldn't make promises for tomorrow, much less until she was old and gray.

She took a deep breath, laid her hand flat on his chest. She could feel his warmth; his heartbeat. "I...." She told her mouth to say the words that would sever the bond and end the problem. "I...." *Just say it's over!* "I love you, too."

He pressed a hand to her cheek and held it there. "Then why?"

"I guess I'm scared. I just lost my Poppa and the thoughts of the future—they scare me. I don't know where my life is even headed. I barely take care of Frosty and me. I don't exactly have a good background. I am certain your family would never like..."

"My family will accept whoever I love. Or they don't accept me." His words were firm.

"But they would be right. You could do better..."

"The hell I could. Don't be stupid, Jane. I told you. I've been telling you. You're perfect for me. I don't want anyone else. I want you."

"But...but...I can't, I mean I don't want to marry."

"Oh, hell. How did you get that out of one simple 'I love you'?"

Jane shrugged and bit her lower lip. She was losing it.

He wrapped an arm over her shoulder and tucked her close to him. "I swear, I wasn't asking for that. I just wanted you to know how special you are to me." His thumb caressed her cheek. "I wanted you to know that as long as you want me, there will be no other women in my life. I swear, I'm not thinking of tying the knot any time soon."

Somehow the assurance brought no comfort. Dream brained,

Jane asked, "Not at all?"

Trip looked like a man being tortured by hostage takers. "Not at all."

Her shoulders dropped forward, her chin dipped. He lifted it with a warm hand. "At least not yet, I'll give you a year or so before I bring it up."

Jane couldn't stop her smile, not even by chomping down on her lower lip.

He hugged her to him. "I promise...we'll take it slow." His hand stroked the back of her neck.

Wrapping her hands around his neck, she rested her head on his shoulder. Maybe she couldn't marry him, but she could have him. And if he was so crazy in love with her, maybe she could, one day, be honest and get him to help her find a solution. He wouldn't want her in jail. And maybe, just maybe, he could sway his mother to her side. A government official would have connections, would know who to pay to help get the identity she needed to be free. Jane's smile broadened. She squeezed him tightly. "You're right. I sometimes get scared because I love you too, and I worry...if I keep letting this feeling grow...it could really hurt me."

"I will never hurt you, Janie. I'd die first. No one," he said as he kissed her temple, "will ever hurt you."

Pulling her to her feet, he kissed her, instinctively spanning her waist, clenching her body to his. A breathy moaned escaped her, warming his lips, and making him smile. Nuzzling against the tender skin below her ear, he whispered, "Is it now safe to say I love you?"

She nodded; heavy eyes closing with the feel of him so close. His hand slid into her hair. "Good. I can't explain this feeling in any way other than being completely, crazy in love with you. And I'm sorry if that scares you. I tell myself to play it cool, but..."

Jane smothered his words with a kiss. Her efforts brought a growl, and strong arms lifted her off her feet and cradled her body against his chest. A giggle erupted from her lips, and her head tipped back as she latched her hands behind his neck as he carried her back to the den.

"I think you will drive me insane. Are you sure your mother was a Brit and not a magic-weaving gypsy?" he asked.

Jane's giggles continued, but she managed to shake her head.

"What am I going to do with you?" His question was good natured, her jubilation evidently infectious.

Pulling herself by circling broad shoulders, she brought her lips to his ear. "You could make love to me."

He took a deep suck of air and dropped her onto her feet. "Don't tease me. I promised I'd go slow, but you go making offers like that, I can't…"

Twisting her hands into the fabric of his Henley, she stepped closer. "I'm not joking. It makes sense. We love each other, right?"

He was quiet, his face serious. Jane assumed he was waiting for her to change her mind, or burst into tears. "Seriously," she said, "I want this."

He still didn't look convinced. He asked, "Right here, right now?"

The room was silent all but for the crackle of burning wood and growing winds. She pulled him toward the overstuffed sofa, luring him with husky words. "I can't think of anywhere more perfect."

He followed like a man stunned by the light of heaven. Somehow when he finally realized he wasn't dreaming, they were snuggled on the couch. Her body, so slight and silky soft, molded to him, her hands clutching his shoulders. He kissed her long and slow, tenderly brushing the hair back from her face. He nibbled on an earlobe, then the curve of her throat and the pulse at the hollow above her collar bone.

Jane closed her eyes and felt his body move over hers. Her curves fit into his bulk like a puzzle piece. His hands caressed flesh as he lifted the soft cotton of her tee and loosened hooks until her upper body was bared to him. He leaned above her and stroked a pink nipple with the palm of his hand. "You're perfect. Absolutely perfect." A shiver passed over her, and she couldn't help but feel exposed. She'd never, in her whole life, been naked in front of a man.

His attention returned to her lips, kissing her until he felt her

157

body relax against his, and her hands gained confidence and sought his flesh, roaming under his shirt, trying to tug it above his chest. In a single move, he grabbed it by the back collar and yanked it over his head. Both of her hands splayed across his pecs failed to cover even a quarter of the expanse. He was brown and firm, thick muscles rippled as he moved.

Cradling a hand that caressed him, he gazed at her, his eyes dark with passion. "I love you."

"I love you, too," she said, wrapping her arms across his back and pulling him close to her.

His fingers trailed down silky skin to the button of her jeans.

His touch set off a blaze in her belly that dried her throat and barely left her able to swallow, much less speak. She closed her eyes, rested her cheek against his shoulder. His hands, so certain in their possession, left her body burning. She didn't know what she wanted exactly. She just knew she wanted him. The feeling was new and delicious and ever so frustrating.

Moving down her body, he planted feathery kisses on her belly. He laid his head, ear down, over her belly button as his fingers traced the lace rim of her panties. "You are incredibly perfect, and as much as I would love to...." His fingers traced lazy circles across her pelvis. "I have to make sure this is really what you want."

"I do. I swear. " Her voice was hoarse.

He let out a fierce groan and returned his mouth to her lips. The heat and texture of his body growing more familiar as she grew bolder in her exploration, her hands moving over him, unable to get enough.

"Now. Trip. I want to know."

He stripped off his own pants. Jane stripped off her panties and tossed them on the growing heap. He kissed her again, this time the urgency was more primal, less playful. She wrapped her legs around his and waited, anxious to know the secrets of the union of a man and a woman.

"You're sure?" he whispered.

"Yes."

He buried his face in her throat as he forced himself to calm down; get himself under control. He kissed her slowly, supporting his weight on an arm as he positioned her body to accept him. She gasped and pressed her back into the couch.

"You all right, baby?"

"It hurts," she gasped. "I didn't think it would hurt."

"You're a...."

Jane nodded against his chest.

"I'll go slow. Tell me if I need to stop." His body stopped. He nuzzled into her neck. "That better?"

Jane nodded. "It's fine," she lied. It still hurt. But she didn't care. She could feel his body pulse in hers. He kissed her neck, moved down to her breast. She cradled his head and watched as his tongue flicked across her skin. His dark body against her snowy white flesh. As she watched him, amazement washed over her. His body was in hers. Burying her face in the curve of his neck, she inhaled the scent of him as she wrapped her arms over his shoulders. Digging her nails into his back, she held onto to him as if her life depended on it.

The loneliness that had been unknowingly weighing her spirit down...lifted. Encircled in arms that felt as sturdy as steel, she was safe. He would protect her. He was part of her...slowly usurping the most precious element of her. Her soul.

Chapter 21

The timer for the chicken went off. Trip groaned and held her tighter. The timer beeped again. Jane giggled. "Better get it. It will burn."

"I don't care—I'm not hungry."

Jane's belly rumbled. The smell of the feast was heavy and alluring. "Really?"

Trip shook his head. "No, I'm starved. I just don't want to move."

The timer seemed to beep louder.

"Oh hell, I better go. Pretty soon it will really let loose. It'll keep beeping until the oven door is opened. Pain in the ass…bossy oven."

Jane grinned as he pulled himself away, crawling over her, slowly kissing her as he left. He bent down and kissed her again. A long beep came from the kitchen. Trip groaned, "Damn thing's half harpy."

"Go," Jane commanded giving him a swat on the butt.

"Oh," he teased as he dressed, "you think since you've had your way with me you can just push me around, huh, lady?"

Jane laughed. "Yes. Yes I do."

He stroked her cheek. "Well, you're absolutely right."

Jane watched him leave. She felt cold and alone with him gone. She jumped up and dressed quickly, not bothering to tuck her shirt in or put on her shoes or socks. She followed the aroma to the kitchen where she found him setting the chicken on the counter.

"I forgot to turn the roaster on. No potatoes. I blame you; you kept distracting me."

"I'm sorry," she said without a bit of remorse. She hugged him around the waist. He tucked her head under his chin and held her close.

"Mmm, you feel good. I could hold you forever."

Jane smiled and nodded, not able to look at him for fear he would see the turmoil the word forever caused in her soul. He's right here, right now. That's all that matters she assured herself.

He kissed her, tipping her head back, his thumb pulling on her chin, opening her lips wider to kiss her deeper. Then he stopped and stepped back. "Wow. I could never get enough of you. But," he let go of her after kissing her forehead, "I better feed you. I'd hate to have you pass out on me and miss out on all my charm."

He opened the fridge. "Let's see. I have biscuits left over from KFC. A salad from Boston Market. And what is this?" He opened the lid, sniffed and sealed it quickly. "Nope, that's a science experiment."

Jane laughed. "Biscuits and chicken and salad. Sounds good."

"Not exactly the dinner I had planned. I was thinking much more impressive."

"You're in luck...nobody has ever made me dinner. I am, um, easy to impress."

"I'm really getting a lot of mileage out of that today," Trip blurted then blushed.

Jane felt the color splotch her cheeks, too. She smiled at him. "You were very excellent."

He gave her arm a squeeze. His hand was warm and loving. He said, "I want very much to do everything perfectly for you. Make you happy to be with me."

"You make me very happy." She grinned, "See? I can't stop smiling."

They microwaved the biscuits, cut sloppy chunks of chicken, and sat down to eat. They ate quickly, over small talk about the dogs and work. Jane reached for butter and knocked over her glass of milk. She leaped up for a towel, but Trip was already to the cabinet and back with paper towels before she could ask where they were. "Your purse." He pointed to her purse on the floor. The milk was running down the edge, threatening to spill over the side. Jane grabbed at it, clumsily lifting it bottom first, dumping the contents on the floor. She started picking up lip glosses and keys when Trip reached down and picked up a little photo book she carried with her.

"May I?" he asked.

She scanned her memory and decided it was safe. She nodded, then sat back down. She apologized, but he waved her off, his attention totally on her pictures.

"This you?" Jane looked over his shoulder at a skinny, bucktoothed girl. She cringed. "Yes."

"You're adorable."

"I'm all teeth."

"You're insane. You are; you were so cute."

He turned the page. "Aunt Tilley." She supplied without being asked. "She raised me until I was twelve. My mother wanted to be a model, or a movie star. She didn't have time for a daughter."

"Sorry about—"

"Don't be," she interrupted. "I was better off with Aunt Tilley."

Next page. "That's Poppa. That's the day I moved in. I took that picture from my new bedroom window. That's him going into his greenhouse. You can't really tell it's him, but it's one of my favorites. I was so happy to be...home."

"Why did it take twelve years?"

"My mum...long story short...she hated Poppa. I believe she hid me to punish him, till she was so broke she had to have something to barter to get herself some money. Poppa was so happy to get me, and he gladly paid her to go away and stay out of my life."

"Wow. I'll stop bitching about my control freak mother."

Jane nodded. "I am thankful she gave birth to me. That's all I will say. She is dead and it is bad luck to speak bad of the dead."

Trip turned the page. "That's my puppy, Oslo." Jane frowned. "I hope someone took him in when I left."

Trip's brows knitted together, but he said nothing. Next page.

"Me and Poppa. My eighteenth birthday." Next page. "Poppa's roses. He loved those roses." Next page, "Poppa and Sasha and me. At my flunking out of Oxford." Jane laughed.

"Your poppa is smiling?" Trip asked in confusion. "You flunked out and he didn't get mad?"

Jane shook her head. "I was coming home. He never really wanted me to go, I think. He just thought it was the right thing to do."

Next page. "Sasha again. She is frowning because she hates pictures. Which is silly because she is so stunning."

Next picture, "That's me being silly. I read that in the old days, women would curl their hair with rags, so I rolled them all over my head. I look like a babushka. Sash thought she was getting even with me, taking a picture when I looked so awful, so I crossed my eyes and stuck out my tongue. I like this picture because I was so happy that day, it was right before Poppa…well, you know, before he died. I didn't have a clue what was about to happen."

Trip's eyes were soft as took her hand in his. "I'm so sorry, Jane."

"Today makes up for it."

Trip smiled at her. Kissed her hand. "Who is the guy in the background?"

"Where?" Jane looked closer. "Oh." She sat back in her chair. "Just Demetry. He was my security. I forget he was always there." She closed the book and frowned.

"What did your dad do?"

"He was a vodka maker. Then he invested in energy. He had a powerful business, and in fallen Russia, he worried for my safety. People sometimes would get stolen for money. We had a few burglars." She laughed. "That's how we got Sasha. She came to rob Poppa, and he caught her."

"And he took her in?"

Jane nodded. "Poppa felt guilty for Sasha. She grew up an orphan. She had nobody, and she is Chechen, and a Russian prison would not be the place for her. A lot of bad feeling between the Russians and the Chechens. And I think Poppa worried that all I had in my life were men, so Sasha made a good addition to the family."

"So, I take it, no sisters? Any brothers?"

"Just a brother. But he and I are not so close. He is a good bit older than me. He is...." Jane thought of Nikki and wondered how to best describe him, sick bastard who would pull the wings off of flies for fun? The guy who married her mother, his father's ex-wife? Jane shivered. There was no explaining Nikki. "He is much older. I barely know him. I am close to Sash. She is my family. I just wish I could make her past hurts go away. Then she could be made happy."

"Can't change the past, but maybe we can fix her up with Frankie? Both of them are surly and bitter. Might make a good match."

"Don't count on it. Sasha distrusts all men."

"And Frank all women...see? They're perfect."

"Why? Not why do you want to fix them up, but why does he hate women?"

"I didn't say hate. He just doesn't trust them."

"Ahh...so why?"

He relaxed his elbows on the counter and said with a sigh, "Ah Frank. That poor bastard has issues. His mother ditched him when he was twelve, his wife divorced him for a banker...hell, even his daughter won't have anything to do with him. His track record with women sucks."

"That's sad. Poor Frankie." She twisted a piece of paper towel between her fingers. "Was he unkind to his daughter?"

"No. Her mom moved her to Sweden when she married. Frank could only see her a few times a year, and he works in...uh...the security business; the step-dad is in banking and is rich as hell. The girl just sort of drifted toward the step-dad."

"How awful." She was quiet for a few minutes, rolling pieces of the paper towel into little balls and lining them up in front of her. "I don't know if Sasha would be good fit. She is not known much for healing hearts, but for breaking them."

Trip nodded. "I figured as much. I suppose I wasn't ever serious about fixing them up."

"It would be nice. Nice to see them as happy as we are. Maybe not with each other, but with somebody. I have a pain in my heart for Sash. She grew up in orphanage until she was old enough to be a runaway. She had nobody."

Trip stood up and hugged her from behind brushing kisses along her neck. "She has you, and that makes her a very lucky woman."

Trip nuzzled the curve of her neck and inhaled her scent. Jane's head fell back against his chest. She closed her eyes and hugged the arms that enclosed her. "Thank you. You are sweet." She squeezed his arms tighter to her. His closeness sent wave after wave of warm current through her body. He spun the bar stool until she was facing him. Brushing her hair back from her shoulders, he planted tantalizing kisses from her ear to her collar bone. Jane's hands moved from his shoulders to meander across shirt-covered flesh until they were touching the bare skin of his neck. His flesh was so warm it heated her body, slowly, thoroughly, making the room warm and her breathing more labored. His lips found hers again, kissing her so deeply she believed she would melt.

She knew what promise his attention held, vague desire gone, she knew exactly what her body wanted. Him. She was lost to all rational thought. His body hard and hot against hers, his hands igniting every spot they touched, his lips teasing and tempting as he kissed her, moving fluidly from her lips to her ears, then down her neck. It was almost more than she could take. She felt his hands move under her shirt. She moaned and pulled him tighter, pulling at the buttons of his shirt. His hand cupped a naked breast. She felt her spine go weak, and her breathing was more and more labored. He pulled back, softly biting her lower lip as if it was torment to stop.

He touched her cheek so gently Jane felt her heart would burst. She smiled and took his hand in hers and kissed it. She had to be honest with this man. She had no other choice.

Tonight she would explain to Sasha. She would somehow make her understand that they could trust him. Jane had no proof, beyond that fact that her heart told her she could trust him with her life.

"Trip, I...." Jane stammered, not sure what to say.

"Do you need more time?"

"It's not that. I just…I feel I must…." Jane's chest squeezed and it took more effort to get air to her lungs. She took a deep breath and said, "There is so much about me you don't know. Things I think you should know before you decide how you feel about me."

"Nothing could ever make me change how I feel about you."

"I still think you need to know about…."

The conversation was interrupted as a storm came in through the front door. A perfectly coiffed, blond tornado moved through the house and took them both by surprise.

"Who the hell are you?" Barbara Coulter asked, shaking a piece of paper in Jane's face.

"Mom!" Trip yelled, using his body to block Jane from her attack. "What the hell's gotten into you?"

Barbara shoved the paper into Trip's hands. "A Jane Mitchell doesn't even exist. I looked her up after Olivia came to me and told me she suspected Jane might be tied to mobsters and drug dealers. I thought she was crazy, but I checked it out just to appease her. There is no Jane Mitchell, besides an old lady in Nebraska, and she sure as hell isn't your girlfriend. So, I asked your *friends* and they were suspicious too. And what's his name…the one from Jersey?"

"Frankie?"

"Yes, Frankie. He said he thought he recognized her friend at the party so he lifted her print off her wine glass, and we ran her through Interpol. Want to guess what we found?"

Trip looked over the Interpol report. In the right hand corner was a mug shot of Sasha, after being arrested for prostitution. Trip looked up at Jane and expected to see shock, but instead he saw guilt.

"She's a prostitute! And *Jane* here, well, I can't seem to find hide nor hair of her." She approached Jane, fists balled, face contorted with anger. "So, just who the hell *are* you?"

Trip stared at the words on the paper. "What's going on, Jane?"

"I told you, there were things I needed to tell you. But my secrets, they're not just my own. They could get other people, innocent people, hurt. I was going to tell you."

Trip turned his back on Jane and walked away, brushing past his mother, shaking off her hand as she tried to touch him, console him. He sat at the table and stared at the report. He flipped through the pages, his brow furrowed, his lips pulled in a granite frown.

Jane took one last look at him and fled. Barbara yelled from the door, "You better run, you little bitch, and we'll see who can move faster, you or the INS."

Chapter 22

It took Trip a full minute to recover. He was in shock. He could hear his mother's voice, her continued harping about Jane. Trip looked over the papers his mother brought for a third time. It was a police report on Sasha. She had been arrested twice. Once in her home country, once in Pakistan. Once for prostitution and once for burglary. "You see what you nearly got mixed up with?" Her answer sounded smug, relieved.

Trip paced the floor with the papers, eyes glancing to the ceiling as he processed the information.

Barbara exhaled hard. She wanted a response from her son. "Well, do I get a thank you?"

"Jane said Sasha tried to rob her family. She told me that."

"Did she mention the prostitution?"

"No. But she said she was a runaway. How else would she have made a living?"

Barbara snorted. "For crying out loud, Trip…you're missing the forest for the trees…." Barbara's voice rose, "She was a prostitute." She repeated herself as if her son was either deaf or stupid. "She sold her body for money."

"I know what a frigging prostitute is! And Sasha being one says nothing about Jane. Mom, this has nothing to do with Jane."

"Birds of a feather."

"Not Jane, she'd never even been…."

"Oh, dear." Barbara approached her son, her voice rising, "She is lying to you, Rowan. Hell, I was a virgin three times before I married your father."

Trip shot his mother a look of disbelief and disgust.

"Oh, don't give me that look, it was the sixties. But it doesn't change the fact that women can, and do, lie."

Trip shook his head. "Not Jane."

"You are being simply ridiculous. Call Craig. He'll tell you what women are capable of."

"What would Tres tell me, Mom?" Trip knew he had hit a nerve. It was his mother's meddling that had disrupted his brother's love affair with his wife, removing Tres from the picture for the first fifteen years of his son's life. This incident was the only thing that Trip ever remembered his mother admitting shame and mortification over.

Barbara's lips worked, but she said nothing for several moments. "So, find out. But keep your eyes open. I am telling you I ran this girl through the CIA data banks and she didn't turn up. It's like she doesn't exist."

"Well, a lot of people fled here after the fall of the Soviet Block."

"All right, so best case scenario is that she's an illegal hanging out with a known criminal. A prostitute."

Trip shrugged. "And you were a virgin three times before you met Dad."

"That's a far cry from prostitution."

"She might have had her reasons. Life is hard in Chechnya."

Barbara shook her head. "I'm calling Craig. He'll talk some sense into you."

Barbara rummaged through her purse for her cell phone. Normally she and Craig locked horns over Craig's view of women. He was the original member of the He-Man Woman Haters Club, a true misogynist—at least he was until he met and married his wife, Mollie. Barbara bit her lip. Maybe Mollie had made him too soft, too forgiving. She surely didn't need Craig telling him to go for it.

While she debated making the call, Trip brushed past her and was out the back door calling for Jane. Barbara rolled her eyes and went to the wine rack. She sorted through the labels until she found a hearty red. She uncorked it, failed to let it breathe, and poured herself a glass. She polished off the glass in two gulps. Poured another, then made a phone call she thought might actually be effective.

*****

Jane saw Sasha's car round the bend in the road. She ran; down over the steep bank that sloped to the road. Briars and rocks pierced her bare feet. She slid in the soft, snow dusted earth, grabbing hold of a sapling for balance. Catching her breath, she stumbled to the road where she took off, running until her lungs burned and it felt like her feet were bleeding. She slowed to a walk as the approaching car slowed to a stop. The old Subaru looked as beautiful as a rare and precious life boat onboard the Titanic. Sasha leaned across the seat and swung the passenger door open and yelled, "Get in."

Once Jane was in, Sasha sped away. Jane took off without her purse, but fortunately, her phone was still in the back pocket of her jeans. Sasha drove; Jane took napkins and pulled briars out of her feet. Neither spoke. What could be said? Jane screwed up.

When Sasha turned onto the interstate heading toward the Dulles International Airport, Jane turned to her, concern furrowing her brow.

"Where are you going? This isn't the way home."

"You can't go home. You said his mother threatened you with a call to INS?"

Jane nodded; she hoped she didn't vomit.

"Well, then you need to get the hell out of town."

Jane nodded. "But what about Frosty?"

"I'll take care of him."

"You're not coming?"

Sasha shook her head and lit a cigarette.

"I don't want to go alone."

"Don't worry about it. I will meet you as soon as I tie up our loose ends. It should, at most, take me a week before I meet you."

"But where will I go?"

"My uncle has a beach home in Mexico. You go there and wait on me. I have to let him know he needs to find a replacement for the apartment building. I can't leave him floating up in the air."

Jane nodded. "No, he's done too much for us. You take whatever time you need." Jane wadded the napkins and tossed them on the floor. "I suppose a few days at the beach would be relaxing." Jane relaxed her head against the back of the seat. "Dammit! I left my purse at Trip's!"

Sasha glanced over her shoulder before switching lanes. "Doesn't matter. I have you a new ID, new passport. Jane Mitchell is no more."

"Great. Did you pack my stuff?"

"I have a bag for you in the trunk. I had it filled and in my closet. Everything is new, but I did take a minute to stuff in those awful flannel pants and Oxford sweatshirt."

Jane's grin was weak, but she was grateful that she'd have something from her old life. Tears burned her eyes. The last of the pictures of her family was sitting on the counter at Trip's. God life sucked so hard sometimes, but what could she do? Nothing. "Thanks, Sasha. I'm sorry for this."

Sasha shrugged and reached for a cigarette. "I was ready for a change."

"Me too."

"Good girl. That's the Jane attitude I'm used to." Sasha sounded confident, nearly bold. "We'll get through this. We always do, right? How much trouble have we escaped?"

"More than our fair share," Jane agreed.

"This is just one more scrape, and we'll beat it too." Sasha tossed a purse into Jane's lap. "Inside is the new passport and stuff—you are now Maggie Kristobel, English vacationer. There is enough dinero in the wallet to cover any expenses, but my uncle assures me he will have the beach house stocked with everything you'll need."

"How did you do all this?"

"I am always a step ahead, working on plans F and G before C ever falls apart."

Jane closed the purse. "I don't know what I would do without you, Sash. You're truly the best friend I've ever had."

Sasha made a sound like "hmmph" and tossed her cigarette out the window as she turned down the road to the airport. She parked the car and hustled Jane from the parking lot to the airport terminal. Jane ignored Sasha's fear of affection and grabbed her for a big hug, "You're like a sister to me, Sash."

"I guess..." Sasha muttered arms remaining stiff at her sides. Sasha had tears in her eyes when she took a step back from her. "Son of a bitch. You have no shoes, no coat." Sasha slipped off her shoes and shrugged out of her coat and offered them to Jane. "Everything will be okay. Someone will be waiting for you when you land to take you to the new house."

"You think I'll look back on this one day and think it was worth it?"

"Was the sex good?"

Jane shrugged. "I only got to do it once, but yeah."

Sasha shrugged. "Well, that's more than some women ever get."

"How could you tell? Do I look different?"

Sasha shook her head. "Your shirt's on backward."

Jane gasped and buttoned up her coat. She gave Sasha a weak smile and turned to the airport where yet another life awaited her.

Chapter 23

Jane's head spun. In less than an hour, she had gone from Trip's arms to speeding car to airport. The clamor of the crowds made her stress level rise as she tried to be calm and be this new person. She had to keep checking her airline ticket to remind herself of her new name. Maggie Kristobel. How was she going to get used to another life?

She stuffed the ticket into the purse Sasha had given her. It was new. As was the luggage Jane had checked at the terminal. Both filled with all new items. The seeds of a brand new life.

Jane Mitchell would. And she would miss none of it, she thought, chin jutted proudly forward. All but Frosty.

Frosty. Jane's heart stopped a moment. She couldn't just leave her baby. Sasha had promised to bring him, hadn't she? Or did she just say she'd take care of him? Like ditch him at the pound? With Sasha, Jane wasn't sure what would be a satisfactory solution. Surely, she knew bringing him with her *was* the only option. She knew how upset losing Oslo made her.

Well, she'd just call and remind her. She couldn't be expected to leave everything. She wiped at tears before they spilled from her eyes. People stared at her as she stepped into the ticket line. A chunky lady in a leopard print coat must have heard her sniffle, so she turned and offered her a tissue and said, "You have bit of a smudge, hon." Jane nodded, then wandered off to find a bathroom where she could compose herself, and call Sasha to make sure she knew how important it was to bring her dog.

Sasha returned to the apartment building, her mind focused on getting herself out of town as quickly as possible. She didn't know how much time she would have before INS was pounding on her door. She didn't doubt they would come. Didn't doubt for one second that Barbara Coulter would have the Capital Police on speed dial.

Sasha punched the elevator button, then stepped back a moment, crossing and uncrossing her arms.

"Bad day, Miss Sasha?"

She answered without turning, "Total shit, Eddie. Total shit." She punched the button one last time, the doors opened, and she stepped inside with nothing more than a scowl for the soft-eyed concierge.

During the brief ride, she thought of what she needed to pack, what she needed to destroy, and what she would have to leave for Eddie to sell. Poor bastard could use some extra cash. As she concentrated on her mental list, she stepped off the elevator and headed down the hall toward her door. She was too preoccupied with her planning to notice that someone was in the hallway with her. As she pulled the key from around her neck, she spotted the shadow. It was large, made by a big man. Her heart thudded in her chest. She turned slowly, barely able to breathe.

Trip. She sighed, a little relieved.

"How the hell did you get down here?"

"Eddie buzzed me down."

"I'll fire that little shit," Sasha said without any conviction. Trip didn't make her nervous. Him she could handle. She resumed unlocking her door. "She's gone. You may as well go away."

As she turned the knob, he stepped toward her. "Go away," she spat as she slipped into her apartment, barely opening the door, hoping Trip didn't dare follow.

"Where is she, Sasha?"

"I don't know, now go away." She attempted to slam the door in his face, but he wedged his foot between it and the frame.

"I'll scream," Sasha threatened.

"Good. Maybe someone will call the police." The words came

from over Trip's shoulder. Sasha's eyes followed them to the figure behind Trip. She remembered him instantly from the party. The man with the scars and the eyes that looked beyond her to the very secrets of her soul. She instinctively feared him. Some men she could twist with lies, some with sex, others, with guilt—every man had his weakness. At least all but a few. There were those few men who were immune to nearly every trick she had in her feminine arsenal. And unfortunately this man was probably one of them.

Sasha sighed and allowed the door to swing open, motioning them in as she turned her back on them and disappeared into the kitchen. She poured herself a shot of vodka, tossing it back and allowing the burn to soothe her. Jane had really gotten them into shit this time. She just needed to get rid of them long enough to get the hell out of here. Trip followed her to the kitchen.

Sasha closed her eyes and shook her head. She was relieved that the other man had not accompanied him in to grill her. He was too calm, his eyes too alert. Trip on the other hand...he was edgy as a cat. Sasha put her glass on the counter and pulled open a drawer and grabbed a fresh pack of cigarettes. As she slowly unwrapped the cellophane, Trip grabbed her wrist and pulled her toward him. "I don't have time for games."

Her eyes fell to her wrist, and he let go. He sighed, his shoulders slumped. "Please, Sasha, just tell me where she is. I have to talk with her."

"Why should I? You hurt her." She tapped out a cigarette and lit it. "Allowed your mother to disrespect her."

"It all happened so fast," Trip said. "I was in shock. And I know that's no excuse, so I want to apologize." He leaned closer to Sasha, who blew a smoke ring in his face. "You have to tell me where she is."

"I don't have to tell you shit." Sasha took a long drag.

"I can help her. She's illegal, right? I can get her a Visa. And I know she has a past, but—"

"A past," Sasha sneered. "Everyone has a past. That's the stupidest phrase I've ever heard. You have a past. Your ugly friend has a past. What the hell? Say what you mean, Mr. Coulter. She may have a past you can't justify to yourself. Things you'd rather not know about." Sasha crushed her cigarette in the ashtray on the counter.

Trip closed his eyes and took a deep breath. When he opened them, Sasha was lighting another smoke. The tiny room was a smoky haze. "Please, Sasha, let me make that decision. Just tell me where I can find her. I have to talk to her."

Sasha took a drag on her cigarette and seemed to relax, she sounded tired, defeated, "Fine. Fine. She's at the airport. She's flying home." Sasha's eyes flickered to the clock on the wall. "You have about an hour before her flight leaves."

"What airport, what flight?"

Sasha shrugged. "Ronald Reagan. And I'm not sure of the flight. One going to Manchester, England."

Trip grabbed her empty hand and squeezed it. "Thank you, Sasha. Thank you."

He bolted from the apartment, calling over his shoulder for Frankie to follow him.

It wasn't until they were in the elevator that Trip explained. "She's at Reagan Airport getting a flight back to home to England."

Frankie shook his head and laughed.

"Something funny?"

Frankie frowned. "Reagan Airport doesn't fly overseas. All flights are continental."

"Son of a bitch." Trip pressed the down button frantically.

"Relax, kid. We'll find her."

"Some spy I'm turning out to be," Trip said with disgust.

Frankie shrugged. "You're too close. Not using your head. That's why it's best to separate personal and business."

"But I don't have a choice right now."

"That's why you have friends. Good thing your mom called me, eh?" Frankie winked at Trip. Trip cursed and let Frankie take the lead.

Frankie didn't knock on the door. He swung it open and allowed it to bang against the wall. That brought Sasha up from the couch with a start. She had her cell phone in her hand and dropped it in her fright. Trip stepped forward and snatched it from the floor. No one was on the line. He checked the call history, instantly recognizing Jane's number. She had called while he was on the elevator. In the few minutes he was gone, he had missed her.

"That's mine," Sasha demanded. Trip ignored her. Her hit redial and was directed to voicemail. He left a message, then snapped it closed and dropped it into his coat pocket.

"Really," Sasha hissed. "This is such bullshit."

"So, call the police," Trip countered, their eyes locked. Sasha backed away moving to the couch and sitting, legs crossed, top leg bouncing nervously.

"Why are you back? I told you what you wanted to know. You're wasting time. You should be at the airport."

"You lied," Frankie said sitting down beside Sasha relaxing against the back of the couch. He took her cigarette from her hand and pressed it between his lips. He inhaled deep then blew smoke rings toward the ceiling.

"I," Sasha began, then thought a moment before answering. "Jane made me promise not to tell you where she was going. I won't break a promise to a friend." She turned to Frankie. "You understand loyalty, right?"

Frankie's eyes narrowed. He studied Sasha's face. She stared back, her cheeks stained scarlet.

Trip's words broke the silent challenge. "When she calls, will you ask her to call me?"

Sasha nodded.

"Thank you. And Sasha, you *can* trust me. I would never hurt her."

Trip turned to leave, gesturing for Frankie to come. Frankie rose but looked back at Sasha as if he were losing the battle. Losing the challenge made his grumpy features even more grizzly.

Trip was nearly to the door when Sasha reminded him he had her phone. "Oh, yeah," Trip answered shaking his head. He reached into his pocket and took out her phone and tossed it to her.

In the elevator Frankie looked across at Trip as if he had grown an extra head. "You're just letting her walk away?"

"Hell no," Trip declared.

"You just did. You really think she's going to get Jane to call you? You let her off the hook."

Trip winked at his friend as the elevator took the down to the main floor. "I bugged her phone."

Frankie looked impressed, "Aha. Maybe you will make a good spy after all."

Chapter 24

Trip and Frankie sat in the parking garage and waited. It took Trip less than a few minutes to set up his laptop, tap into a satellite feed, and lock in on the bug he left in Sasha's phone. In no time, he had the volume turned up with Sasha's lusty voice coming over the speakers. Frankie shook his head as if agreeing with Trip that she wasted no time. Trip hit record and punched a couple of buttons to begin tracing Sasha's caller. If it was a landline he'd have the number immediately. If it was a cell phone it'd be only a few minutes. The search wheel kept spinning. And spinning. Whoever Sasha was talking to was speaking on an encrypted line. Trip felt a chill run down his spine. Frankie lit a cigar and frowned. Who the hell was Sasha? And who was Jane?

While Trip let the computer try to trace the call, he switched his attention to the conversation. It was a man on the other line, he sounded over fifty. Both were speaking Russian. The man was calm, while Sasha sounded panicked. He told Sasha to calm down. She took a deep breath, sounded like she was about to cry, then poured out her story in that one single breath. The man barked a few words, then broke the connection.

"Well, what the hell did they say?" Frankie asked.

Trip ran a hand over his hair. "It was a guy…Viktor…shit. My Russian is barely good enough to be a damned tourist, you know? How the hell—they talked so frigging fast. I could barely keep up." He rewound the tape, listened again. His jaw clenched and his frown deepened.

"It's just too damned hard—and the dialect is crude."

"Give me your phone, kid." Frankie held out his hand and took Trip's cell phone. He gave Trip a grin, removed his cigar to say, "Charlie. He's a Cold War relic. He'll know enough to get the gist of this." Frankie winked at Trip as he turned his attention to the phone. "Hey, Charlie, you rat bastard. I've got a job for you." Frankie took a puff and chuckled. "The hell you're on vacation. It's an easy one, you whiny little prick, turn off your porn a minute and help a guy out." More chesty laughter. "The hell you aren't. Come on, you know you're gonna do it. Just stop busting my balls and interpret this phone call." He flashed a thumb's up to Trip. "Russian. Hell, I could have told you you were rusty, but you're all I've got." Frankie listened a minute, then said, "I can't use an official translator. Damn straight it's illegal. Oh, now you're curious. I'll up the intrigue for you, it's a woman, sexiest friggin' woman you've ever seen. Long red hair, long legs. Possibly a phone sex chat. All right, I'm going to let the kid play it for you."

Trip and Frankie waited. The phone call took four minutes. Charlie listened to it three times before telling them, "The woman told the guy that Anya met some dumb bastard who blew her cover, so she sent her to the beach house. She is scared that the police will be at her door any minute to haul her back to Russia. He told her to be calm, remember to ask for Mr. Black of Cosa Nova if she gets nabbed. Then the girl got upset because Anya's prints were through Interpol. Now here, man, she flips out. It's too damn shrill for me to make all of it out, but the other guy tells her to be quiet and calm down…not to worry. He tells her to stay off the phone—it's being traced—she says what of Anya? And he says, don't worry, she's still dead. The girl told him 'thank you, Viktor' and then he hung up."

Frankie thanked him and hung up the phone.

"They're going to kill her, Frankie. Jane has to be Anya. And they're going to kill her."

Frankie frowned. "Let's be calm."

"They said, 'she's still dead.'"

Frankie nodded, thinking, his face wrinkled in thought. "We

have to find out who Mr. Black is."

"How the hell we going to do that? Who the hell would Mr. Black be?" Trip asked.

"That's a typical cover. CIA uses Mr. Black, Mr. Smith—you know, real clever names like that. Cosa Nova is the key. Let me call my contact at Langely and see if he can find out who this person is."

Before Frankie could make the call, Trip opened his car door and stepped out.

"Where are you going, kid?"

"I'm going to talk to Sasha. That bitch is going to tell me how to get hold of Jane if I have to strangle her."

Frankie shook his head. "I'll talk to red—you go to Dulles. That's the only airport close enough for her to drop Jane off and get back home by the time we got there."

"You're right." Trip got back in the car as Frankie stepped out. "Shit." Trip pounded the steering wheel. "I should've thought of that." As Frankie rounded the front of the car, Trip said, "Thanks for dealing with Sasha, don't let her steal your soul."

Frankie held up his cigar in salute, then said with a sly grin and an evil wink, "Don't worry for me, kid. She's just a lady in distress…and she may need…my comfort."

Trip shook his head, not really caring what Frankie had planned. He just needed to get to Jane.

He broke land speed records getting to the airport. Once there, he knew he was looking for a needle in a haystack. He rushed to the service desk, spied the sweetest looking attendant, then made his approach. "Excuse me…." Trip cleared his throat. When the lady turned, he flashed his best smile, then feigned embarrassment by looking at the floor as he spoke. She moved closer, bending her head closer to him so she could hear his quiet words. "I," Trip said, then stopped. He covered his face with his hands a second before facing her. "This is really embarrassing."

"Go ahead," she said gently.

Trip felt hope swell. This woman was an eager helper. "Ma'am. I just lost the best woman in the world. She's mad at me—I lied to her—and now," he did his best to sound choked up, "I'm going to lose her."

"Oh." The response was simple, but dripped with sympathy.

"If there was some way…oh hell, I don't even know what flight she is trying to take. She has family all over the map. There is no way I could find out what gate she'd be at."

"Just a minute." The lady held up a finger. She turned and called out, "Sandy." She then turned back to Trip and said quietly, "Sandy's head of security."

A sturdy, middle-aged woman in a brown uniform appeared. The agent told her his tale. Sandy frowned at Trip. "You cheat on her?"

"No, ma'am." He mumbled. "I joined the Marine Corps without talking to her about it. She's convinced I'll get myself killed. And her dad just died, so she's emotional."

"Well," Sandy scoffed, "What the hell were you thinkin', boy?"

"I didn't realize."

"Didn't realize. Men never realize." She pulled her walkie-talkie off her hip, "Attention all security. Looking for…."

Trip whispered Jane's description to her, Sandy repeated it. Finished, she shook her head at Trip and offered him a lecture on women as they waited.

*****

Frankie walked right in as if he lived there. "Honey, I'm home."

Sasha dropped her glass of vodka on the kitchen floor, where it shattered. "Dammit. Eddie let you in again? I swear to God that little shit is going to regret this. You could have called, you son of a bitch. I could have had a heart attack."

Frankie grabbed her by the arm and pulled her close. "You admitting you have a heart?" Her eyes were wide as she stared up at him. Frankie kept her within arm's reach as he explained through gritted teeth, "You are going to tell me what is going on here."

She wriggled against his grip, but quickly abandoned the idea of breaking free. "Nothing is 'going on.' Jane just went home."

"You're lying. We tapped your damned phone. What are you up to? Why did you say Jane was dead?"

She said nothing. He wrapped a hand in her hair and pulled until she looked up at him. She clawed at his hand that gripped her arm. He pulled her hair tighter. Sasha felt her body warm and an electric tingle coursed through her veins, which only made her hate him that much more.

Frankie leaned close, his lips grazing the sensitive skin of her ear. "Don't lie to me, lady. I want answers. Is someone going to hurt Jane?"

Sasha's features softened a little. Her green eyes clouded with tears, the stubbornness and hard lines melted into fatigue and worry. "I sent her away to keep her safe. I would die for Jane. What Viktor said is she's *already dead*. She's officially dead. Suicide over a year ago."

"Stop playing games with me. I want the truth."

A tear spilled down her cheek. "Let me go and I'll tell you everything."

Frankie eased his grip on her hair, but didn't release her. Instead, he pulled her in tight to him. His hold was gentle yet strong and assuring, she stiffened, but then gradually relaxed against his body. She closed her eyes. He forced her cheek onto his chest. "I can't do this anymore," she whispered. "I promised…I promised Viktor I would keep her safe, but…." She gripped his shirt with the clutch of a person teetering on a cliff. "But I'm scared. Something is wrong. I can feel it in my gut. I just know."

Her body trembled. Frankie squeezed her tight, stroked her hair like she was a scared child. "Tell me everything, Sasha. I can help you."

"You are a spy, aren't you?"

"Sort of. We work in private security. We keep people safe from bad guys and secrets. We're good at what we do."

"I knew it. I told her so."

He tipped her chin gently until she was looking at him. "I want to help you."

She nodded, her tongue flicked out, moistening her lips. She couldn't help but realize Frankie had the most honest eyes she had ever seen. His brow was furrowed with worry. For her. If only her life was different, her history not so sordid, maybe she could find a—

She interrupted the thought. Frankie was here to help Trip, to help Trip find Jane and nothing more. She was losing her mind. Fear was making her crazy. She closed her eyes and pushed her thoughts toward what she could share with Frankie.

His voice was low, his presence so close, she could feel the warmth of his breath on her skin, smell his aftershave mixed with the smell of expensive cigars. "Who was on the phone?"

"Viktor."

"Who is Viktor?"

"Jane's father."

*****

Jane heard someone call her name. Her heart sped up, and she clutched the ticket in her hand. The ticket with her new name. The person calling for her was calling her by her old name. She turned toward her caller. It was airport security.

"Ma'am," the young man, Brandon, according to his badge, said. "Are you Jane Mitchell?"

"Um, yeah…how did you…?"

"Security said to look for a pretty blond with blue eyes."

Jane looked across the stream of people. There were plenty of other blondes.

Brandon nodded and grinned from ear to ear. "I'm really good at being lucky."

Jane nodded and said, "Seems you are."

Brandon pointed behind him. "There's someone at the front desk for you."

Jane looked at her ticket, none of her identification fit the name Jane. She swallowed hard and gripped her purse straps to still her shaking hands. She followed the guard wordlessly. She caught sight of Trip's head because he stood a full shoulder height above everyone else around him.

He ran to her, lifting her from the ground. "Jane! I thought I

186

lost you. I'm so sorry, so damn sorry." He kissed her cheek, her hair. "I love you, God how I love you."

"Still?"

"Always." He kissed her, hugged her to him so tightly she could barely breathe. But who needed oxygen when you had love? Jane felt her heart soar.

"I love you too," she whispered. "I'm sorry I lied to you."

"It's okay." He let her slide down his body to her feet. "I've got you. I'm not letting you go."

"But...."

"But nothing." He took a step back and looked down at her. His brow furrowed. His fingertips caressed her cheek, brushed loose strands of hair behind her ear. "Listen, you are in danger. I intercepted a phone call, and I heard Sasha say..."

"What do you mean?" Her brows drew together. "You intercepted...."

"She said you were dead."

She didn't hear what he said. She needed him to answer her question. "What do you mean you intercepted a phone call?"

"That's not the point...."

"Yes. It is." Her voice rose. "What does it mean intercepted? You overheard her? What?"

"I tapped her phone to find you. She was talking to some guy named Viktor. And they were talking about killing you."

Jane pushed herself away from him. "Who are you? What do you mean you tapped her phone?"

Trip looked stunned, tried to grab for her. "Who's Viktor, Jane?"

"My poppa. He's my father. And he's dead." She spat. "Killed by a traitor like you. He pretended to be a friend. Then he killed him."

"You can trust me, Jane. I love you."

Jane moved farther back. Trip made a step toward her, but she put her hands up like she was ready to block him if he came any closer. Trip scanned all the people watching, including the helpful security guards who were now getting antsy. His tone was urgent.

"It's me, Jane."

"And really, who are you?" Her head shook side to side. "I know Sasha. I know Poppa. They would never hurt me. They love me. You? I don't even know who you are. Sasha told me not to trust you. She told me you were a spy."

"Jane, I love you. Come with me. We'll go see Sasha and ask her to explain what I heard."

Jane's eyes narrowed and she backed away from him. "How do I know where you might take me? Go to hell, Trip."

"Jane." He breathed and stepped toward her cautiously like he was coaxing a jumper from a ledge.

"Take another step and I will scream."

"Please," he begged.

Jane took another step back, then spun on her heel and ran. Trip started after her, but was instantly grabbed by security.

Chapter 25

"What do you mean, 'she's dead'?" Frankie demanded.

"She is dead," Sasha answered matter-of-factly. "Legally dead. She died last year. Announced in papers, she was put in coffin and buried. Dead. To the world? She is dead."

Frankie frowned, and his eyes narrowed. "Don't play games with me Sasha. What the hell are you talking about? Are you telling me Jane's an imposter?"

"No, Jane is who she says she is—well, with the exception of her name. It's really Anya, not Jane. And her last name isn't Mitchell, it's Sarkhov. She was drugged, then revived, then I took her from the country where she would be safe."

"Safe from who?"

Sasha shrugged. "Viktor's not certain. He has suspicions, but he needs proof."

"And Viktor is Jane's father?"

Sasha nodded. Frankie went to open his mouth, but shut it with a snap as his phone rang. He shot Sasha a look of annoyance. She folded her arms over her chest and looked away. She pretended not to listen, but she couldn't help but hold her breath and focus on Frankie's low voice. She could barely hear, his head was dropped and his words were few. A couple of *are you sures?* and that was about all. He snapped his phone closed and looked up at her and took a deep breath. "So, Viktor Sarkhov is dead too, eh?"

She bit her cheek and nodded. "Legally."

"So we got two goddam dead people running around...the

question is why? And who the hell was Mr. Black, who seems to be the only son of a bitch who's truly dead."

"Mr. Black isn't dead."

"The hell he isn't. They found him floating in the Potomac."

Her head shook. "No. That's not…."

"I just talked to my inside guy at the CIA. Viktor Sarhkov—shot dead by a KGB informant…. Or well, so the official story says. And Mr. Black dead by suffocation probably three days ago, body recovered this morning."

"But I talked to him a few hours ago."

"Black ain't talkin' to anybody, sweetheart. I suggest you tell me everything, and you tell me fast. Your contact could be a double agent or God knows who."

Sasha stared at the walls as if she expected a solution to materialize on them. "I was asked to keep Jane safe."

"And you will…if you trust me."

Frankie grabbed her arm. "There's no time for this, and you know it."

"I should call Viktor." Sasha grabbed her phone and dialed. Her foot tapped on the floor as she waited. No answer. She dialed the number again. Still, no answer. "I don't understand. I talked to Viktor right before you came. He always answers."

"Holy shit, lady. Don't you get it? Whoever you talked to this morning wasn't Black. Whoever it was is probably the same guy who killed the real Black. I'm assuming he knows where to find you?"

Sasha nodded slowly. "The courier brought me Jane's new passport."

"So, whoever killed Black knows exactly where Jane is headed?"

"Oh my God." She paced, her mind swirled. "Oh, I…I have to get to Jane."

"Hopefully, Trip has her by now."

"But I told him the wrong airport!"

"We figured it out. Nice try, by the way."

"I promised I'd keep her safe. I owe Viktor. I'd be dead or

worse if it weren't for him. He bribed party members to get me set free, even after three arrests."

"So, that's how you made it out. I figured as much. Beautiful woman like you…"

"It wasn't like that. Not Viktor. He treated me like a daughter, or a niece. He was good to me. He just wanted someone he could trust to be there for Jane. His compound was all men. He worried Jane would get too rough; thought she needed a woman around."

"So he springs a thief and a…."

"Whore?" She grabbed her pack of cigarettes and dropped into the couch. She picked at the cellophane wrapper. "I don't know why Viktor trusted me. Especially not with his daughter. I wouldn't."

"I wasn't going to say that." He sat beside her. "And you have kept her safe."

"Until now." Tears burned in her eyes. Her hands were twitchy, and she tried to pull a smoke out, but she couldn't settle them enough to be useful.

Frankie took them from her, pulled one out, lit it, and handed it back. Taking it with a nod, she reached for the ashtray on the end table and cradled it in her lap.

"Any idea who might want Jane dead? For real dead?"

"Any number of people would kidnap her for ransom, but the only one that would want her dead, to just be dead."

He tapped himself out a smoke. "And that would be?"

"Damn it. I hate to say. If I am wrong, then Viktor would be pissed I ever said it."

Frankie made an exaggerated sweep of the room. "It's just you and me, babe."

Sasha snorted.

"Bugs? You think the place is bugged?"

"Of course not!" she whispered.

"Then who? God damn it! How long do you think we have until someone comes for you? When Trip gets Jane off that plane, whoever is looking for Jane will come up empty-handed and they'll come where?"

"Here."

"Of course here. And they'll find us sharing smokes and talking about the mysteries of the free freaking world. What the hell is going on?"

Sasha's hands shook. "Viktor is a Russian businessman." She cleared her throat. "But some of his businesses are less than totally legal. But he is good man."

"Get to the meat, Sasha. We may not have a lot of time."

"Okay, okay. I'm not sure what you want to know."

"Why is Viktor dead?"

"His business was being corrupted. Someone within was trafficking in little girls and women. KGB came to Viktor and told him their suspicions. Viktor was furious, and he wanted to the bottom of the problem quickly, so KGB starts to work with Viktor...under disguise."

"So, he was working with the KGB?"

Sasha nodded. "Yes. And they were following the threads back...from brothels to orphanages to Viktor's business. Viktor told me he was pretty sure who was involved, then strange things started to happen...weird accidents for him and Jane. Viktor told me it was getting too dangerous, that he was closing in on the guilty, but couldn't say unless he was absolutely certain." Sasha took another drag.

She closed her eyes a moment and tried to stay focused. "The KGB agent, he suggested the fake death. They figured with Viktor gone, whoever was involved would be bolder. Viktor wasn't convinced." Sasha sighed. "But then, the last day...Jane's dog, Oslo, ate a plate of cookies off of Viktor's desk, and the dog fell over dead." Sasha's closed her eyes at the memory. "The little thing didn't even twitch. Just died. Cookies were filled with poison."

"So, of course, Viktor decided to die." Her leg continued to bounce, but it slowed a little. "Viktor and Demetry quickly hatched a plan. They *fought* over wages...the commotion brought Jane to the room in time to see Demetry fire at Viktor. Well, then Jane launches herself at Demetry and out the window they both go. Jane was knocked unconscious."

"KGB gave her drugs to make her look dead. She even had a

funeral with casket and all." Sasha rubbed her forehead. "She wasn't supposed to remember any of that, but she's been plagued by nightmares ever since, I wanted to explain but I couldn't. All that really mattered was that she stay hidden."

Sasha looked up at him, her voice clear and strong, "Viktor told me to get Jane out of Russia. To keep her safe until he said everything was all right. And everything was all right until she met your friend." Her eyes narrowed. "I told her none of you could be trusted."

"So, Jane has been hiding here while the world thinks she's dead?"

"Yes. But Jane doesn't know she's dead. She thinks she's wanted for Demetry's murder."

Frankie shook his head and grunted. "Why the hell would you guys lie to her?"

"To protect her. You don't know Jane. She lunged at a man with a gun! If she thought people were getting hurt, she'd try to help." Sasha's head shook. "And that would be dangerous for her. She is not capable of dealing with such evil." She looked at Frankie hard. "And these people...who steal children and women? They are pure evil."

"I agree. It was actually a pretty good plan."

"Yeah! Until that bitch ran her fingerprints!"

Frankie rubbed his eyes with the palms of his hands and asked, "So, who is Mr.Black, and why would someone want him dead?"

"He is our CIA contact. He gets me passports and money when I need it. He brought the stuff for Jane a while ago; said his liaison, Mr. White, would bring me one in a bit."

Frankie leaped from his seat and dragged Sasha with him. "Pack your things, Sasha. I need to get you the hell out of here."

Sasha paled. "I...don't...."

"Get what you need. I mean it." Frankie pulled a gun from a holster behind his back. He checked the clip and took it off safety. He went to the front door, stepping over and crunching the glass on the floor as he walked. Locking it, he slid the chain lock in place. "How soon did he say he'd be here?"

Sasha looked at the clock on the wall. She chewed her lips as she thought. "He said two hours…and that was over an hour…."

"Just get a bag and let's go."

Sasha headed to her room, stopped and called, "Frosty. Frosty! Come to Auntie Sash." The dog came squirming out from under a chair. "Come on, baby. We've got to go." Sasha grabbed at the dog, who in turn grabbed a ball, growled, and took off. He hid under Jane's bed. Sasha's voice was brittle as she got down on her knees and begged, "Please, Frosty. We must go!"

*****

Jane kept looking over her shoulder. She expected Trip to reappear, to confuse her even more than she already was.

Jane's heart pounded in her chest, and she was having difficulty taking a deep breath. She stood in the ticket line, her hands shaking so badly she had to grip the straps of her purse to still them.

She kept repeating Trip's words in her head. He tapped Sasha's phone. That made him a spy, which made Sasha right. She bit her lip. So he was probably using her. But for what? Did he know she was wanted for murder? And if so, why not just arrest her?

He had to be after something else, but what? Maybe they thought she knew something about her father's business. And the millions of dollars he had tied up in it. But wouldn't Nikki be a better person to check into? Or could Trip be with the Bratva? Maybe Poppa had done something to anger them? No. Not Poppa. He was loyal and trusted, even his rival red fellas respected him. He was a name to know, even by public officials. No one would have anything against him.

No one but Nikki.

Jane's mind raced putting the clues together. Maybe, just maybe, Nikki didn't have Poppa's money. Maybe he thought she had it. Maybe he was using Trip to weasel his way into her life and find out if she had the money.

That would explain getting between her and Sasha. Sasha was too clever and would see through ruses and lies. But why would he tell her Poppa was alive? In the midst of all of her current turmoil, the little girl in her had a tiny spring of hope. What if he was alive?

But what would make him hide from her? Make her suffer from the loss?

No, he wouldn't do that to her. If he was alive, he would get her out of trouble with the KGB. Jane remembered their last night together. Poppa had asked her to walk with him.

"You are a grown woman, Anya. Grown enough to understand a few things. Things you must accept to be safe should something happen to your poppa."

"Don't talk like that, Poppa. It's depressing. Let's talk of a holiday…maybe go see Aunt Tilley?"

"No. Anya. You need to listen. Nikki is returning home tomorrow. He has gotten himself in trouble with some very bad people." He stopped walking as if they revelation wore the strength from him. "He has done some things that are unforgivable. He is coming to me to have me clean it all up, but I don't know if I can. And if rumors are true…." He shook his head and started walking again.

Jane grabbed him by the arm. "What rumors, Poppa?"

"Terrible things, *dorogaya dochka*. Terrible things. If these things are true…" He shook his head and looked to the horizon with a sigh, "then I can think only that your brother is pure evil. A demon." Tears clouded his eyes. He cursed and looked away. Jane grabbed him and gave him a hug. He squeezed her tight. He was strong for an older man, his body hard from boxing in the gym.

"No, Poppa," she assured him. "Nikki is just a man."

He nodded, his whiskered chin rubbing her cheek. "I hope you are right, little one." He stepped back and smiled at her. He wrapped an arm across her shoulder and walked on toward the pond. "Still, I have an ill omen for the future. Hopefully it is just the imagination of an old man. But I want you to promise me that no matter what happens, you will be strong and be smart. Trust Poppa, eh? No matter what, trust Poppa."

She smiled up at him. "Of course."

"You are my light, little Anya. As much as Nikki is my dark, you are my light. But both of you are my children so I have to try and save your brother."

"I understand. We will help him together."

Jane had thought he meant some sort of intervention, but now she had doubts. Maybe there was more to her father's plan to save Nikki from himself. Could he have faked his death to help his son? That was absurd. And Trip had said her father was out to kill her. And nothing was more ludicrous than Sasha and Viktor planning to kill her.

She was next in line. She handed her ticket and ID over to the man at the metal detector. He looked at her papers, then at her. He frowned and asked her to step out of the line. Jane looked over her shoulder. Maybe she should run? Trip might still be waiting on her, but she might have a chance of talking him into letting her go. But then, maybe he was the one who had turned her in.

"There is an urgent message for you, Miss Kristobel. I was asked to stop you at the gate."

"Oh." That was all Jane could manage to say. She followed the airline attendant to a small white room with a single heavy door. A tall man with blond hair and glasses smiled at her and took her suitcase. "Anya? I am Mr. Black. Your father sent me to take you somewhere safe."

*****

Trip saw Jane get pulled out of line at the same time as Frankie's hard-edged words told him Jane was in danger. She and Sasha's contact had been killed and replaced with a mole. Trip scanned the airport for any breach in security he could slip through. The whole time every fiber of his body screamed with the tension.

He spotted his weakness. A group of flight attendants were coming on duty. They walked in a clump, their rolling suitcases humming on the floor behind them. Trip stole a suitcase from a mother busy with a couple of toddlers and stepped into the clump. He smiled down at a lady on the edge of the pack. She blushed and looked away. "Where you flying today?" he asked with a wink and enough charm to weaken her knees. He flirted with her until she slid her badge and opened the door for them. Trip broke away from the pack with a promise of seeing them later, ditched the suitcase, and searched the narrow hallways for any sign of Jane.

He caught sight of the back of her head. She was being led by a tall blond man through a door that led to a private parking lot. Trip called her name. She turned and took a step behind her escort as if to shield herself from Trip.

"Jane, you need to come with me. You're in danger."

Jane shook her head. "I don't know you."

"Yes, yes you do, baby, it's me. I'm not lying to you. Look in your heart, you know I love you."

"You lie. I don't know you. You tap phones and tell me things I know," Jane's voice cracked. "That I know can't be true."

"Just back off, son, I'm a federal agent." The blond-haired man flipped open a badge, then shut it again. "I'll let Ms. Sarkhov call you when we have her somewhere safe...then you two can work this all out."

Son of a bitch. That was Trip's only conscious thought as he pulled his gun out from his shoulder strap. He pointed it at the man and said, his voice quiet and calm, his hand steady, gun aimed straight between the agent's eyes. "Mr. Black, I assume?"

Jane nodded.

"Let her go or I will drop you right where you stand."

In a move swifter than a lightning strike, Mr. Black pulled his own gun out of his pocket with one hand and yanked Jane from beside him with the other...using her as a shield. He jammed the gun into her temple. She cried out in pain.

Black cocked the hammer and started backing away. "Stay back, boy. Nothing I hate more than trying to get brains out of wool."

"Let her go," Trip demanded.

"Don't think so, son. This lady's worth more than you'll make in your lifetime."

He pushed the heavy door open with his hip and backed out into the parking lot.

Trip felt like he was gut shot as he watched Jane disappear into the sunlight, her eyes boring into him as if begging him to help.

Jane kicked and bit Black's arm. He responded with a vicious headlock that cut off her breath. She dug her teeth in deeper until she felt the pop of skin and the iron taste of blood. His grip tightened, until she couldn't breathe. Relinquishing her bite with a strangled gasp, she kept kicking him with flailing feet. Her efforts slowly weakened as his strangle hold and her exhaustion brought her mind to a blank and her body went limp. He flipped her up over his shoulder and carried her to a limo waiting in the parking lot.

Trip ran at the fire door and hit it with such force that it banged off the outer wall. He watched helplessly as Jane was tossed into the back seat of the limo. When the door was shut, Trip seized the moment and squeezed off a shot. The man's body jerked, and he clutched at his shoulder. Trip fired again. Another hit.

Black turned on Trip and unloaded his full clip. The bullets pinged off the concrete walls, chipping the paint and ricocheting on the asphalt. Trip ducked behind the door and watched helplessly as Black got into his car and sped away. Trip ran out into the parking lot and shot at the tires. One blew, causing the car to careen left, then right, then steadily off down the road.

With zero chance of catching them, Trip turned and headed back into the building only to be met by an armed security SWAT team. "Perfect timing," Trip lamented, dropping his gun on the ground and putting his hands in the air.

Chapter 26

"Leave the dog," Frankie ordered.

Sasha shook her red head and dropped to her knees. "Frosty, please come to Auntie Sash. Please." Tears burned in her eyes, blurring her vision. Damn dog. Flea-infested little rodent felt as important to her as if he were a child. Swiping a hand across her face to rid herself of the tears she realized her hands were cold and shaking.

"Damn it, dog," Frankie spat as he flipped the bed on its side. Frosty dropped his ball, backed his furry little body in a corner and barked. Sasha scooped him up, gathering him in her arms. "Bad boy." Her voice quivered as her body began to shake. "Jane would never forgive me if I lost the mutt." Sasha clutched the dog as if hugging him close would keep them all safe.

"I'm ready."

"No purse? Clothes?"

"I…uh," Sasha looked around the apartment. She had no intention of setting the dog down to pack. Nothing here was irreplaceable. "No, I'm ready to go."

The frown that Frankie sported so well reappeared, and he grabbed a purse on the counter. "This yours?"

Sasha nodded as she kissed the dog's ear and cradled him against her cheek.

Frankie tucked the purse under his arm and grabbed the leash hanging by the door. He snapped it on the dog's collar and wrapped the strap on her wrist. "Just in case he gets down."

She nodded. "Good thinking."

He walked her to the elevator with a protective hand at the small of her back. Pushing the button, he looked down at her. "You okay? You look really pale."

"I'm fine. Can you call Trip? See if he got her off the plane?"

Nodding, he pulled his phone out of his pocket. Sasha had a sick feeling in her stomach as she watched his face go grim. Covering her mouth with a cold, shaky hand, she decided she didn't want to know what Trip had to say.

He hung up, and she knew it was bad when he grabbed her and pulled her close. Closing her eyes, she leaned against him. If Jane was gone, what did she have? Frank's voice was low. "She wouldn't go with him."

Sasha's voice was small and weak. "But she's okay, right?"

Frankie's shook his head. "They have her."

Sasha's knees went weak, and she collapsed against his chest. His arms tightened around her. "You've got to be strong, Sasha. We're going to get her back, I swear. I'm going to take you somewhere safe, and then I am going to go help Trip. We'll get her."

"Promise?"

"I promise." Red-rimmed blue eyes looked up at him. A shaking body stilled in his arms. Without giving it a single rational thought, he kissed her.

He held her face in his hands as if he could transfer knowledge and calm with a look and a touch. Sasha started to feel calm, but that ended with the popping sound of gun fire. Sasha's body jerked, a hysterical scream slipped from her lips, but was quickly muffled as Frankie clamped a hand over her mouth.

He whispered in her ear, "Sounds like they're in the lobby. Is there another way out of the building?"

Sasha's eyes were wide, her pulse quickened in her throat, but she nodded.

"I'm moving my hand. Don't scream. Understood?"

She nodded. As his hand lifted, she whispered, her voice hoarse and breaking into tears as she asked, "Eddie. Do you think they hurt him?"

Frankie's brown eyes looked at the stalled elevator. Eddie must have shut it down by hitting the emergency stop at the desk. Several more rounds of gunfire sounded above them. "I don't know. We best get the hell out of here."

"There is a back door, in the apartment. It leads to the alley."

"Come on." He dragged her by the hand back through the apartment, pausing only a moment to put his ear to the door. He gave Sasha's hand a squeeze and placed a finger on his lips. She nodded and scratched the dog behind the ear until he relaxed and nearly fell asleep in her arms. Frankie inched the door open. The alley was quiet. He swung it open far enough to look out. A single armed watcher was stationed by the back door. Wordlessly, Frankie grabbed him in a headlock and dragged him into the apartment. The man barely struggled, his body went limp, glassy eyes stared back at Sasha as his gun dropped to the floor.

"You just knocked him out, right?"

Frankie grabbed the gun and slid it into his coat pocket. "Sure," was his simple answer.

Grabbing her hand, he silently led her out of the building, around the dumpster. They inched along the wall until they reached the back of the building. From there they traveled through one back alley to another until they were several blocks away.

Frankie looked over his shoulder and sighed. "I don't think anyone followed us."

Sasha looked back where they came from. Her heart thudded, and her throat was dry, partly due to the pace—partly due to fear. She hoped they didn't have anyone on the roof watching the streets. Clinging to Frankie's hand, she no longer cared about being brave or being strong. She was too tired to go an inch more. Frankie tucked her under his arm. Sirens howled in the distance, moving closer with each passing second.

"Sounds like the police will have the apartment under control. Let's get you somewhere safe."

"Can I stay with you?" He looked grim, and his head started to shake. Sasha gripped his shirt. "You can't leave me! I don't know who I can trust. A-and, you might need information. I could help."

"Fine. But do as I say, got it?"

Sasha nodded and wiped at drying tears.

Frankie made a call, and within minutes a car arrived. He helped Sasha get in the back seat before sitting shotgun. The driver, a thin man in his twenties, seemed nervous. He kept adjusting his rearview mirror, his Adam's apple protruding with each anxious swallow. "Mr. Coulter is at the airport."

"Then take us there."

The man nodded and fidgeted in his seat. He glanced at Frankie before turning onto the interstate. As cars whizzed by, the driver added, "They have a tactical team on sight and ready."

"Any idea where they took the girl?"

The driver shrugged. "Don't know, sir. I was just told to get you there. This is my first time out of the office, well, besides to get coffee."

Frankie rolled down his window and pulled out a cigarette. "You mind?"

The man shook his head. Frankie lit his smoke. He offered it to Sasha, but she shook her head no. Her confident features long ago melted into a countenance of fear and desperation. Her eyes looked big and hollow as captured prey.

The driver took them through several security check points until they were in a private parking lot at the back of the airport. They were greeted by a tiny woman with her long brown hair pulled back in a ponytail. She must have been waiting on them, because she approached the car as soon as it pulled into the lot.

"Mr. Bonmarito?" the woman asked as soon as Frankie stepped out of the car.

Frankie nodded.

"Agent Radgman, you can call me Kristine. Please, come with me."

She led him into the building, down a corridor to a freight elevator. She punched a button and soon they were headed to the belly of the airport. Escorting them off the elevator, down another corridor where she used her thumbprint to open an airlock door. It led to yet another hallway with a door at the very end of the corridor that was guarded by two heavily armed security guards. She nodded to the guard on the left. He punched in a code and the door swung open.

The room was filled with people. Trip sat slouched in a chair, one hand resting on the table, the other running nervously over his skull. A man paced the room, talking on a cell phone. Cell phone talker yelled, "I don't give a rat's ass about the chain of command. Get Viktor the hell out. No, I wouldn't report the move. There is a breech. Someone fingered Black. It has to be someone on the inside."

While the guy on the phone continued his rampage, Frankie seated Sasha in a chair in the corner of the room. He pulled a chair up next to Trip, giving his leg a firm pat. "What the hell's going on, kid?"

"They've got her, Frank. I should have stopped him, but I couldn't." Trip held his head in his hands. "I shot at the car. I tried to get Jane to trust me. Why the hell wouldn't she just trust me?" Trip looked caged, edgy. His words and movements were anxious and choppy. "Dammit, Frank, why didn't she trust me? Now, who knows where she is. This is such bullshit. This morning she was safe. I let her run away, and I let that son of a bitch take her."

"You didn't let him do anything. You say you got a shot off?"

Trip nodded. "Too late. I would've shot earlier, but he had her in a head lock with a gun to her head. I wasn't sure I could get a clean shot, so I didn't take it. I should…"

"You should have shit. He'd have blown her head off." Frankie sat up straighter. "I guarantee it. Even a clean shot between his eyes could've caused a spasm and he'd have pulled the trigger."

Trip sighed and rubbed his eyes. "That's what I thought. Anyhow, I followed them out to the parking lot…after he put Jane in the car…I shot the bastard…twice." He held up his fingers in Frankie's face. "Twice. Right in the heart. Bastard gets right in his car."

"Probably a vest."

Trip nodded. "Shot out a back tire, but still he drove away. Just drove the hell away."

Sasha gasped from the corner. Frankie looked back at her and said, "It'll be all right."

She bit her lip and nodded, hugging the now squirming dog tightly.

"So, what'd you get from the license?" Frankie asked.

"Not a damn thing. Government car issued to the real, very dead, Mr. Black."

"What do these egg heads know?"

The tiny escort, Radgman, coughed loudly and dropped a dossier in front of Frankie. "You field guys think you're the only ones who work?" She sat down beside him. "Egotistical bastards." She flipped the file open. "Let's see how quickly I can get you up to speed…seeing as how you guys have insinuated yourselves into a situation, that I must say, was running smooth as glass before you got involved."

"How the hell did we…?" Frankie asked.

"Shut up, Frankie," Trip said. "I just want to know what the hell is going on."

Radgman nodded. "A year ago, the department, with the help of the KGB, was investigating a child trafficking organization hiding in the remnants of Chechnya, Kosovo, and so on. The investigation brought us to Yekaterinburg City, and to Viktor Sarkhov's mostly above board smuggling business. Viktor checked out, but still so many things pointed to his operation…it couldn't be ignored. There had to be a connection, so we bribed a man inside."

"Demetry," Sasha offered from the corner.

Radgman looked back at her and nodded. "Yes. Demetry."

"So," Radgman continued, "within days, Demetry says, Viktor is on to him,"

"Hah. You can't fool Viktor," Sasha added.

Radgman ignored Sasha's comments. "So Viktor questions him. Demetry caves. Then, to our surprise, Viktor wants in. He wants to help. So Viktor was brought in and started working for the CIA. I figure he wanted to maintain his credibility as a *businessman.*"

"His honor."

"Credibility, honor…would you like to tell this story?" Radgman snapped at Sasha.

Sasha shrugged and leaned back in her seat.

"So, anyway…like I was saying…Viktor started doing his own investigations and quickly found out the people involved were very close to him. And that a branch of his company was funding an orphanage. An orphanage with international connections. This orphanage was supposed to be monitored by the—"

"The UN," Sasha interrupted. "What a joke."

Trip turned to Sasha, "You know all this?"

Sasha shrugged. "Just guessing."

Radgman sighed hard. "The problem was bigger and more dangerous than Viktor ever dreamed. And the puppet master in the horrid affair was not just close to Viktor, but was his only son. Nicolai Sarkhov had made connections with powerful people…dignitaries and politicians. So many household names were suspected and could be exposed that there was a strong push to shut the investigation down, for national security."

Radgman snorted. "But Viktor refused. He swore everyone would know, that just shutting the business down wasn't enough. The guilty, no matter what their station in life, needed to pay for their crimes. That threat to go public put Viktor, and his family, in the crosshairs. Some very powerful people want him dead."

"So, why the hell didn't he…?" Trip turned to Sasha. Frankie grabbed his arm and kept him in his seat.

"Didn't what?" Sasha shook a finger at Trip. "Didn't keep Jane safe? We tried. She was dead. Dead. No one looks for dead people. Not until their goddam names are sent through Interpol and everyone who thinks she's dead gets suspicious."

"I never."

"Well, your mommy and your girlfriend did."

"And it seems…," Radgman contended, "…that Mr. Black was also somehow outed. How? We're not sure. He was the only plant we had in Nicolai Sarkhov's operation. We assume Nicolai somehow figured out who Black was working for, and we suspect, had him killed."

"So, the guy who kidnapped Jane is working for her brother? This Nicolai?"

"Nikki. A true-life evil half-brother," Sasha offered. "I figured Viktor suspected him. Probably wished he was wrong, probably why he needed very strong proof."

"But why would he hurt Jane?" Trip asked. "She didn't do anything to him."

Sasha shrugged. "All I know is there were at least two attempts on Jane's life. There was an ignition bomb on her car and someone filled a plate of cookies with arsenic. Viktor first thought someone felt the heat of the investigation and wanted to send him a message, but then Nikki attacked Jane."

"Her brother attacked her?" Frankie asked.

Sasha nodded. "Nikki hates Viktor...and he hates Jane. He hates Viktor because he thinks he killed Tracy...and he hates Jane because...well, because he is a lunatic and blames her for her mother's death."

"What the...." Trip shook his head, his confusion obvious.

"Tracy. Tracy Dugan. Viktor's second wife...Jane's mother...Tracy had an affair with Nikki, then married him."

"So, Jane's mother married her stepson. Gross. But what the hell's that got to do with Jane?" Trip asked.

"Tracy hid Jane from Viktor for eight years. And Tracy was a heartless bitch to her daughter. Viktor despised her for it. So when Tracy overdosed, Nikki assumed Viktor was behind it."

"Was he?" Frankie asked.

"I wish," Sasha said.

Trip cracked his neck and rubbed the balls of his fists to his stinging eyes. "Okay. So, we know Black is dead, Black's doppelganger has Jane, and most likely it is her sicko brother we're looking for, right?"

Sasha nodded. Frankie flipped through the pages of the dossier. "But where?"

Mason, a chubby guy glued to his computer screen in the corner of the room gave out a whoop. "We have contact. Just got an agent update—our Mr. Nikki Sarkhov is en route from Kennedy Airport flying under the name Gunther Krauss. Airport records show he is flying into this airport. Should be arriving…," he looked up at the clock "…twenty minutes ago—what the—whatever happened to real time? Friggin assholes. Anyhow, a car is supposed to be tailing him…. Maybe we'll get an update on location. I'll check with dispatch." He spun his desk chair back around, pressed his head set to his ear, and started making calls.

"Jane was taken twenty minutes ago." Trip paced the room. "He must have been in the car. Where the hell would he take her?"

He looked around the room, scanned each face for an answer, all he saw was pity, disappointment, and in the face of Sasha, pure panic.

Chapter 27

Hearing was the first of her senses to recover. Mumbled voices in a nearby room—no, closer. They were in the same room, but they were talking away from her. An airplane soared overhead, a bird twittered. A door or window squeaked open. Jane lifted an eyelid ever so slightly. The harsh sun made her eyes sting. She couldn't tell who was at the door; it was a man. Medium build, well dressed. There was another man, his voice a deep baritone outside the door.

Mr. Black, Jane realized as awareness slowly crept back into her skull. The words spoken by Mr. Black were hard to decipher, his voice was too low, too mumbled. The man in the door cursed in Russian. The man told Black, "Go to the car and wait…and make sure no other cars followed…put the damned body in the trunk."

Mumbled response.

"Oh, Jesus, can't you think of anything on your own, you stupid bastard." A long sigh, then the man spoke again as one would speak to a child. "Put him in your trunk."

Mumbled response.

"Damned superstition! You just killed a man, you stupid asshole. You don't think that's bad luck? You can't leave his body in the friggin' street. Hide it!" He slammed the door. "Damned fool."

Jane struggled to move.

"Shit," the man cursed. He grabbed her arm; she tried to twist it away. It felt like a bee sting in her neck. Then, everything went dark again.

Elizabeth Seckman

She woke to more cursing. This time, Jane recognized the voice. Her heart squeezed as she tried to decide whether or not it was a good thing or a bad thing. She opened her eyes as he turned and closed the door and came into the room. "Nikki?" she whispered, her throat sore from the choking, her thoughts sluggish from the drugs.

"Little sister." He sat, cross legged in the chair across from her, polishing his revolver with a white hotel wash cloth.

Jane sat up. She rubbed her throat and crossed her legs under her. She looked around the room. It was a hotel room with the same burgundy carpet and paisley bedspread as the millions of other American hostelries. She didn't know what Nikki had planned, and she trusted him naught, but she figured it would be in her best interest to play dumb. "Oh, Nikki. You are a sight for hurting eyes." She smiled at him and sighed.

"Sore, darling...the word is sore." He laughed and tucked the gun in his coat pocket. "You really should have completed your studies at Oxford."

Jane shook her head. "I was never that smart. You were always so much more clever than me."

"True," he admitted. "But Father didn't see the point in sending me to college. Prick."

Jane flinched but composed herself and said nothing.

"What's going on, Nikki? Why did that man try to kill me?"

"Nando?" Nikki laughed. "Silly girl. He was just trying to help you. That man chasing you at the airport?" Jane nodded. "He was trying to kill you. Not Nando."

Jane rubbed her throat. "He choked me."

"You were screaming and biting and kicking…. He had to calm you down."

"Oh. I guess." She picked at her thumbnail. "I suppose you're right. He could have just shot me."

"True...see, you are a little clever, too." Nikki winked at her.

"What is going on, Nikki?"

"Seems Poppa has been playing his games again. He's clever too. He faked his own death—and yours I might add—to escape the law." Nikki stood and walked to the bed, sitting down beside her. "But unfortunately, none of us can escape justice. So, all of Poppa's plans are unraveling. Pretty soon the police will arrest him for conspiracy to harbor a fugitive."

"What fugitive?"

"You, darling sister. You killed Demetry. Then father faked your death. Very elaborately I might add. It was a beautiful service. I think Sasha took care of the details. I cried my eyes out. When they lowered you into the ground...I couldn't believe what I was seeing. I..." he pulled out his cell phone, "...even have a picture of you and Poppa's graves." He handed her the phone. "Tragic, wasn't it?"

Jane closed her eyes. "That explains the dreams of being locked in a box...."

"You can thank Poppa for all of our nightmares."

"How did Poppa do that? I saw him die, saw Demetry shoot him."

"He must have been wearing a vest, but somehow he survived. But then rash little you throws Demetry out the window, so you, my dear, are a murderess."

"So Poppa isn't really dead?"

"I'm shocked he didn't tell you. He let you suffer the grief. Hmm. I'm a little shocked."

Jane shook her head. "No. I thought he was dead. I thought I was wanted for Demetry's murder."

"Well, you are... now that you're alive." He put his phone back in his pocket. "Father's attempts to keep you out of the gulag were so narrow-minded. How can a dead woman continue to live? Has it been fun hiding, sweetie?"

Jane shook her head and applied a pout.

Nikki gave her a sympathetic grin and a pinch to her nose. "Have no fear, sweetheart. I can help you. I have connections now, Anya. I am more powerful than Poppa ever dreamed of being. I have friends who can make all of your troubles disappear. Friends in the American government, the Russian government; hell, even at the UN. I will get your name cleared, and then we can be together. Just you and me. We will be wealthier and more powerful than you ever dreamed of being."

"I…" Jane looked confused. "I don't need money or power, Nikki. I just want a normal life."

"Stop being pathetic. Weak. Jesus, you're mother ruined you. Thank God, my mother was a good, strong Russian woman; too bad you had to be crippled by English blood. Your mother was beautiful, but never could be strong."

"Nikki? How can you say that? I thought…you loved her?"

"You know, Anya, you are trying my patience. I want to help you. I want to keep the only family I have left."

"But you said Poppa was alive?"

"At the moment." Nikki looked at his watch. "Or maybe not. A friend in the justice department helped me weed out Mr. Black from my ranks after I showed her some pretty naughty pictures of her and a congresswoman. She got all nervous…you know how uptight Americans are."

"You blackmailed her?"

"Dammit, Anya, stop it. How can I trust you if you can't take the truth?" Nikki leaned closer to her. His nose almost touched hers. "The world, little sister, is an evil place. Either learn to deal with that or get out of it. Let's start with some hard truths about your mummy."

Jane swallowed, but said nothing.

"Your mum was a whore. She danced for Poppa while he was married to my mama and screws the old man until he can't see straight. Which I will give her credit, the bitch knew what she was doing… when she was motivated. Then my mama dies. Coincidence? I don't think so. Next thing you know, the whore is in the house and taking over the place before my mama is stiff in the grave. But that wasn't good enough for her. She grew tired of the old man. She wanted someone young and energetic. I was only fifteen when she started sneaking into my room, teaching me things I had only read about. Such a conundrum for a boy." Nikki laughed, his head thrown back.

He grew quiet, placing his index finger to his lips. "Truth be told, part of me hated her, yet I would have done anything for her." He looked off in the distance a moment before adding, "Well, would have done anything to keep her coming to my room." He laughed. Jane flinched at the sound.

Jane bit the side of her cheek. Her heart pounded in her chest; her throat was dry.

"Then she left. Ran away. Left me lusty and thinking I was in love. So she took off with my heart and Poppa's money." Nikki laughed. He touched his chest with his fist. "I suppose I didn't need a heart.... It only held me back."

"Nikki. Don't be..."

"Shush, shush, shush, little girl. I am telling you truth. You need to know." He put a finger to her lips. "Anyhow, when I turned eighteen, I left Poppa's house, and I went after Ms. Tracy Dugan Sarkhov. I found her in London. And I found out about you. Tracy said you belonged to your Aunt Tilley, but I could see the resemblance, even though you were just a baby. You look just like her, you know?"

Jane nodded and smiled as she debated whether or not her brother had any sanity left. His eyes were wild. His voice was shrill and clipped like he would, at any moment, break into full wail and howl like a rabid dog.

"There was even a small part of me that wondered if you were my own. God forbid." Nikki touched Jane's cheek with his fingertips.

Jane gasped. She squeaked as calmly as she could, "I know who my father is, Nikki."

"Sure. If you say so."

Jane cleared her throat and asked, "So you knew I existed, long before Poppa? Why didn't you tell him about me? When I was a little girl?"

He shrugged. "Never thought of it. Well, and then when father got his empire back.... I told you about your mother stealing all the money, didn't I? How she left Poppa with barely enough to make payroll?"

Jane shook her head.

"Well, she did. Robbed him blind. But he is…ahem…was a crafty old bear and he was making money again in no time. So, I had riches and suddenly, I had a sister. Now, what's the point in splitting all the money in half? Besides, Poppa didn't miss what he never knew existed."

"But I…"

"Don't start whining!" he barked and slapped her on the cheek. "God, the incessant whining—your mother was the same. I want to get along with you, Anya, but not if you act like a pathetic little whiner!"

"Go to hell, Nikki. I have never been a whiner!" she snapped.

"That's better." He patted her stinging cheek. "I need to know I can trust you. That we can do business together."

"Why share with me now?"

Nikki laughed. "Good question. And the answer is…because I," he tweaked her nose, "have more money than God. I have more power than God. And because I am feeling sentimental." He looked at his watch again. "Surely by now, my sweet, we are orphans."

"No, Nikki. You can't. You have to stop this. You can't kill Poppa!"

"Well, technically, I'm not. He's already dead, remember? No one will even give a damn. Poppa will be killed by the very people he paid to protect him. And you…" He brushed a piece of hair away from Jane's face. "You look so much like your mother. So beautiful. I miss her, Anya. She was the only woman I ever loved, that I felt the stir of desire for. You can't imagine how lonely I have been since she died." He took her hand in his. "But she left me a gift. A girl with eyes like hers; with a smile like hers."

"I'm not my mother, Nikki. I'm nothing like her."

He shook his head. "It doesn't matter, when I look at you…I see her." Leaning forward, he tried to kiss her. She turned her face away and tried to scoot away. He grabbed her legs and pinned them to the bed. "Two choices, Anya. Life with me, on my terms. Or death."

Jane hid the revulsion that washed over her like a rancid wave. "But I am your sister."

214

"My sister is dead." He pulled her toward him and kissed her. His lips felt wet and cold against her own. He pulled back and looked down at her. A satisfied smile pulled at the corners of his mouth. "You will have whatever new life you want. Hell, I'll even get you your degree from Oxford. We don't want our kids to be shamed when they hang out with the children of senators and diplomats, now do we?"

Jane shook her head no.

Nikki reached out and undid her coat button. "Show me you love me, Anya."

Jane clutched the fabric. Her hands shook. "I…I am…."

"Ahh, Father did keep you locked up, didn't he? A nervous little virgin?"

Jane nodded. "And I, uh, need to use the bathroom."

"Go ahead. We have forever." He stretched himself out across the bed. Jane smiled at him as she clambered off the bed and practically ran into the bathroom. She shut the door and locked it. The walls were all solid. No window to crawl through. Jane started to cry. She couldn't think. She felt like puking, but swallowed the bile and willed herself to think.

Emergency. What was the American number for emergency? Nine eleven; it was nine eleven. She pulled out her cell phone. No eleven. Son of a bitch. She would call Trip. She'd rather he arrest her than she become Nikki's…she shivered, unable to finish the thought. She dialed his number, then turned on the tub water to hide the sounds of her talking.

Trip picked up in an instant.

"Jane, baby, where are you?"

"I don't know. A hotel."

"Are you safe?"

"No." The word was choked. She couldn't stop the shaking of panic. "It's Nikki. I'm at a hotel. I'm scared."

"I'm putting a trace on your call, Jane. I am going to find you. Do you hear me? I am going to find you."

Jane nodded. She couldn't speak.

Nikki knocked on the door. "Time's up."

"One more minute." She kicked the phone behind the toilet.

He tried to turn the knob. "New rule: no locked doors."

Jane looked toward the phone and wondered, how long would it take for Trip to find her?

"Open the door, Anya!"

"I'm almost..."

He didn't wait for her to finish. He threw his body against the flimsy wood. The entire door bowed, the veneer cracking and groaning with each blow. Jane screamed as she pressed her back against the splintering door. Then screamed again and again, hoping someone, anyone, would hear her.

*****

Trip clutched the phone in his hand. The room was deathly quiet, so the sounds of Jane's screams echoed in the room.

Then suddenly they stopped. Trip could hear breathing on the other end. "Jane, baby? You all right?"

Then the connection ended. The room was deathly quiet until someone let out a tired sigh, followed by another's plea for God to help, then a strangled cry from Sasha, who turned and bolted from the room. Frankie followed her; the heavy door slammed behind him. Trip scanned the faces in the room for an answer. All he saw was pale and helpless looks staring up at him—all but Mason. The chubby man clicked away on his laptop as if he never heard the call. Trip's jaw clenched with irritation at the sound. His eyes narrowed, and he was a breath away from taking the laptop and smashing it against the wall.

Then as loudly as a head-on collision on a highway, Mason spun his squeaky chair around, ripped off his headset and announced with a smile, "I got the ping! Here's the address."

Chapter 28

He dragged her from the room with just one hand clamped round her throat. She grabbed at the doorframe, but had to let go. The pressure on her throat was making it impossible to breath, so she put every bit of effort into trying to pry his hands loose. Nikki squeezed tighter. Jane's feet kicked wildly left and right until she made contact with the wall behind her. Blood pounded in her temples, so she tried in vain to crawl up the wall to relieve the pressure.

"Who did you call?"

She couldn't answer, couldn't scream…only a watery gurgle.

"You just couldn't stay dead, could you? You always have to complicate things! I could have given you the world. The world, Anya! All you had to do was love me."

"Go to hell." It was barely a whisper; the words were hardly even intelligible.

"Not before you, little sister. And before you die…I want you to know…your whore friend is going to die too. Just because you've totally pissed me off. I was going to sell her back into the sex trade she loves so much, but maybe I will have her cut into tiny little pieces. Listen to her scream. You think she'd beg me for mercy?"

Jane's eyes rolled in her head and a merciful blackness almost consumed her, but Nikki released his grip, and her greedy lungs sucked a raspy, cool breath of air. Her body crumpled to the floor, and she coughed, her throat felt like fire.

Kneeling in front of her, he took her chin in his hands and lifted her face to his. "I'm also going to find out who was on the phone, and I'm going to put a bullet between his eyes, *Jane*. He sounded far more concerned than a simple acquaintance. What kind of game have you been playing while hiding from me?"

"No games, Nikki. It was just a number Sasha told me to call if I was in trouble."

Red faced, his words exploded from his mouth. "So, why did he call you *baby*? Why do you lie to me?"

"I'm sorry." She covered her ears with her hands to muffle his words. "I won't lie anymore. You are scaring me. That's why I lie to you. I…I…love you, but you are making me feel very afraid."

His shoulders relaxed, and he smiled. "Ah, sweet Anya. Come here." Tucking her body into his, he held her, rocking her like a child and kissing the top of her head.

"Do you know…when you shoot someone in the head, there's a red shower. It's really rather beautiful. When my men kill Poppa, it's going to be with a bullet to the face, and I've ordered them to set a canvas behind him to catch the spray. That's art, little sister."

"Jesus, Nikki." She tried to push away from him.

Squeezing her to him, his arms felt like a vice. Her brother was double her size, a big man like her father. He sighed. "I didn't figure you'd appreciate it. Knew you were playing me, pretending to love me. No, little sister, I know where your loyalties are, so no matter how much I wanted you with me…you have to stay dead."

Her throat burned, and she swallowed hard, trying to speak carefully. "You're right. I don't see it. But Poppa was good to me." She stopped pushing against him and pulled him to her for a hug. "But he was never kind to you like he was me. I'm sorry for that. I hated my mother. You were right, I didn't care that she was dead. She was cruel to me. Said mean things to me all the time." She nestled her cheek against his shoulder. "I do understand your anger, Nikki. Really, I do. And I do love you."

Nikki gripped her body tight and buried his face in her hair. "He was going to turn me into the police, Anya. The police. I'm his son. His own flesh and blood."

"I hate to believe that, but you must be right. Poppa must have changed."

"Or maybe you weren't seeing clearly."

"Or that." She gulped, took a deep breath, and continued, "He had no right to make me think I was wanted for murder. To hurt Aunt Tilley like that."

"She was devastated. I held her hand at your funeral.... Wondered if she would collapse from the pain."

"He had no right. And neither did Sasha."

Pushing her away, he looked down at her as if judging her sincerity. His face softened, and he cradled her cheeks in his hands. "I won't let them hurt you again."

Giving his hands a squeeze, she leaned forward and kissed him. As his lips explored hers, one thought flashed through her mind— she would go to hell for this, but she had to do something, anything, to buy some time. A tear slid down her cheek as his hand moved up her shirt, touching soft flesh that belonged to another. A fire started to burn in her chest as the street fighter's blood reminded her that a Sarkhov never surrenders. As he trailed kisses down her throat, she pulled off her shoe and brought it across his temple with as much force as she could muster. Again and again she hit him, causing him to back away and cover himself like a wounded child.

"I hate you, Nikki! I despise you. I loathe you. I can't even stand to let you touch me long enough to kill you." She spit on him, kicked him with her still-shoed foot. He grabbed her leg and jerked her off her feet. Falling to the floor, she hit the ground fighting.

Digging her nails into the soft tissue of Nikki's face, she mercilessly pinned flesh to bone, then ripped, dragging her nails from his ears to his nose. He yelped and cursed, blood draining instantly from the marks.

As he gingerly touched his damaged face, Jane took the moment to leap to her feet and kick him with all her might, not knowing where her blow would land. He roared as her foot landed on his groin. She ran, a little off balance, and bumped into the dresser on her way to the door.

Looking back at him, he stayed curled up, coughing. The door was locked. Deadbolt, lock, slider. As trembling hands undid the locks, she could hear him getting to his feet. Looking over her shoulder, she saw him pull the gun from the back of his waist.

Her heart raced, but she forced her hands to be calm.

Snapping the last lock free, she swung the door open. Instead of a clear path to freedom, a body of flesh blocked the door. She shoved hard, ready to punch and kick some more. He grabbed her by the arms and tossed her like a rag doll onto the concrete concourse. She lay there on the ground looking up at him, bewildered and stunned.

"Run!" he ordered as he drew a gun from his jacket. She saw the weapon and crawled backward, petrified to turn her back on the man. "Run!" he shouted again, giving her shoe a kick.

Pow! Pow!

Gunfire. She covered her ears and let out a shriek. In the silence that followed, she looked at her chest for blood, but there was nothing. The man in the doorway flinched. Then she saw the blood. It poured from his shoulder. He fired back into the room, as he shouted to Jane, "Get the hell out!"

More shots. This man was evidently her rescue, but he was losing. His body jerked again, then again. His eyes were wide open as if by instinct. He retreated until he was backed up against the metal railing. Another step and he dropped the twenty feet to the parking lot below. Someone opened a door and screamed, then slammed it closed again. Nikki stepped out of the door and grabbed Jane by the hair and dragged her to her feet.

"You stupid bitch. See what you've done? This could have been so easy. Now look. Police will be called. An innocent man is dead. Does it make you feel better, Anya? Make you feel important?" He dragged her toward the hotel steps.

Jane kicked him in a high judo slam to the chest.

He absorbed the kick with a grunt, then yanked harder on her hair. "Enough, Anya. Poppa taught me the tricks as well." He then let go of her hair, spun in a half circle, then brought his foot up under her chin.

She felt her teeth clip together, felt the pain explode in her chin. Touching her hand to her chin, she pulled it away dripping in blood.

She felt the rage rise in her. She dipped her shoulder and rammed her body into his chest, knocking him off balance and causing them both to tumble down the steps.

Landing on top of him, his head hit the concrete, but hers was spared. Jane heard the sirens in the distance.

How far were they? And were they coming here? She didn't know.

Nikki appeared to be unconscious, so she searched around and under his body for his gun. She found it. She checked the clip. Plenty of shots left. She would hold him here. Someone would call the police. She could run, but what if he got away, went after her father, Sasha, and Trip?

She worked her way over to the wall, scooting herself back, resting her head against the cool stucco. Her face hurt. Her teeth hurt. And it hurt like hell to swallow. But she was alive.

Nikki started to rouse. He looked up at her and smiled. "Bravo, little sister. You win." He drew himself to a seated position, his ears perked to distant sirens. "I've learned my lesson, Anya. Let me go before they get here." Tears sparkled in his eyes. "I won't hurt you, I swear. I will go away and you'll never hear from me again."

"Hah!" Jane wiped at the still dripping blood. "You've already hurt me." Her voice was hoarse and she could barely talk.

"I was angry. I didn't think you deserved the Sarkhov legacy. But now I know. I know you're strong, and I know you do deserve it. I respect you now."

"Did you respect Poppa?"

"He *didn't* love me!" Nikki's face looked contorted as he shouted the words at her. "He never loved me!"

"So, you killed him?"

"I didn't."

"You told me!"

Nikki took a deep breath and said calmly, "He's not dead…yet. Let me go and I will make sure he is set free."

"I can't trust you. You're sick, Nikki. I am your sister. What you asked of me in there…is sacrilege."

"Don't waste my time with morality lessons based on fairy

221

tales." Leaning his head against the wall, he added, "Just let me go."

"No, Nikki. You're insane. You have to be put away so you can't hurt anyone."

Nikki's laugh frightened her.

He looked at her through narrowed eyes. "You think putting me in jail will keep you safe? Trust me, Anya, I've hidden enough cash and I have enough connections. I can blackmail half of Washington, London, Paris…. Don't you know?" He pointed to himself. "I am a titan. I swear to you, lock me up, I will kill everyone you love. Even whatever scraggly little pets you harbor." He laughed and rolled his head against the wall. "No, little sister, you better just kill me now. I swear to you on all that is unholy…tormenting you will be my life's work." His face was grave, sincere. "So, either show me mercy and trust my honor or shoot me right now. Those *are* the *only* options you can live with."

Nikki got to his knees and crawled at her, his face within inches of Jane's. She lifted the gun pressing it to his forehead.

"Go ahead. Shoot me. Don't be cruel and lock me up like an animal. I beg you."

Jane's hands shook. She told herself to pull the trigger, but she was looking in his eyes. Eyes as clear and blue as her own.

She closed her eyes, cocked the hammer…but those eyes were still there.

She sighed and relaxed her grip on the gun. He smiled and gave her a kiss on the cheek. "Thank you, Anya. I wish things could have been different. I wish we could have been friends." He leaned back on his heels. "You are too trusting. Always remember that." He stood to leave turning his back to her, looking back only to wave good-bye. Jane dropped the gun on the sidewalk and let her tears fall.

She covered her eyes with her hands and let the sobs wrack her body. The calm was gone, all that was left were raw nerves and pain. She needed to get to a phone, call Sasha and her father. And Trip.

She felt him. His body blocked the sun and casted a shadow over her. Instinct told her to grab the gun, but she was a second too slow. She shook her head and cursed her stupidity. She looked up at him, "Why, Nikki?"

"Because I am the bad guy? Because I don't like loose ends? What reason will make you happy? How disappointed will you be when I tell you it was for the money and the power? With father gone, I control everything. No Viktor Sarkhov and his *code of honor* to get in the way of business."

Cocking the hammer on the revolver, he sighed. "But I never wanted you to die. Not the first time, not this time. You're all of her I have left."

Jane beat her fists against the concrete. "Shut up! I'm not her! I'm nothing like her! If you're going to shoot me, just do it."

"Don't be so testy. You were the one who asked the question in the first place."

"Go to hell."

"You first." Nikki placed the gun against her forehead.

Jane took a deep breath. She never thought about dying, never gave any consideration to her body being breakable, so she never really had a preconceived idea about how she would react to impending death. She supposed she should see her life flash before her eyes, be gripped by fear, or be lost in prayer.

One simple phrase went through her mind—*well, this sucks.* Squaring her chin, she looked her brother in the eye. He might end her life, but he would never get the satisfaction of hearing her beg. He might have cried like a baby for mercy, but she'd die a thousand times before she gave him that pleasure.

Maybe, if she was lucky, she'd get to haunt his ass.

Chapter 29

The gun shots echoed in the nearly all concrete hotel breezeway. A second shot rang out.

It didn't hurt to be shot, but then it didn't ease the pain in her battered body either. Jane slowly opened her eyes. Nikki must be toying with her.

Looking up at him, his eyes were wide…so wide, she couldn't stifle the little scream that rose to her lips. He grabbed at his chest, his gun fell beside her. Bloody foam bubbled from his mouth, his wide eyes going glassy with death. His body collapsed, face smacking off the cement, mouth open, but unable to take another breath.

She looked beyond his lifeless form…standing at the top of the steps was Trip.

She closed her eyes and rolled her head back against the wall. His arms were around her in an instant…so warm, strong, and safe. She wanted to explain, but suddenly her body started to shake, and uncontrollable tears filled her eyes and spilled down her cheeks.

"Shh," he ordered, kissing the top of her head. "It's all right. Shh."

She tried to lean toward him, but the pain in her head sliced through her, causing her ears to ring. She closed her eyes, suddenly feeling groggy and light-headed. She fought the gathering darkness, willed herself to stay alert. She needed Trip to understand she loved him, that even if her identity was a lie, how she felt wasn't. Even if he was a spy, she loved him.

If she fell asleep now, he would be gone when she woke. She gripped his arm, he held her tighter.

"I love you, Jane. Stay with me."

She allowed the words splash over her warm and comforting. She tried to force her eyes open, to gain focus. But she couldn't. Her head hurt too badly. It throbbed and rang making it difficult to concentrate. She let her head drop against his chest. The sound of his heartbeat drummed against her ear. Tears rolled from her eyes as the comfort of black oblivion surrounded her.

"Jane." Trip felt panic. His training did little to calm him. He couldn't tell where the bullet hit. There was too much blood. The bruises and marks on her face left little doubt that Nikki had beaten her badly. He recognized head trauma. Knew she, at the very least, had a concussion, possibly a subdural hematoma. Her pupils were unstable, eyes rolling like a horror movie, into the back of her head.

"Baby, don't leave me. Janie, open your eyes and look at me. You have to stay with me, baby. I love you."

She willed them open, but it was exhausting and the light was painful. The pain made her feel dizzy like she had been spun. But she focused on his eyes. He was crying. He didn't need to cry. She opened her mouth to talk, but the fog in her mind rolled back in and she couldn't concentrate. She stopped struggling. She felt him wrap her close to him. His voice in her ear was soothing. A tender hand touched her cheek; tender kisses on her temple.

"Trip," she whispered.

"What baby?"

"You saved me."

*****

Her body went limp. Trip tried to rouse her. Panic rose when he couldn't. "Wake up, Jane!" he cried. He checked her pulse. It was weak and erratic, but it was there. The arm he cradled her with was soaked in blood. Gently, he brushed the hair from her face. Nikki's bullet grazed her ear and skull. It looked like a flesh wound; he prayed it was a flesh wound.

He never should have let her go. When his mother attacked her, he should have known she would bolt. He should have thought of that. He let her get away, let her come to this. He kissed her forehead. She was so warm. *Please God, please...he prayed. Don't take her from me. I have to make all of this up to her.* He was tortured by the memory of her eyes. Eyes that looked to him with pain as he first made love to her, eyes that looked to him to make it all right. She allowed him to hurt her with the trust in him that he would bring her to a place of joy. And then he failed her. He touched her hand; it was like ice. Panic gripped him.

Police skidded to a stop in the lot below him. He could hear them circling the cars with the dead bodies in the lot. "UP HERE!" he yelled. He heard footsteps coming toward the stairwell. Two uniformed officers bounded up the steps. Trip barked before the first man cleared the stairwell, "Get an ambulance here fast."

"One's en route," the officer answered. "Should be here any minute." The officer checked Nikki's neck for a pulse. "This guy's dead."

"So is the guy in the parking lot," the other officer informed him as he came toward Trip, his holster unsnapped, hand on his gun.

"My gun's laying there. I shot the piece of shit there. I need an ambulance. I think she's going into shock. There's a bullet wound to the side of the head."

The first officer reached into Nikki's pocket and pulled out his wallet. "Nikolai Sarkhov. You know the guy?"

Trip shook his head. "Not personally."

He flipped through Nikki's wallet. He looked over his dead body then at Trip, "A dead Russian with a UN security pass, a suit that would cost me a month's salary, and another dead suit on a Honda down below. So, is the girl Russian?"

"Yes."

"She dead?"

"No, dammit. Weren't you listening? She needs an ambulance."

The second officer squatted beside him. "She shot? She's losing a lot of blood."

"Head wounds always bleed a lot," Trip snapped.

The officer looked across her body to Trip. He frowned, sighed, then said, "Yeah, sure, she'll be fine." He spoke into his radio on his shoulder, "ETA on that ambulance?"

"Three minutes... you should be hearing it, officer," the dispatch responded.

Trip listened. He could hear its howl. Such a beautiful sound. It came closer and closer until he could see the awkward box roll up, red lights flashing. Her crew jumped out. The officer stood and waved them up to the balcony.

The first officer put Nikki's wallet back in his pocket and turned to Trip. "So, I assume this man was fighting with the woman?"

"Yes, then I shot him."

"You kill the guy down below too?"

Trip shook his head. "No, he was there when I got here."

"And you don't know who he is?"

Trip shook his head.

"So, who's the girl?"

Trip looked down at Jane. Her pulse beat weakly in her throat. Who she was didn't really matter right now, he just had to get her help. "Jane. Her name is Jane."

The police officer nodded. "I'll have to see your ID. A detective will certainly want to talk to you."

Trip nodded. Paramedics cleared the steps like angels flocking from heaven. Trip allowed them to pull her from his grip as if watching from another planet as they prepped her for transport. They moved quickly, efficiently, within minutes they had IVs running and had her carefully strapped her to the gurney.

"Be careful with her. Please," Trip said.

"We'll do our best, don't worry. Any allergies?"

Trip shook his head. Another tear fell. He wiped it away.

"Any medical history...?"

"I can't say for certain. I, we...haven't been together very long."

The paramedic smiled at him, a smile filled with sympathy. She spoke so earnestly, Trip felt his heart calm just a little. She said, "We'll take good care of her. We'll be taking her to County General.

You know where that is?"

He nodded. She smiled at him again and they were gone.

A detective in a button down shirt moved to the left, so they could get the gurney down the steps. He moved toward Trip slowly, looking over the scene as if he was bored. He nodded his head in approval offering a good work kudos to the officers. He kneeled in front of Trip, his hand extended in greeting. "Rowan Coulter?"

"Yeah." Trip shook his hand and offered his ID. The detective waved it off, turning instead to the officers. "Boys, put up a barrier, don't let any press in. Touch nothing and wait. You're about to see a secret ops cleaning crew go to work." He winked at Trip. "Gotta love workin' in DC."

"Do I need to go in…and answer any questions?"

"I'm sure you'll be debriefed later."

"Good. I need to get to the hospital.

"When then, get the hell out of here, son."

Trip didn't ask twice. He paused only a moment when the uniformed officer apologized for the delay and handed him back his piece. Trip didn't have time to wonder how often this sort of thing happens for the cops to be so well versed at dealing with the situation. All he cared about was getting to the hospital.

Trip called Frankie, who was already aware of what had happened. "That was Buddy Ray on the hood. He was the first agent on the scene. That bastard killed a good man. Sorry I couldn't get there myself, brother."

"I'm good. It's Jane. Frank, she…." In his haste, Trip cut across a lane of traffic, a horn blew, he ignored it.

"She'll be fine. You better pay attention to the road, man. We'll meet you at the hospital."

*****

Trip paced the waiting room. There was no one to tell him what was going on. Jane's care and status were guarded like national security secrets. Trip drank coffee and paced the floor. The minutes ticked by slowly, painfully. His anxiety was distracted by a commotion coming from the elevator. Trip wandered out of the waiting area to the hall to see what was going on. A swarm of men in dark suits escorted a large, stocky man with a thick neck and salt and pepper hair. The bear of a man carried a bouquet of roses, an array of colors orange, white, pink, red, and purple. He spoke to the man closest to him in Russian and the man headed to the desk, Trip assumed they were looking for information on Jane.

Trip stepped forward and was immediately accosted and moved back by three of the suited men. Trip twisted his body free, announcing to Viktor he was the one who got Jane to the hospital. Viktor brushed off his guards and approached Trip. He looked him over from head to toe then asked, "You did this to my daughter? You are the one who killed my son?"

Trip said nothing. Viktor spoke the truth. What could he say?

Viktor continued, "I had her safe. You put her in danger. You made my daughter run in fear. Now she is here."

Trip started to apologize, but the man who was sent to get information returned. He whispered to Viktor. Viktor cursed and scowled at Trip. His eyes were hard and Trip had little doubt if Jane died, Viktor would probably have him killed.

Chapter 30

Trip didn't know what to say, but he knew he had to say something. He couldn't lose Jane. Not to death, not to an angry parent.

"Mr. Sarkhov." His voice was bold. Viktor's head tilted slightly, as if intrigued or annoyed that the young man had the moxie to demand his attention.

Viktor didn't utter a single word, but Trip took his raised eyebrow as permission to speak. "Mr. Sarkhov?"

Viktor responded with a glare.

"Sir, I love your daughter. I would never hurt her. And if her knowing me is what brought Nikki to her, well, sir, it was unintended."

"Unintended?" Viktor bellowed. "How do you 'unintentionally' blow my daughter's cover?"

"I didn't know she was undercover. I didn't know she was in harm's way. She worked at the apartment, how was I to know? Trust me, had I known, I never would have left her alone. But how was I supposed to know when *she* didn't even know what the hell was going on?"

Viktor's eyes narrowed. "You blaming me?"

Trip's jaw clenched. "I suppose I am. Way I see it...you're as guilty as I am. Both of us lied to her."

"I tried to keep my daughter safe."

"Intentions, sir?"

"Why you...." He took a step toward Trip, his fist clenched. A woman called out, "Stop it, Viktor!"

They both turned to find Frankie and Sasha coming down the hall. Sasha ran to Viktor and touched his arm. "He didn't hurt Anya, Viktor. Nikki didn't find her through Interpol. My friend, the senator…I got a call from him. Mr. Black was found out days ago. Nikki was watching him, tracking his every move. And when I made my weekly contact, Nikki was listening. He had the real Mr. Black killed him and replaced him with one of his men. That's how he got to Anya."

Sasha's cheeks blazed. She glanced at Trip and took a large breath and then added, "If Trip's mother hadn't scared Anya with Interpol? She and I would have been sitting ducks. We would have let him into our apartment, and he probably would have killed both of us. At least this way all the plans were fouled up and we were put on edge. And…." She looked at Trip. "Anya does love him. She will be mad enough that you lied to her. Don't rid her of her boyfriend as well."

Viktor's jaw muscle twitched. "Why didn't your senator warn you?"

"His intel is days behind. He warned me with a phone call as I drove to the hospital. I'm telling you, Viktor, we would surely be dead if we hadn't been spooked."

Viktor's face relaxed and he let out a long sigh. He turned to Trip. "You love my daughter?"

"Yes, sir. I do."

"And your intentions?"

"I would gladly marry her…if she felt the same…and with your blessing, of course."

"I would have to know you before I gave any blessing. But…." He patted Sasha's cheek. "I trust Sasha. If she says not to run you off, then I won't. But I will be watching you."

Viktor turned and started to move away. Trip took two strides forward and stepped in front of him. "And, sir. I also want to extend my apologies about your son. I," Trip lowered his eyes, "I would honestly do it all over again to save Jane, but I still want you to know I feel bad that you lost your son today."

Viktor's face flinched in a frown, his eyes glassed over ever so briefly, then he nodded and patted Trip on the shoulder. "You saved my daughter. And you saved me having to see my son locked up like an animal. God have mercy on his soul, and I hope He finds some good in him. Certainly there was some."

"Absolutely, sir," Trip added.

"Well, if you want to keep kissing my ass…find me coffee. I need to sit." Viktor growled and plopped himself in a waiting room seat. Viktor looked as comfortable as an elephant on a pin cushion. Trip nodded and headed off for coffee.

Frankie stopped him and gave him a rare smile and a punch to the shoulder. "You did good, kid."

Trip shrugged. "What I did almost got her killed. If she hadn't met me…."

"If she hadn't met you, no one would have known Black's cover was blown and she and Sasha would also have been found floating in the Potomac…and we wouldn't have gotten the amount of intel we did get. Because Jane's cover was blown, we caught them with their pants down…literally and figuratively. Investigators have leads on tracking organizations that front charities…people donate money to them for God's sake…and they are the ones exploiting the damn kids. They will be shut down. We have the names of high-ranking officials in multiple countries who will go to jail before they go to hell. And…Jane is alive."

"But my…"

"Serendipitous, my friend. Nikki was onto Mr. Black. He was within hours of taking out both Jane and Sasha."

"How do you know that?"

"Sasha has a connection with Senator Mosely."

"The southern guy?"

"Yeah. He's on a child welfare oversight committee and has been getting info from Sasha, who unfortunately knows a lot about it. Anyhow, Mosely put his own mole in Nikki's organization, and it was that guy, Deuce, that Nikki sent with a group of henchman to kill Viktor. Deuce took them to Viktor, all right…and a freaking SWAT team. They're all in custody…singing like birds."

Sasha nodded. "If Nikki had the opportunity to set us up, it would have been ugly. I assure you, Nikki would have made us suffer, and Jane would have suffered most. Nikki is crazy."

"Was," Frankie said as he put an arm around her shoulder and squeezed. Sasha smiled up at him and blushed. Trip wasn't sure what happened to the bitchy red head he had come to know and love. Her face was softer, her eyes red rimmed from tears and she seemed to be leaning on Frankie. Trip looked Frankie over and decided he must not mind. Maybe his jokes about hooking them up weren't so far-fetched.

"She does love you," Sasha said to Trip. "I never saw her so happy." Sasha broke into a sob. Her hands shook. She pulled a tissue from her pocket. "Sorry. I am tired. I am not crying."

Trip nodded, not sure whether or not to point out that she was indeed crying. Frankie pulled her tight. "This has been a rough one. I'm going to take her to get something to eat. Then she needs to rest."

"I am fine," Sasha sighed. "I need to see if Anya is okay."

"You're worn out. Your mission's over; time to take a break. You did what you were supposed to do…. Now let's get the hell out of here and let this guy go see about the girl. You'll keep us posted, right?"

"Of course." Trip shook Frankie's hand, and then went to take Sasha's, but couldn't help but pull her in for a hug. "Thank you, Sash. You couldn't be a better friend. Jane's lucky to have you." Sasha nodded against his shoulder, tears choking any words she might try to utter. She took a step back, blotted her eyes. "My bitchiness to you was never personal."

"I understand. Take care of her, Frank." Frankie nodded, and they were gone.

Trip got the coffee, but when he got back, Viktor was gone. The only person in the room was a hulk of a man in an ill-fitting black suit. He stood. "Mr. Sarhkov went to see about his daughter. He says you wait here."

"She's all right?"

The man shrugged and scowled.

Trip went to the window and watched the cars pass below.

The man's cell phone rang. He answered it and said yes, or *da*, a couple of times, then turned to Trip. "Come with me. You can see her now."

Viktor met him in the hallway. He looked Trip in the eye and stated, "They say you are a spy?"

"Not exactly, but yes, I work in covert surveillance. For private security, not the government."

"What you think of that, Demetry?" Viktor turned to the huge man beside him. The behemoth shook his head and frowned.

"Deceit come easy to you?"

"No, sir. It's just a job. I mainly do computer work. I, uh, admit, I was looking for excitement…"

"My daughter is excitement?" Viktor's voice echoed in the hall.

"No. No. Sir, Jane is…"

"Her name is Anya. She will be Anya. She is safe now. No more deceits."

"No, sir. I was saying…I wanted a more exciting job…J…Anya is special. She was the one who told me to follow my heart. She is why I even went into covert ops. I swear, she is in no way excitement."

"So, you are saying daughter of Viktor Sarkhov is boring?"

"No. Jesus. I just…I love her. I love your daughter. She is perfect and beautiful and I want her."

"Want her? How? You think she is simple Russian whore? Think she has to have a man to be something? Not my daughter. My daughter is strong, and smart, and…"

"Perfect. Sir, she is perfect. And I don't want…I mean none of my intentions are anything less than noble."

Viktor looked him over. Then crossed his arms over his chest and nodded. "Come. I have left her and I need to get back. You can see her. I will get to know you. Then I will decide what your intentions will be with my daughter."

"Ah. Thank you, sir."

He turned the knob and led them into the darkened room.

Demetry slipped past them and stood like an immobile sentry in the corner. Viktor took the chair by Anya's bed. He took her hand in his and said quietly, "I don't know if you can hear *milaya moya*, but Poppa's here." He motioned for Trip to get a chair. "Poppa found your friend in the hall. He wants to say hello."

Trip's heart squeezed and he felt like he could vomit. He expected her to be awake. Expected her to be sitting up in the bed, her usual vibrant self. Instead, she laid helpless, tubes connected to her arms and in her nose. Trip looked to Viktor for an answer, but he paid no mind to Trip. He sat holding his daughter's hand as he crooned to her in Russian. From the corner, Demetry cleared his throat and spoke. "They gave her a shot to keep her asleep. She breathes on her own. They have to rule out brain trauma."

"*Da*, yes," Viktor supplied. "Her MRI was good. The bullet wound barely nicked the scalp, though it took a bit of her ear. She had so many bruises to the head, they want to be certain she doesn't have a bleeding brain. By putting her in coma, they say they can...*will* stop brain swelling. Besides she has a broken arm and two broken ribs. She is more comfortable this way."

"That son of a bitch," Trip seethed. He sat beside her. He touched her cheek. It was warm. "Jane?" No response. He leaned closer, his lips brushed against her ear. "I love you, baby. Don't you dare leave me." A tear dropped on her pillow. He rested his cheek on the bed beside her so he could feel her warmth, smell her skin. She would be all right. She had to be. He closed his eyes and was haunted by the images of a smiling, happy Jane. Remembered as she was this morning, smooth and naked under him, trusting in him to share herself completely. He could still feel her breath on his lips, feel her hands locked around his neck as he made love to her. This couldn't be happening. This was just a nightmare. But the beeping IVs and the antiseptic smell of the place told him the harsh reality.

He could lose her.

No. Viktor said she would be fine. But then, how many times had he heard that? He remembered the housekeeper telling him as the ambulance carted his dad away when he was a little boy that everything would be all right. And it wasn't. He only had six years with his father, six months with Jane. He needed more. Needed a lifetime to satisfy him.

He tried to brush the thoughts away, but he couldn't. He didn't want to cry in front of the man he needed to respect him, but he did. He hid them as best he could as he sat in silent vigil with Viktor and Demetry as the sun set outside the window.

Chapter 31

Midnight approached and there was no change in Anya's condition. Trip looked across the bed at the haggard Viktor. He looked years older in the middle of the night than he did earlier in the day. Trip whispered into the half-lit room, "Mr. Sarkhov. Why don't you get some rest? I'll stay here. I swear she'll be safe."

Viktor shook his head no. "I have to explain to my daughter why I lied to her. I cannot take the chance that she will be angry with me."

"I could call you at the first signs of her waking. You need sleep."

"I am afraid that if I leave here, I could lose her. She is all the family I have."

Trip looked at him with sympathy. "I understand. You just look tired."

"Well, you look like hell too, boy. You willing to leave?"

"If you aren't quiet, I'm going to make you both leave." The voice below them was small and weak. They were both up and out of their seats in a flash. Both saying her name...Anya. Jane. She opened her eyes a sliver, then closed them again as if the effort was draining. She smiled. Then nodded back off to sleep.

Viktor and Trip waited, both suddenly alert and watching for signs of liveliness.

As the dawn broke, she started to stir a little more, her hands squeezing theirs as they held onto her. At 7 AM, the doctor came to her room, checked her charts, her vital signs, and her pupils. He sighed and nodded. "I'm not going to give her any more sedation. She seems fine. All the scans seem normal. You guys will be here?"

"Yes." *"Da."* They answered in unison.

"Good then. Let me know when she wakes and we'll check her neurological functioning." He wrapped his stethoscope around his neck, stuck his pen in his pocket, and left without another word.

Trip and Viktor looked at each other, their faces hopeful, yet scared by the possibility of more complications. "She will be fine," they assured each other in unison.

Demetry went to get coffee and breakfast; and to make the mandatory call to Sasha with an update. He brought back a bag of breakfast food. It sat unopened on the hospital tray. The coffee cooled untouched. The noise in the hallway increased as more staff arrived at work and visitors trickled into the building. Sasha and Frankie came and went. Nurses checked in and the doctor came back. He checked her over, frowned and left.

Viktor's brow furrowed. He rubbed his chin with his hand. Scratched his head. Then he announced, "Demetry and I are going for walk. Last night, she smiled when you talked to her. Talk to her again."

He motioned to Demetry and they were gone. Trip moved out of his seat and sat on the side of her bed. He brushed her hair back from her face and spoke quietly, "Jane, baby. Can you hear me?"

Nothing.

He tried again a little louder. "Jane. I don't know if you can hear me, but I love you. I...." He wasn't sure what to say. He just spoke what was in his heart, "I'm sorry if I hurt you. I'm sorry that I ever lied to you." Stroking her cheek he kept talking. "I love you and I'm so scared right now. I'm scared that I'm going to lose you."

He had to take a minute. Glancing out of the window, the clouds still moved steadily across the sky. His fingers smoothed her hair; his words came hoarse and choked from a constricting throat. "I know it sounds crazy, but I can't do this whole life thing without you. I need you."

No response from Jane. He rested his head on the bed beside hers and whispered, "Hey, God, I know I'm like this brat kid who only calls when I need a favor, but damn it, she's a good woman. Please?"

He choked on the words. He couldn't wipe the image from his mind of her body being lowered into the earth. It was a morbid thought, but one his mind couldn't shake. Tears fell freely down his cheeks, landed in wet splotches on her blanket. He didn't know how long he sat there, begging, praying, telling her of the happiest moments with her, his plans for their future. He was almost out of words and hope, when a hand touched his cheek. His eyes flashed open and his head spun toward the hand.

"What is wrong, Trip?" Her voice was weak, but she spoke. "Why are you crying?"

"What's wrong?" His tears mingled with an exuberance that could only be called euphoria.

"Yes. What's wrong?" she asked. Her face was contorted with concern. Her thumb brushed against his wet cheeks.

"I thought I'd lost my best friend."

"Frankie?"

"No, you. You were supposed to wake up hours ago."

"I was?"

"Yes. You were."

"So, you..."

"I was petrified. Scared shitless."

"Over me?"

"Yes, you." He kissed her hand.

"Trip, there are things I need to tell you." She tried to sit up and winced. She lay back down on the pillows. She touched her throat with her hands. "My throat hurts."

He dried his eyes and got her a glass of ice water. "You've been through a lot, baby. We will talk later."

She was quiet a moment. "I remember. You came for me." She closed her eyes a moment. "Nikki? What happened to Nikki?"

"He's gone." Trip's brow furrowed deep.

"Did you kill him?"

Trip nodded. "If there had been any other way, but he was ready

241

to take a shot at you… well he did…it was my bullet that made him jerk and miss hitting you between the eyes."

"I remember now. Poor Nikki."

"I'm sorry, Jane."

"It is not your fault. I just wish my brother could be a different person, you know?"

Trip nodded. He gripped her hand harder. He was afraid she'd hate him…throw him out of her life.

"Was I dreaming? I heard Poppa's voice."

"He is here. Him and Demetry went for a walk."

"Really?" Her eyes sparkled. "So Nikki was right. He did fake his death. He is alive?"

"Yes. He's alive and he has been here all night. I made him leave…he looks tired."

Jane laughed. "You made Poppa leave. I doubt that. He is up to something." Jane looked around the room and breathed the heavy scent of roses. "Ahh, Poppa's roses. Those and a man declaring his love for me…what a way to wake up."

Trip leaned down and kissed her gently, careful not to hurt her. He rubbed his nose against hers. "I'm so sorry for everything. I never should have lied to you."

"I lied to you too, Trip. I understand." She touched his cheek, tears sprang to her eyes. "I love you too much to care. You could tell me you were Stalin and I would still love you."

"Viktor is worried you will be angry he lied to you. And I think Demetry is a little on edge too, though it's hard to tell, he's so talkative."

"Sounds like Demetry, but I knocked him out a window, he's…."

"Fine. Alive and kicking. Still working with your father. There were blanks in the gun he fired at Viktor. When you attacked him, they worked it into the plan."

"It wasn't very nice of them. I suffered horribly thinking my poppa was dead. Thinking Demetry was a traitor."

"They were afraid if they were honest with you, you might not maintain the ruse of being dead. That you might tell people you were alive so they wouldn't suffer."

"Oh, no! I hadn't thought of that! Aunt Tilley. She must be crushed. Has Poppa told her? She needs to know. She doesn't have anyone but me. It was bad enough for her to think I was a criminal, but to think me dead...."

"And it seems Viktor was right."

"Right?"

"You would have told."

"Only Aunt Tilley."

"And that would have been one too many." He held her hand. "Seems Viktor knows you, too well. I'm certain Nikki was watching Tilley, probably had her phone tapped."

"Oh, Nikki. I never trusted him, but never dreamed he was such a bad guy."

"The worst. Frankie and Sasha told me your dad helped shut down several front orphanages that were feeding children to the sex trade."

She clutched her stomach. "I will be ill. Tell me you lie. No one does that?"

Trip frowned.

Jane closed her eyes and frowned. "Why are people so evil?"

"Your dad did what he had to stop it. When Nikki thought his family was dead and he was free to operate the business on his own, he got sloppy. Your dad didn't hide to hurt you. He did it to protect you. The good people beat the evil ones."

"This time."

"And next time. There's more good than bad in this world."

"You really think that?"

"I do."

Gripping his hand, she sighed. "I hope you are right."

"It's just one bad man can do a lot of harm, and it took several teams of people to stop him. Hell, even Sasha's fat friend was in on it."

"Fatty?"

"Yep, seems Fatty is a champion for good."

"So, he's not cheating on his wife?"

Trip shrugged and let out a chuckle. "Hell if I know about that, but we'll call the man innocent…he saved your father by planting his own mole, so he deserves the benefit of the doubt."

"Fatty did what?" She pressed fingertips to a tender forehead. "Oh, never mind, I will sort it all out later. All this thinking makes my head ache."

"You said I was to be first called." A voice from the door boomed.

"Poppa!" Not a single feeling beyond elation spread through her veins. She held out her arms, calling him in for a hug.

"I'm sorry I killed you." He stepped into the room and hugged his daughter. "And as soon as we started looking into the vile business… accidents started to happen. Too many accidents to be by chance," Viktor explained.

"Trip explained everything. You are a wise poppa, always looking out for me." Tears overwhelmed her and her body shook. He felt so warm and sturdy under her arms, like the most wondrous wish come true. Nikki said he was alive. Trip said he was alive. But the full reality of her father returning in the flesh to hug her was more than she could imagine.

"I'm sorry." Viktor's words were choked.

Jane shook her head. "No, no. I am happy. I'm so happy. These…I swear…happy tears!"

Jane held onto his hand as he pulled away. She looked past her father to Demetry. "Sorry I killed you, Demetry."

"Is okay, little mouse."

She grinned at him, her heart glad that her bodyguard and companion since she was but a wee girl was someone she could love and trust. She turned to Viktor. "I am glad you are alive too, Poppa. I was so sad without you."

"I am sorry, *milaya moya*…these were dangerous times."

"It's all right, Poppa. I am just glad to have you back." She smiled at him, glassy eyed and radiant. Trip gave her shoulder a squeeze. She looked up at him and his heart flip-flopped. He couldn't help but lean down and kiss her. Her hand wound its way under his collar, stroking the strong flesh of his neck.

"Whatever happened to waiting on my blessings, son?"

Trip grinned down at her and said without looking back at Viktor. "Your dad can't decide whether or not he likes me."

Jane bit her lip and cringed. She looked up at her father who winked and smiled. Jane whispered in Trip's ear, "How do you make people love you so much?"

"I must just have a way with Sarkhovs." He glanced up at Viktor, cleared his throat as he stepped back and said, "But I better not press my luck."

Epilogue: Six months later

Viktor kissed his daughter's cheek, then took a step back and smiled. "You are lovely, *devochka*. I never got to see you as a baby, but you will always be my baby girl."

Anya smiled. "Yes, of course, Poppa." She adjusted the roses in her bouquet. "These roses are lovely, but I can't wait for you to get back to growing your own."

"*Da*. I am buying a house on the beach. I am going to live where I am warm, where I can garden in the sunshine, not a house."

"You're not going back to Russia?"

"Course not. My baby is here. You will have little ones. I will be…what is American? I will be Grand Poppa. Sounds good." He sat his girth on a chair by the window and looked out over DC. "No, Anya, I am staying here. Maybe I go to island like Trip's family. I like it there. Not so far from my Anya."

"Oh, Poppa!" Anya cried and kneeled down to hug him. "I couldn't be happier." Tears burned her eyes. She pressed at her eyes gently not wanting to mess up the make-up Sasha had so carefully applied.

There was a tap at the door. Anya gave her father another glowing smile, then hurried to answer. It was Trip's mother. Anya blushed a little, but stepped back to allow her to enter. She brought her two daughter-in-laws with her. The ever cheerful and difficult not to love, Mollie; and the ever quiet, yet equally as difficult not to love, Jenna. Barbara cleared her throat and nodded a greeting to Viktor. She then turned her attention to Anya. "Anya. Dear. I wanted to give you a gift." She handed over a velvet-lined box.

Anya opened it to find a diamond-encrusted bracelet with a single red stone in the middle. "It is a garnet," Barbara explained. "Rowan's birth stone. He is my last single child and I gladly give him to you."

Jane touched the red stone affectionately. "Thank you," she said quietly.

"Thank you." Barbara gave her hand a gentle squeeze. "Thank you for not holding it…"

"Enough." Anya held up her hand to stop the apologies. "We are family, no? Family forgives. Family understands."

Barbara turned to Viktor, who had risen upon her entry, and shook his hand. "And you, sir, thank you for raising such a wonderful daughter."

"I must not take all the credit. Her Aunt Tilley had a big hand."

"Anya has spoken of her. Too bad she couldn't make it to the wedding. But I understand why she and Rowan wanted to hurry and marry before he left on another assignment."

Anya frowned. "Yes, I wish Aunt Tilley could be here too. But I have my new family…and Poppa…and Sasha. Sasha? Where has Sasha gone to? Where is the maid of honor?"

Jenna's cheeks flushed. "She said something to me, but I don't remember. The boys were shooting each other with fake guns and using the ring pillows as shields, so I was pre-occupied. Dear Lord, I hope they settle down before the ceremony. Mollie?"

"She helped me diaper the girls, but I don't recall her saying she was going anywhere. I assumed she was coming back here."

"She will be here. You can trust Sasha to keep her word," Viktor assured.

Anya nodded slowly, bride nerves suddenly fluttering in her belly. She tried to maintain a pleasant conversation with her future in-laws, but couldn't keep from looking over their heads and scanning the crowd every time the sanctuary door swung open. She let out a squeal when she spotted a glimpse of red moving toward her.

Sasha blushed as she approached and Anya teased, "I thought

maybe you snuck off from me…again!" Anya hadn't let her off the hook for sneaking away and marrying Frankie without so much as a word to anyone. And then she hid the fact that she was expecting, forcing Anya to interrogate her for the truth after she so very noticeably gave up vodka and cigarettes.

It still amazed Anya. Her usually attachment-free friend was married and expecting while she and Trip were still in "dating" mode as mandated by her father. She hadn't had a moment alone with Trip for two months. Demetry was always with her, trailing right behind just like at home. He sat a row behind at the movies and a table away at dinner. Anya hadn't managed much more than a peck good night since she left the hospital. She told her father it was because Trip was headed out of country for the hasty nuptials, but quite honestly, if she didn't get some alone time with Trip soon, she was going to go insane!

"I always have good reasons for what I do, Miss Anya! I was rounding up lost family," Sasha said as she pulled a short, plump middle-aged woman through the door.

"Aunt Tilley!" Anya hopped up and down like a happy child before running to her aunt and throwing her arms around her, patting her back with her bouquet of roses.

"I wanted to tell you I was coming, but then Viktor said to surprise you. I wouldn't miss this for the world. I would've come some months ago, but there was a mix-up with my passport. Seems I was placed on a watch list. Seems your Nikki had me tagged and watched by Scotland Yard. Can't say I'm crushed that the bloke is dead, horrible sport he always was."

"You're here. Thank you. This is so perfect. I am so happy."

"I brought you your grandmother's pearl earrings. Isn't that a tradition in America too? Something borrowed? I was to wear them when I married, but…" She looked flustered then fussed on, "No matter. You will do them proud."

"You need something blue." Mollie chimed in. "But I was busy with the girls and never thought about it."

Anya shrugged. "No matter."

"Not so fast." Jenna grabbed a blue marker from a Sunday

school desk and pulled down Anya's long white glove. She drew a tiny bouquet of hearts, inscribed it with "forever" on her wrist, then pulled the glove back up to cover it.

Mollie ticked off the criteria, "We have the borrowed and the blue...now, something old."

Viktor pulled a coin from his pocket. "I found this digging for dinosaur bones as a boy. My brother told me it was gold. I have always considered it a good luck charm." He handed it to Mollie and she directed Anya to slip it in her shoe.

"Something new?" Jenna reminded.

"I have my bracelet." Anya shook her glittering wrist in the air.

"Looks like you ladies have covered all the bases." Barbara smiled at the three ladies, her eyes a little glazy, but her jaw firm.

The wedding planner popped her head in the room. "Okay, guys, need you to take your places. We're about to begin." She looked at Anya. "You ready?"

She nodded and turned to Viktor who took her arm in his. Aunt Tilley and her new family gave her hugs as they headed toward their seats. Sasha kissed her cheek and grabbed her bouquet from the table. "I guess I go first."

Anya nodded. An electric thrill ran down her spine. It was time! She turned to her father. "So, do I look all right, Poppa?"

"More lovely than a princess. I am proud of you, Anya. You are a strong and beautiful woman. I owe your Aunt Tilley much. I am going to ask her to stay with me in the states. I can buy a house with many rooms. No need for her to live alone. "

They walked toward the door of the sanctuary. "Poppa, that is a wonderful idea. Do you think she will?"

He shrugged. "I don't know, but I think I should have asked long ago."

Anya raised an eyebrow at her father.

Viktor laughed and patted her hand. "Nothing to tell, daughter. Your aunt always respected your mother. But she is gone. Time to move on."

Anya grinned. She gave him a kiss on the cheek as he lifted the veil over her head and concealed her beneath its gossamer shimmer.

As the wedding march grew louder, Anya felt a tremor of fear. There were hundreds of people out there and she didn't know more than twenty of them. Her knees started to shake. What if she tripped; what if she forgot her vows…and God forbid, what if she slipped up and cursed? Her mouth was dry and her hands shook as she took her first step into the great expanse of the cathedral. Her father squeezed her arm gently, but it did nothing to quell the panic. Everyone was standing, looking at her.

She moved on shaky legs to the aisle. Looking past the multitudes of people and the flash of lights as photographs were snapped, to the man waiting on her. He smiled as he waited…on her, to begin their future… together. The sounds and sights of the church melted away. She felt like she floated to the altar, carried by unseen angels who glorified in the day with her. When Trip took her hand in his, it was sturdy, warm, secure. He was hers forever…now if only…forever could ever be long enough.

Elizabeth Seckman

End of Books:

Hello reader! Welcome to the last page. There are so many good books choose from, I'm thrilled you chose this one. For that, I thank you. Words can't express just how grateful I am. Of course, I hope you enjoyed the story.

How about you? I'd love to hear what you think. You can find me on Facebook *https://www.facebook.com/pages/Elizabeth-Seckman-Author/361427683923220*) and my blog (www.eseckman.blogspot.com).

I know you're busy, but if you'll take a minute and write a review for this or any of my books, I'd love to offer a little more than thanks. Each month, I'm giving away a $10 Amazon or Barnes and Noble gift card for reader feedback. If you write a review on either site (Amazon or Barnes and Noble), email me the link to that review at eseckman@ymail.com (please write Reader Review in the subject line) and I will randomly select one winner per month for the give-away.

Blessings!
Elizabeth

About the Author

Elizabeth divides her time between her beach cottage and her scrupulously clean house in the hills of West Virginia. Ooops. That's fantasy Elizabeth. The real Elizabeth spends her days schlepping after her four boys (five if you count their father) and the assortment of pets they swore they'd take care of.

She does live in West Virginia; the house is clean when the mother-in-law visits; and she does have serious dreams of living at the beach. Elizabeth is a Marshall University graduate with a degree in counseling. This has proven very beneficial when dealing with the make-believe friends she hangs out with all day (she calls this 'writing').

Follow her blog at: http://www.eseckman.blogspot.com

Before You Go...

Share your voice and help guide other readers to these wonderful books. Even if it's only a line or two your reviews help readers discover the author's books so they can continue creating stories that you'll love. Login and leave a review.

www.ingramcontent.com/pod-product-compliance
Lightning Source LLC
Chambersburg PA
CBHW050024180626
46810CB00002B/559